I0831789

Rose From the Basement

Jerome J. McCarthy

Rose From The Basement

Published by The Real Life Series Publishing Co., LLC.

ISBN-10: 0-9800083-4-4
ISBN-13: 978-0-9800083-4-0

PUBLISHER'S NOTE
This is a work of fiction. Names characters, places and incidents are either th product of the author's imagination or are used fictitiously, and any resemblanc to actual persons, living or dead, business establishments, events, or locales entirely coincidental.

First Printing December, 2010

Graphic Design and typesetting by Jerome J. McCarthy.
Cheif editor Marla A. McCarthy
Contributing editors Sonja M. Hunter, Aaron L. Ashley
Printed in USA by Lightning Source

Unless otherwise identified, Scripture quotations are from the King James Version of the Bible.

Inquires should be addressed to:
The Real Life Series Publishing Co., LLC
PO BOX 1563
Keller, TX 76244-1896

www.TheRealLifeSeries.com
info@thereallifeseries.com

DEDICATION

This book is dedicated to the most important and influential woman in my life, my wife Marla. I am thankful for the life lessons she has taught me through her unwavering commitment to God and our family. All that I learned about females and relationships is because of her. She is also responsible for my growth as a man of God, husband and father. I am truly blessed to be one flesh with my best friend.

I would also like to acknowledge the strong women that sowed into me and blessed my life that are now gone to be with the Lord - Linda J. McCarthy (mother), Laura Mae Council (grandmother), Deborah A. Hollins (mother-in-law). You are deeply missed and your legacy still impacts me. You may not physically be here, but you occupy residency within my heart.

Table of Contents

Introduction

Too often we go through things in life similar to our children, yet some of us choose to mask our flaws behind our perfect-parent veil. Others choose to ignore the situation outright and operate in silence. We need to realize that young people are traveling down the same back roads we have been down before. In order to reach this younger generation, it is imperative that we are transparent and let them know we have been where they are. We need to show young people that there is a map (the Bible) that will illuminate their path and guide their footsteps. We must place our embarrassment (ego, position, pride) aside and minister to them at a level they understand. I would rather share my past, be embarrassed and face ridicule than to know that I could have possibly kept a young person from going down that same path I did. I think they are worth that risk!

Understanding that each female experiences and is exposed to things at various ages, I encourage you to take the time to interject your own situations with your daughter, step-daughter, sister, niece, cousin, or young female you are mentoring. For my adult readers, please remove your cloak of perfection and be honest with yourself. We all made bad choices in life, but it is never too late to change our walk. If you see a young person veering down the wrong path, don't let them make the same bad decisions we did at their age. You may not look at yourself as a mentor, but by saying a few honest words, you may very well change the course of their lives.

Rose From The Basement is a novella written in love to the daughter I never had, my nieces, cousins, goddaughters and other young women in my life. Young readers, I implore you to grant me your attention and be open-minded. I know abstinence is not a cool or popular topic, but I ask if you find yourself anywhere within the pages of these characters, and you have an inner desire to go against the grain and not conform like others around you, that you come to agreement with me that a change should be made so that you may experience a peace-filled, joyful and victorious life. Be Blessed!

- Jerome

Chapter I

Track Meat

A brisk wind whirled through and rustled the loose paper and dirt that accumulated in the streets of this sedate, small, blue collar town. West Pointe was a post card All-American community so intimate in square miles that one mishap from an irresponsible teen could taint an entire family name. With a population of approximately 14,000 the town was basically comprised of old money and wealth passed down from previous generations. The foreign freight company, U-SEND, was the only major corporation in town which employed one-third of the residents. The pay wasn't competitive but it afforded stability, kept food on the table and offered decent benefits. Aside from the local grocery stores and restaurants, the remaining residents commuted to surrounding metropolitan cities for employment.

The temperature was moderately breaching the mid 60's this particular day and the frequently visited spots in town were all desolate. Occasionally an overpriced carnival would pillage through town, but the majority of the time there were a minimum amount of community activities offered. Due to the economic climate of this town the residents of West Point appeared erratic with spending habits, but one sure thing you could count on was the town congregating for high school games. People sowed heavily into West Point high school athletics and anticipated a high return on their investment. Football had become a second religion behind Christianity, but during the off season other sports sustained their faith. Whether it was baseball, basketball or track, the ultimate goal was to be left standing the victor...with your foot firmly welded against your opponent's throat.

The athletic event for this particular day was the track meet versus the neighboring small town rival Athens. To express their contempt, West Pointe often referred to the residents of Athens as townies who looked like they drunk bad water. Athens would retaliate claiming West Pointe citizens were hatched, not actually birthed. Initially it was taunting used to stir up competitive juices, but over the years it evolved into an ugly rivalry as many parents disgusted with the course of their life decided to live through their children via athletic competitions.

The fans eagerly anticipated the final race because it had bearing on the outcome of the track meet. The runners positioned themselves to prepare for the Women's 200M. Some of the females jumped up and down to invigorate their muscles, while others sat on the ground and stretched to stimulate their tendons. As the chatter from the stands grew louder, the women continued their individual pre-race customs. Candice was in lane seven sporting a brand new expensive pair of Nike track shoes her uncle bought online and mailed to her. It was rare to see her in something so flashy due to her family's financial situation.

Candice used to have a fervent passion towards track and field. Ever since her earliest memories, she appreciated the strength, agility and grace displayed by track athletes. It truly was a beautiful sport in her eyes as she watched and admired how various veins and striations revealed themselves within the architecture of their muscular frames while athletes participated in various events. She often told her mother that she thought it was cool that women could be strong and cut, yet feminine at the same time.

A modest, humble, yet confident athlete herself, Candice knew in her gut no one would come within 1.5 seconds of her in this race. Now slightly covered with a light perspiration, she firmly placed her ankle in the palm of her hand and stretched her quadriceps as she looked forward toward her destination. To intimidate her competitors and give them a glimpse of what was to come, Candice took off in a 10-yard sprint. After she slowed down, she walked with her hands on her waist while slowly rolling her neck to loosen herself. This was a ritual she performed ever since she won her first race at age seven. Right before her races, her eyes became focused on her goal, and all she could hear was the air expelling from her chest as she blew by. She developed the ability to completely block out all but two sounds; the gun going off at the start of the race and her mother screaming – *Go Candy!*

Candice learned a lot while running track. How there were some people on the sidelines rooting for her, the reality is some did not. It taught her to be like a racehorse with blinders and not pay attention to negative energy. She stayed in her lane, set her own goals and continued to move forward; a lesson on the field that would eventually carry over into her life.

There was a lot of hype built about this match up because rumors were circulating that Jada, the star athlete of Athens track team who recently committed to LSU, had been training with a former Olympian. Her previous meet results, along with the pace she was on, suggested she may eventually make the qualifiers. Candice was new to this town so she didn't quite understand the severity of the rivalry, but she sensed the thick intensity in the atmosphere. People had been chattering about the face off between the future Olympian and the up and coming new girl in West Pointe. Candice never listened to the hype. She always dreamed about going to the Olympics, but first things first. Even though track temporarily allowed her to escape issues within herself, she had a lot of family drama going on and had to make sure things were okay at home first. She glanced over at her All-American competitor and began to assess the situation.

Ok Candy, you can do this girl. You've been here plenty of times before. Yes, she looks fast, but heck she is a senior, and I am only a sophomore. If I come in 2nd I will be doing good. No…you know what, that is not good. Heck, who says I can't win? Shoot, bump her. I have every bit as much as a right to be here as her. Why am I short changing myself? God gave me this ability and I plan on using it. You did bless me with this ability God, didn't you? I don't know sometimes. Why do I have this gift, but my family has to go through so much? I don't have money to visit colleges or get all the nice new things like most girls to pamper myself. There is just so much going on with my mom and family. She works so hard, and it seems like she never gets rewarded for it. I guess I could fall into a rut and feel sorry for myself and say history would repeat itself so why bother running…but no. I am a different person. Get your game face on Candy and suck up all the sob stories. This is life and you have to deal with it. You have to win this one; there is no exception. Do it for Moma. I am sure it would cheer her up.

"Runners, to your block. Mark. Set…"

There was the normal hesitation before the race as the young women dug their fingers into the track anticipating the ear piercing crack triggered by the starter pistol. One of the rivals became too anxious and jumped the gun. The announcer advised which lane the false start occurred in, and with the new rules implemented this year, the next person who had a false start would be disqualified. The runners got back into their blocks and patiently awaited the second calling.

"Mark. Set…"

Pow. The pistol echoed sharp like a 60's western movie and the race was off. Candice started out the blocks late to ensure she didn't false start. The girls were staggered with four clear forerunners. As the first 40 meters passed, Candice's God-given ability kicked in and like nitrous, she propelled herself into the pack of four leading women; one of which was her teammate. It appeared to the crowd that she was gradually accelerating, and she started to break free. Cheers from the locals grew louder as friends and family chanted "Go Candy!" Candice crossed the line and put on her brakes as she awaited the announcement of the results. A short time passed, and the announcer revealed the standings. As she anticipated, she finished 1.5 seconds ahead of second place.

This was the last event, so the PA announcer recited the summary of events. Candice's placement, along with her performance in the 4x100 relay helped her team beat Athens. Candice walked past Jada, who was standing in the midst of her other Athens teammates, and was surprised when she went out her way to make eye contact and speak.

"Hey, Candice, right?"

"Yep, that's me," Candice responded in an apprehensive tone still guarded fearing a foul comment brewing. To her surprise, she received a congratulatory pat on the shoulder.

"You have some serious talent. Keep it up, and you'll escape this God-forsaken town. I will be seeing you soon, I am sure of it!" Jada uttered while winking and trying to mask her disappointment of second place.

Even though Candice constantly contributed to the team, there were girls on the team who didn't like her. She usually received more love from her competitors because they respected her talent. Her teammates' hatred towards Candice wasn't based on personality because she was kind to everyone, but merely due to her being attractive and athletically gifted. They also considered her to be a threat because she provided competition in regards to the attention of guys at their school, therefore they resented her presence and attacked her anytime they could. Candice would attempt to be nice, but high school girls can be downright cruel; a lesson she learned about female character at an early age.

There was an incident in junior high where a girl was jealous of Candice's hair and attempted to place a wad of gum in it. Candice had just started her cycle, and laid her head on her desk as she was experiencing extreme cramps. Apparently the young girl was upset that a guy she liked commented about Candice having pretty hair, therefore she decided to eliminate her threat. What she didn't count on was a passive, quiet Candice retaliating. On the edge of sanity, the gum temporarily made Candice lose her mind as she picked up her social studies book and whacked the girl in the face so hard she shattered her eye glasses and broke her nose. Given the trouble the other girl caused in the past, Candice was only suspended three days. During the ride home Candice explained the situation to her surprisingly calm mother. She shared some stories from her youth and reassured Candice that women act that way well into adulthood so she has to constantly guard herself and monitor her friends.

Candice enjoyed when she had open conversations with her mother and the wisdom transferred allowed her to maturely handle herself against fickle females. She always vowed she would never harm another person physically, however she would protect herself at all costs. As she walked past some of her gossiping female teammates, they began to speak in a tone deliberately audible enough for Candice to hear as they attempted to discredit and tear her down.

"Look at her. She thinks she is all that. I bet that is not even her hair."

"I know girl. She is not as cute as she thinks she is. And what is up with her always winning by that margin? I am not a hater, you know I give respect when respect is due, but come on now. You know her mother probably dating somebody from Balco or something."

It hurt Candice's feelings that she wasn't accepted by her peers even after her contributions, but she learned to develop thick skin as this was her third high school in two years. Her mother, Lisa Richards, was a recent divorcee and due to finances had no choice but to sell the house and move her daughter and herself to an affordable apartment. A few months passed and things appeared to be making a turn for the better when Lisa was hit with another setback; she was diagnosed with a benign ovarian cyst. There was surgery performed to remove the grapefruit-sized tumor, however Lisa had little time to recover due to the stress of being a single mom and trying to hold her home together. In her attempts to be strong for her daughter, her will was broken again as she found out her ex-husband didn't agree to his end of the settlement and dropped her from his health insurance. Between backed up utilities and creditors calling in an attempt to collect on the hospital debt, Lisa had no more energy left to fight her ex, nor anyone else for that matter. She made a decision to save her sanity and move back to her hometown to live with Candice's grandmother.

Candice was upset they moved, but she was more distraught her parents had separated. The move served as a constant reminder that kept pricking at her heart and she often sat in class thinking about her parents. *How do you just end a marriage due to irreconcilable differences? What in the world is that? You don't just quit a 16-year marriage when things go bad! That makes no sense to me how can you be incompatible after you have been around each other so much? For the life of me I can't understand that. Why dedicate all that time and effort into some-*

body if they are going to just leave in the end? I refuse to go out like that!

Candice attempted to cope with her feelings as best she could, but her know-it-all attitude at times inhibited her ability to see life from her mother's perspective. Within time she learned more about what really happened, and eventually she grew to understand the gravity of the situation and stopped giving her mother so much grief about it. Her goal was to excel in sports and academics so she could provide a way into college for herself and lift the burden from her mother. The move annoyed Candice at first but after she considered the loneliness of Lisa, she felt it may be good for her mother to actually be around her own mom. Besides, Candice always got a kick out of her spunky grandmother and her remarks. She began to think this may be a new beginning for their family.

Unfortunately that thought didn't have time to take root. To add to their eventful year, two months after they were settled in Candice's grandmother passed away in her sleep, thus leaving Lisa with additional bills due to funeral arrangements and other medical expenses not covered by Medicare. This was the poker hand of life Lisa was forced to play with, and often times she felt as if everyone else around her had a full house. Lisa made every attempt to shield her daughter from their financial woes, however sometimes her circumstances became so overwhelming she would slip into a minor depression, which oftentimes bled into her daughter's demeanor.

The track meet ended, and the coach briefly spoke with the team congratulating them on their efforts and giving Candice recognition for coming close to the state record. Candice walked over to the bench and grabbed a towel to wipe the curly hair which now clung to her brow and side of her face. As she took a sip from her water bottle, she felt a pair of strong arms wrap around her waist and lick her neck.

"My Candy. You are even sweet when you sweat."

"Boy stop. That is nasty."

"What? I can't help it if my woman is fine. Give me some love."

Candice's boyfriend Andre laid a kiss on his exhausted girlfriend.

"So what are you about to do with your sexy first-place self? You hanging out with the team?"

"Boy please. For what? So they can poison my food? You know those heifers don't like me and I don't have time for their wishy washy ways. One day they want to speak and the next they have issues with me. Whatever! They can all jump off a cliff for all I care. Try to be nice to them and they just want to act stupid."

"Candy, do you think you are over-reacting a little bit?"

"Dre, you have no idea how catty chicks can be. You can wear red and they look at you and just go crazy like *Oh my Lord. She's wearing red. That is my boyfriend's favorite color. She's trying to steal my man!* You have no idea how deep a female's brain can go and these are some petty high school girls we are talking about. I know guys think they are so smart cause they conquer all these dumb broads and have them falling all over them, but most guys are clueless to how psycho these chicks are nowadays. How they plot and scheme is ridiculous. I just keep my distance because I have too much going on in my life and I really don't want to have to beat one of them ho's down over some nonsense."

"You are so feisty girl. I like that face you make when you get upset. It is turning me on."

Andre paused and gave Candice that look which alerted her that an appeal was coming.

"Since you aren't doing anything, why don't you come over? My dad is going to be working late tonight, so I will have the house to myself for hours."

When Andre was seven years old his mother left for another man, so he currently lived with his father and younger brother. Andre never spoke about it, but it hurt his feelings that he hadn't heard from his mother in years. To mask the pain, he kept busy with athletics and women.

Candice loved Andre…as much as she understood about love at the time. She truly felt he was the man she would grow old with. Because they both were in situations where a parent left, she felt they shared a unique bond. However lately she felt uneasy as he had been making sexual advances that she was not ready for. Part of her felt guilty for not taking the steps to please him. After all, he was a big-time popular athlete and one of the most popular seniors. Here she was a mere sophomore and new to the area. Girls were lined up waiting for Candice to mess up so they could jump in her place and try to fill the void she was not ready to dive into.

Like usual, when Dre made these suggestions, Candice tried to avoid going over his house as best she could.

"Baby, can we just go to the movies or something? I really don't want to be cooped up in a house this evening. Maybe we can go to Applebee's or something? We can get a nice basket of wings and then I can feed you your apple crisp."

Andre navigated his fingers around his girlfriend and passionately kissed her again. He allowed his hands to crawl down the small of her back and palm her damp rear.

"Dre, stop baby. People are watching."

"They don't care. All of them know you are mine anyways."

"Yours, huh?"

"What's up with you girl? You don't like P.D.A.?"

"No, I don't mind public displays of affection, but you just said I am yours like I am a piece of meat."

"You are. My sexy track meat. I want to take a bite."

Candice thought his lines were corny, and even though he embarrassed her at times, she still appreciated the attention she received from him. It also amused her to watch other girls' reactions when they were together. While Candice would be in her boyfriend's arms, petty females would stare and cut their eyes at her. It helped to ease her frustration with these bickering girls as she knew their jealousy was eating them up inside. Candice had the guy all the girls wanted and she had to admit that it felt good.

"Candy, I get the feeling you are trying to avoid me. Don't you want to spend some time with me? I thought you loved me?"

"Boy don't be silly. You know I love you."

"Well if you love me, then why don't you want to express your love for me? Don't you think it is time for us to go to that next level? I mean I feel how your body reacts when we touch and kiss. I know you are ready. Come on. I promise I will be gentle."

"It's not that. I am just not ready. I want my first time to be special. Call me old-fashioned, but I don't want to be rushed or anything. I don't want to lose my virginity in the back seat of a truck or on a funk-nasty couch. I don't want to be on some musty sheets or on the floor getting carpet burn on my butt. Maybe I am just being a hopeless romantic, but I want this to be something I remember. I also don't want you to be disappointed in me either."

"As blazin' as you are, trust me I won't be disappointed. And some of the things I have planned for your body, trust me you won't be disappointed either. I can't wait to see you completely naked. I mean, I have seen your shirt off and that made me have wet dreams for weeks. I dreamed about that sexy stomach of yours lined with my sweat. Then one time, I flipped you over on your stomach and…"

"Come on Dre, chill. I just had a long day. Track season is over, and I just want to go home, take a shower and rest. Maybe go to a movie or dinner, but not that…not right now baby. Do you understand where I am coming from? I love you, but just not today."

While testosterone was ravaging his body and raunchy thoughts pillaged his mind, Andre tried to mask his disappointment behind the veil of a tight-lipped smile. Even though he had every girl after him in school, Andre had never been with a girl as beautiful and intelligent as Candice. She had this wit about her and this glow that made her different from anyone he ever met. Andre also had never been with a girl who told him no to sex; something that aggravated him about Candice, yet intrigued him at the same time.

"I can respect that Candy, but you are going to have to come out of that shell eventually. Don't make me wait forever. I am a growing boy and I will be going to college next year…hopefully. I just want to share this moment with you and have a memorable summer between us. There are so many things I want to show you…so many places I want to make love to you. This will be my last summer in this psycho town, and I want to go out with a bang. I want that bang to be with you Candy. I love you and would never ask you to do anything that would intentionally hurt you. We just need this if we want to have a real relationship. All relationships progress and this is the next step to a serious commitment. When I go off to school, I need to know that you are on my team."

Candice hugged Andre tightly but felt uneasy about his subtle ultimatum. The couple talked for a few minutes and then Candice located her mother to drive her home. In the car on the way home, Lisa praised Candice for her efforts, which was the result Candice wanted. But she was too hurt to enjoy her mother's elation because her mind was consumed by the conversation with Andre. They pulled into the driveway and she kissed her mother prior to going upstairs to take a shower.

One new perk Candice had living in her grandmother's house was she had her own attached bathroom. She locked her door then turned the shower on the hottest setting. While undressing, she looked at her naked body in the mirror and thought about Andre's comments regarding seeing her nude. The young athletic teenager skimmed over her body gently using her hands trying to discover any imperfections or anything that stood out that would make her uncomfortable if she were naked around Andre. The two got into a hot and heavy session once before where Candice allowed him to remove her shirt. She felt herself getting flushed with heat but grabbed his wrist to stop him as he went to slide his hand down her pants. Candice felt bad about the situation because teasing him was not her intention. She truly cared for him but got caught up in the moment and regretted not being able to please her boyfriend. Andre did not help matters either with the guilt trips that he kept laying on her.

Now reminiscing about the session, Candice wondered how her life would be if she actually gave into his demands at that time? Would she be experiencing the guilt and anguish she felt at this moment? Probably not, but at what cost? Or maybe she would experience a pain, just a different one. Her thoughts played tennis back and forth as her optimistic side scored and the chair umpire declared – love. She felt butterflies in her stomach like the kind she would always get on the morning of a track meet. With steam rising from the shower and creating a sauna like environment, Candice entered and allowed the hot water to both relax her muscles and mute her voice as she began a conversation with herself; a habit which had become her way of coping with the difficult decisions and emotions she had to process at her young age. She used these conversations as therapy sessions since she was unable to trust many of her thoughts with anyone else.

"If he loves me like he says, why can't he wait? I just don't understand. And what's up with the comments about college? Be on his team? What the hell? I actually thought we would have a future together after school. Maybe he could go professional in football while I train in track. Or worst case scenario we graduate from college, get good jobs and build a house together out west. A nice home with French doors and shutters and a lattice fence like you see on television. I'd have a nice rose garden out front and for our anniversaries Andre would go out and pick them and line our bathtub and bedroom with fresh petals. Heck, maybe we'll buy an ocean front home because I am sure we will be doing well financially. We'd have maybe one or two kids…Andre Jr., and a girl named Anita after my grandmother. Oh, and don't forget about the puppy. You know, the cute little puppy he is going to put in a big box with a red ribbon bow on it and give to me at Christmas. Am I psycho for thinking like this? Planning all this stuff out? No Candy, that is what all females do. Besides, their situation is different from yours anyways. You are being realistic; they are all just off in La La Land trying to cash in on a bankrupt fantasy.

"Yea, this could work between us. Dre gets me like nobody else…we just vibe together. Like when we dance, when we talk, when we spend time together. I can't explain it, but if this isn't love I don't know what love is. I understand his angle somewhat because he is just going through some changes. I know guys get besides themselves when they go to college, but I guess I never really thought about him actually being with someone else. Is that a possibility? Is he dropping hints that he is going to leave me when he goes off to school? I don't get men. I mean, I know he is horny and all, but is that supposed to make me feel better…guilt me into sex? Hey, I am big-dumb-smooth. Come let me whisk you away and use you as my sex toy for a passionate summer before I go off to the university and screw a gang-load of skanks until I concoct a brand spanking new STD and spread the strand along the east coast.

"Lord, why am I in this position? Not to sound all dramatic, but all I want is to be loved. Why can't he just hold me and kiss me? I don't know much about you other than when I used to overhear my grandmother pray and us going to church occasionally, but there is nothing wrong with wanting that, is there? I want his affection but not like this. Then again, what other choice do I have? I can't just let him go to school unsatisfied or he will sleep with someone else. I guess I am going to have to eventually give in, otherwise I will lose him forever."

Chapter II

Happily Ever After

Princess of the Plum Plum Pickers was the moniker given by office workers because of her intense work ethic, however friends and family address her by her middle name, Rose. To the rest of the world she is known as Edith Rose Hughes, the successful CEO of Rozi Cosmetics. Headquartered 45 minutes from her hometown in West Pointe, Rozi Cosmetics was one of the first mineral makeup companies on the east coast. Not only is Rose well-known in the community for her success as an entrepreneur, but for her hefty contributions to the local recreational facility.

Rose is the second born child out of four children. She has an older sister, a younger sister and brother. Prior to her achievements in the business world, Rose was married to the vice-president of a family owned logistics corporation. She suffered a bitter divorce which propelled her to step out on faith with her dream and start a cosmetic company. She used the pain inside as drive to keep her aggressive. Now five years removed from her ex, Rose often reflects back on that period of time and wonders what she did to make him leave. Even though she used the hurt and pain to start a company that assists women in looking their best, oftentimes her past consumes her thoughts and makes her feel ugly inside.

Rose sat at her desk preparing to leave for the day. She had a 45 minute commute home and wanted to beat the traffic. As she walked toward the door, her desk phone began to ring. She stood motionless deciding whether or not she wanted to answer it, and after the third ring she dropped her items and aggressively snatched the phone off the receiver.

"This is Rose."

"Hey Big Sis? Glad I caught you. Sorry I am asking this so late, but can you do me a huge favor?"

"What do you need Rochelle?"

"Tomorrow is Terry's birthday and I want to surprise him. I have so much to do and it is hard with this kid…a kid who can't keep secrets. Can you baby-sit Tonda for me? I will bring you dinner and a movie."

"Sure girl, I don't have anything planned. You don't have to bribe me…I love spending time with my niece. She is a riot. Do you want me to come by, or are you bringing her?"

"I will bring her. Thank you so much!"

Rose looked forward to spending time with Tonda. She was tired of retiring to an empty home, so she welcomed the company. Not to mention, her niece's comments were so honest and humorous that it was some of the purest joy Rose was able to experience at the time.

The evening presented itself, and Rochelle dropped off her eight year old daughter. Rose hugged her sister and grabbed the bag from her arm.

"Now look Tonda, you be good for Auntie. You mind your manners and don't break anything. Don't eat too many sweets and try not to stay up late. And oh, I almost forgot. Make sure that you take your…"

"Enjoy yourself girl and get out of here. She will be fine." Rose interrupted. "You have all day to do the mom thing. This is Auntie time, now scoot and go have fun with your man."

"Rose thank you so much. Love you."

"Love you too."

Rose shut the door then instructed her niece to put her bags up. While Tonda changed into her pajamas, Rose went to the kitchen to prepare dinner. As she opened her Subzero refrigerator, the remains of her last obsessive compulsive bout revealed neatly organized rows of beverages and leftovers. She grinned thinking about the time she wasted color coordinating and rearranging items by height, then began to expel ingredients onto the counter. After cleaning them thoroughly, she chopped up the fresh cilantro, jalapeños, red onion and tomatoes, then added salt and lime juice as she prepared her homemade pico de gallo for their nachos.

Tonda skipped down the stairs with her oversized house slippers on and leaped from the bottom step. She playfully landed on both feet, then ran to hug her aunt while asking if she could help. Rose smiled and began showing her niece how she constructed her infamous chicken nachos, which were always a hit at family gatherings. After the marinated chicken was lightly seasoned and cooked, Tonda and Rose began topping the nachos to their liking. When the layers of cheese melted, she threw a dab of sour cream on the side, took the tray with the mound of nachos and walked it over to the couch. While smacking and licking her fingers, her niece wiped her chunky salsa and saliva-dripped hands on the pant leg of her pajamas, grabbed the remote, and turned to the Cartoon Channel.

"Your TV is so nice. What is this, plasma? I want to have one like this when I grow up."

"I am sure you will Tee. Just work hard in school, and you will be fine."

Rose felt this was the response she should give, but she knew life was a lot harder than the after school special one-liner she just recited. There will be roadblocks, unseen obstacles, and did I mention men, who will completely throw your life off track and dissect your heart in what seems like a classroom of all your peers. As Rose dazed off thinking about the trials of life, she was amused by her niece's innocence.

"Look Aunt Rosie. These are called Powder Puff Girls. You should try to do your hair that way. You have worn it that way for so long."

Rose began to reminisce on her marriage. She used to be very adventurous and change her hair regularly as a way to spice things up. This was, however, during an era her niece couldn't recall. From colors, to various styles, Rose was willing to try anything once and often times would impromptu role play with her husband. After her divorce, she became more conservative with her choices; her boldest change being highlights.

"Go to my room and get my brush, and you can design my hair however you see fit."

Tonda retrieved an armful of hair supplies, strategically aligned them like a professional, and began playing hair stylist with her aunt.

"Aunt Rosie, I like this cartoon. I think that would be a good name for kid's makeup."

"That's cute baby, but children really don't need to wear makeup. Enjoy your time while you are young. You will have plenty of time to cover blemishes when you get older."

"Hmm. If not makeup, why not make some products to help young kids clean their face?"

Rose was amused at how bright her little niece was.

"You know what Tonda, you may be on to something there. That is a good idea. Maybe I need to get you your own office in my building."

Rose and Tonda continued to watch television until they both retired on the plush sofa. In the morning they spruced up, then Rose treated her niece to pancakes at the IHOP. They enjoyed their extended breakfast prior to Tonda's reunion with her parents. After Rose returned her niece, she habitually slid back into her same diligent routine of work and fitness.

*   *   *

Rose hadn't heard from Rochelle in a couple weeks, which peaked her concern. She rearranged appointments for that afternoon and drove over to check in on her baby sister. When Rose knocked on the door she was greeted by her stout brother-in-law Terry, who greeted her with a hug.

"Hey Rose."

"Hey old man. How you doing?"

"Oh, I am not that old…yet. I still have about half a decade before I get to your age."

"You are really trying to get hurt, huh?" Rose snickered.

"So what do we owe this visit?" Terry inquired in a welcoming tone.

"Oh, nothing at all. I was just in the neighborhood and thought I'd stop by and check on my sis and niece…see how everyone was doing."

"Ro is at the hair salon, but should be getting home pretty soon. Come on in."

Terry opened the door and escorted Rose towards their den.

"Can I get anything to drink for you?"

"Whatever you are having is fine old man. As long as it is not prune juice."

Rose's wisecrack called attention to his belated birthday. Terry took the elderly jokes in stride as he walked into the kitchen to prepare a beverage for his guest. A few moments later he resurfaced with a steaming hot white plum tea prepared with a teaspoon of honey.

"I love herbal tea. Thank you so much."

"Not a problem at all. Hey Rose, thanks for keeping Tonda last weekend. We really needed the time alone. You know Rochelle has been going through some things lately and…let's just say that time helped."

"It is no problem at all. I can keep her anytime y'all need time alone. Besides, she is so adorable. Glad she took after my sister."

"Woman please, that is all from my side of the family!"

Rose and Terry drank their tea while joking with one another. Midway into the conversation, Terry's cell phone chimed. He politely raised his index finger.

"Excuse me one second."

Terry turned his back towards Rose and spoke in a tone just faint enough for her to hear.

"What's up man?…Not today, but maybe tomorrow. I am taking Tonda to the zoo like I promised her…naw, just me…giving Ro some time alone…she getting her hair done right now, I am just here chillin' with her sister…no man, I told you before, I am not…naw dude because that would be on me…look, bout to go…later."

Terry flipped his phone closed with his thumb then turned towards Rose.

"Sorry about that. That was my stupid friend."

"What was he talking about, if you don't mind?"

"Man, you're nosey. Must run in your family," Terry responded with a hint of sarcasm. It was a frequent occurrence during their conversations, however over the years they developed a unique affinity towards one another.

"We weren't talking about anything important. He wanted me to hook him up with you. That is absolutely not happening."

"That sounds important to me. Why not? What is wrong with him?"

"Trust me, he is my boy, but I know what he is after. He is a good person but right now he is fighting his calling and sometimes, oftentimes, falls victim to his flesh. Besides, I look at you like my little older sister and it is not going down like that."

Terry and Rose knew each other since high school. They were in marching band together, and after one of their home games she introduced Terry to her baby sister Rochelle. They dated off and on for years and married shortly after college. Rose looked at Terry as a brother and she often came to him when she had questions regarding the opposite sex.

"Probably best then. I have the worst luck with men. I know not all men are bad…just all men within a twenty-two mile radius of wherever I roam. Maybe it is just me. That is one thing I can say all my failed relationships have in common…me. I make the worst decisions when it comes to men."

"You shouldn't be that hard on yourself. Dating is not easy, especially not in this day and age. Even though you want to believe you can forgive someone for their past and accept them as they are, it doesn't mean there aren't consequences from their past that still affect you."

Rose enjoyed these conversations she had with her brother-in-law. Having a male's perspective with no ulterior motive was refreshing. She envied Rochelle at times for landing a good man, however she had boundaries and never crossed the line. Terry was a respectable man who she could ask questions and receive honest answers.

"This is what I don't understand about men. I feel I am a decent catch.

I have a nice career, no kids, and I am in shape. I don't think that I am that bad on the eyes, for my age my body is nice and tight, and I am not necessarily a slouch in bed either."

"That is where you are getting confused sis. Sex doesn't have anything to do with it."

"Well, you could have fooled me. I haven't met a man who hasn't approached me with that in the back of his head, but I understand that it is just natural and men need that release."

"See women approach this thing all wrong. It is not all about sex. Sex will catch a man's attention, but it won't keep him. If you offer sex freely or make it readily available then yes, most men will take it. But sex alone will not provide you with the long-term commitment and a fulfilling relationship that you seek. Contrary to belief, a man needs to be mentally stimulated. He needs a woman to challenge his intellect. He needs a woman who will be there for him to share his goals and dreams. He needs a woman who he can tell his inner most secrets to and trust she won't use them as leverage against him later on. Yes, sex is a needed, healthy part of a married relationship, but trust me if you can't mentally arouse him, he won't stay around long. Men can get sex from anywhere. Women pass it out like windshield flyers these days."

"I guess. Maybe the guys I have messed with have just been sexual deviants. It is darn near impossible to find a good man that warrants the investment of my time. It seems like you have a good head on your shoulders, but most men are not like you. For instance, I have this one woman that works for me who lives with her boyfriend. They have been engaged for eight years now. I don't understand why does it take so long for men to make up their minds? I think half the time men don't even know what they want."

"I understand what you are saying sis, but let's dig to the root. The real problem is neither sex wants to observe God's original purpose and plan for male and female relationships. What it all boils down to are men and women manipulating to get what they want out of a relationship and not necessarily what the other partner needs. So to address your question, all men know what they want, but may not necessarily know what they need."

Terry adjusted his position and rested his foot on the ottoman.

"Say for instance your employee. From the sounds of that situation, he is keeping his options open until something better comes along. I worked with this girl who lived with her boyfriend and her five year old daughter from a previous relationship. Because she had a child she felt she couldn't get anyone better, so she held on to him even though she was unfulfilled in the relationship by his lack of everything. He didn't do anything but take from her. One day this girl and an older woman in our office were at the break room table talking about marriage, relationships and whatnot. The younger girl expressed her frustration with her boyfriend delaying their wedding plans and not taking any strides towards marriage commitment. Every time they talked about marriage, he would avoid the conversation or change the subject. The older woman responded with a question. With a scolding, yet loving tone she asked - *Why would he want to marry you if you are giving him all the things a married woman does? You are cooking for him, cleaning up after his nasty draws and giving him sex. Why would he want to marry you and pay for cookies when you giving them away free? Where is his incentive?* Now of course there is more to marriage than sex, food and laundry, but you get the point. Women these days don't keep their legs closed long enough to even find out what the man they are dating is about, then before they know it… bam…they have gotten themselves in a situation where they are emotionally and spiritually attached to someone they don't even know. Someone who doesn't meet any of the criteria of the man they wanted."

"True Terry, but what you fail to realize is it is harder than it seems. I am sure there is a man for that girl, but if I were in her shoes I don't know what I would do. It has to be hard raising a kid by yourself…then to actually find someone who wants to spend time with you? Asking her to give that up to go back to a lonely lifestyle is a lot easier said than done."

"I am not saying that it is easy by any means. What I am saying is most women have perception issues. If you change how you view yourself that would solve half of your relationship problems. If you realize how valuable you are then you wouldn't put yourself in compromising positions. And when I say you, I don't mean you in particular…I mean women as a whole. If you want to dedicate your life to being in a relationship with a man who constantly shows you he has no intention of treating you right, then so be it. That is your choice, and you have every right to. But in my opinion, life is way too short to waste years upon years on a man who is unwilling to move forward. You have to make room for a door to open for a real man to enter your life. A man with intentions of living each day to the fullest with you and treating you as God intended."

Rose tried her best to locate a chink in his armor for a rebuttal, but nothing came to mind. She knew he was making relevant points, nonetheless she felt her argumentative nature rising.

"I hear what you are saying, but it is still hard though Terry. You are talking about changing a way of thinking that has evolved for years. Men aren't the easiest creatures to understand by any stretch of the imagination, and women have just adapted and learned how to get what they want."

"They get what they want, but at what cost? How many women are happy manipulating to get their way? Name me one woman who has orchestrated her relationship and I guarantee she is not happy. Name me one woman who stole another woman's husband and they had a fairytale ending where they lived peacefully together for 30 years then died in their sleep holding hands. Women make up these scenarios in their mind until they believe it and don't realize how delusional they've become. Things are so crazy nowadays that some women make detailed plans for how their boyfriends will propose to them. You have women competing with and trying to upstage their friends' weddings. Or my all time favorite…women get pregnant thinking the guy will marry them and they will live happily ever after. That is all just foolish ways of reasoning. The way I look at it you have two options. You can be transformed through the renewing of your mind so you can understand God's purpose and intention for relationships, or stay complacent in your walk and keep going through the same thing. The choice is really simple."

Terry's words struck a nerve with Rose. She always had a handle on business and finances, but relationships were her achilles heel. She often stated she was a walking oxymoron because her business intelligence was near genius, but her discernment of men was remedial at best.

"Tell me this, since you have all the answers. I agree women do some stupid things, but why do guys act like butts all the time? They are like constant contradictions…they say one thing and then do another. It just really annoys me how men treat women like they are expendable. Men approach women like they are an appliance. They have the attitude like - *if you act up, I will just replace you with a better model*."

"See Rose, what you fail to realize is…from a selfish, get-what-I-want-perspective…it is more beneficial for men to be a jackass towards women than a good guy. This whole male, female thing is so complicated. People are so used to functioning within dysfunction that relationship roles have been distorted. There are women out there who are more receptive to being treated like crap from a loser than they are open to a chivalrous man attempting to be a gentleman."

Rose's stubbornness moved to the forefront as she pre-determined to debate regardless what was said.

"I don't think that is necessarily true."

"You don't? When a guy acts like a complete jerk to a woman, or acts like he may actually leave, what usually happens? He gets her attention, sex, meals, whatever she has to do to keep him in her life. Now reverse that. A guy is opening doors, cordial, doesn't ask for sex on the first date, then what? Females don't know how to react and they let those guys go."

"Man, whatever Terry."

"Whatever nothing, it is the truth. When I was in college, during that year when your sister was trying to rediscover herself, I dated this girl who worked at the university bookstore. We hung out a few times and when we finally kissed I decided to be a gentleman and not grope her body. We had only known each other two weeks at this point. Later in our relationship we reminisced on the first month we dated. Do you know this girl had the nerve to tell me that she initially thought I was gay because I didn't try anything with her? I chose to respect her body and not fondle her, so that made me less of a man? That comment took me back and let me know how bad society had gotten. It made me question how women define men and what they accepted from relationships. Her brain was conditioned to associate me being physical with her to love, attraction and commitment."

"Terry, it is hard to read men. How many guys really want to be with a woman just for her? I mean, seriously. Most men women meet eventually want sex, and if you don't concede then you end up like me...alone. I am not saying it is right, but it is a lot easier to take some steps to secure a relationship, versus going the traditional moral high road and praying someone will fall into your path."

"I love you Rose, but like Cliff Huxtable told Theo in one of my favorite Cosby episodes, that's the dumbest thing I've ever heard in my life! No wonder you get D's in everything!"

"Shut up," Rose chuckled while playfully throwing a throw pillow at Terry.

"Seriously, you need a tutor for relationships. When you built your company, you didn't put all that hard work in and set all those guidelines with dreams of failing and it crumbling apart. That is foolish to enter a venture with that mindset. You knew what it would take for that company to be successful, so you stuck with a blueprint for it and were diligent. You made sure that if something didn't align with your plan, you wouldn't waste any time on it. If you approach your business in that manner, then why wouldn't you approach men and relationships the same way? Why would you settle for someone who doesn't align with your plan whatsoever and keeps you from obtaining your desired end result? Why would you set yourself up for something you know will crumble…just for a few days or weeks, or if you are lucky months, of a man's attention? You are depleting your spirit allowing these men to come in and constantly take, take, take from you."

"You don't understand."

"Apparently not. I don't understand. Some women have so much potential, then go backwards settling for a man who is not about anything… just to say they have a man. My sister has dated some men that made my head hurt trying to figure out what she was thinking. Seriously, some of these guys I'd sit there and think wow, how drunk was my sister when she met you? So from my experience, no I don't understand. I don't understand how women settle for mediocrity. How's that saying go? I can be happy all by myself. I'd rather be happy and alone, then in a relationship and miserable."

"Well men…"

"Let's not talk about men. We can say men are dogs and talk about all the ignorant stuff they do for the next two hours. Let's focus on women and their part. Like I said before, women need to stop rewarding men for being foolish and set some standards. Hell, you don't get a Scooby Snack for shh…"

Terry caught himself as he realized Tonda was in the next room over.

"You don't get a Scooby Snack for shipping on the carpet."

"Shipping?"

"Scooby-Doo…snack…dog crap…never mind! You know what I meant. I am a work in progress, so forgive me."

Rose liked the fact Terry was so real and honest about his flaws even though he was a man of the cloth. In a time of hypocritical people, Rose liked surrounding herself around real folk for a change.

"Back to what I was saying. My point is it starts at an early age. In high school, what do women do? They go after the bad boys. Women don't understand the influence they have over men. If girls in high school would take a stand and say they are only attracted to guys who are actively working towards attending college, what do you think would happen? These young boys that I mentor are acting out trying to do what they feel gets the attention of these young girls. If women say they like fast cars and big money, then that is what guys go after. If women say they want a dangerous guy, then that is how guys will act. Women need to raise their standards and expectations and let these men know their lifestyle is not acceptable. If women didn't express an interest in a man's money or vehicle and focused on him as a person…meaning his character, his walk with God and how he treats women in his family…what do you think would happen?"

"I appreciate your optimism, believe me it is refreshing, but like I said, you are talking about trying to change the way people have thought and behaved for years. It is not going to happen."

"I didn't say anything about changing *them*, I am talking about *you*. I remember when I was in 5th grade, the teacher told us all to stop talking or the entire class would get into trouble. There were a few kids who kept talking and playing around and this upset some of the other classmates. The born-again quiet classmates felt it was their saintly responsibility to stand on a soap box and say *shhh* to remaining chatter boxes. By the time three or four people started saying *shhh*, the classroom was once again loud and people began to argue. Safe to say the class all got into trouble."

"What is your point Terry?"

"My point is I sat in that class and didn't say a word. At that moment this revelation came to me…and I have used this in my life up until this day. I thought to myself, if people learned how to stop worrying about what is going on around them and took care of themselves and shut up, then they wouldn't put themselves into certain situations where they get into trouble. Too often when a troubling situation arises, we get caught in the game of pointing fingers to defer our faults."

Even though Rose was reluctant to listen, she knew Terry had her best interest at heart and respected his opinion. She tried to suppress her stubbornness and be open to learning more about men and what she was doing wrong in relationships. She slowly drunk the remainder of her tea while trying to absorb everything her brother-in-law was saying.

"All that to say, you can't worry about what the next woman is doing, or what someone is whispering in your ear. You have to take care of yourself. When everything around you is going haywire, set aside time and work on rebuilding you. Heck find Jesus, straight up. I know that is not the popular answer or the one people want to hear, but read your Bible and grow closer to God. Your relationship with Him is more important than a relationship with a man."

Terry was growing to become one of the most popular youth pastors in their region. His church was located in the city of Jackson; the same residence of Rozi Cosmetics. Rose enjoyed the church services, however she never felt compelled to join and hadn't visited since she last attended with her ex-husband years ago.

"I have to admit, I haven't been to church since Troy."

Rose could have very well kept that comment to herself, but she wanted to defer accountability and be reprimanded.

"See, linking with the wrong man is some serious stuff. My sister went through something similar. She was in a situation with this man where she let him draw her further away from God. He had her believing that as long as she was just a good person that she didn't have to really adhere to the guidelines within the Word because God is love and is a forgiving God and only God judges me, yada, yada. He basically tried to convolute the Word to coincide with his behavior at the time to make him feel better about what he was doing."

Rose reflected on her past and eerily saw herself within the story of Terry's sister.

"Yea, I have to admit that was me. Terry, I was so in love and called myself being a good wife. At first he made excuses that he didn't like our church because it was small, so we went to a different church. We get there and then he complained about the preacher and the amount of money he was getting. It was always something. Because I loved him so much, I did what I felt a good wife should do and support and follow him."

It was apparent something Rose said was disturbing as Terry sat straight in the chair and elevated his voice.

"Maybe I am just taking this personal, but I find it funny that people have so much of a problem with preachers sowing into lives of others 24/7 and getting compensated for it, but then turn around and think it is alright for Gates, Trump or these Fortune 500 CEOs to have money and spend it how they see fit. Pastors are on call day and night. They sacrifice time alone with their family dealing with other people's mess and shouldering their burdens. Psychologists get paid for it, but let a pastor have a nice watch or car then there is a problem?"

"Wow, that pinched a nerve. Calm down. I didn't say I agreed with Troy. I was just making a point that I just really let myself go with him. I cut myself off from my friends and family calling myself being a good woman. I understand about leaving your family and cleaving to your spouse, but in retrospect I see he was just trying to cause dissention between me and my people. It was like he got off knowing there was tension in our family and we weren't getting along. He selfishly just wanted me at his disposal."

Terry's distaste for his former brother-in-law was evident by his rigid facial expression.

"You know how I feel about him. I never ever ever liked that fool Troy, or heck any of your boyfriends for that matter, but I just tried to be a good brother-in-law and support you in whatever decisions you made. Rose, I will never try to coerce you into coming to church because to me it is more important that you develop a relationship with God versus getting stuck on religion, religious practices or religious institutions. The most important aspect of any relationship is communication. If you open the lines of communication back up with God, I truly believe He will lead you in any decision you make, from men to the body of believers that is right for you."

"I know, and I appreciate that. I just don't know what to do at this point. I have grown so far from God I don't know if He even listens to me anymore. I know He protects me and has blessed my business tremendously, but that business was birthed through the pain of my divorce. It is like I always have to go through something hurtful to get deliverance. My finances have always been in order, but when it comes to relationships, it is like God walks in the other room while I am talking to Him."

"That is two-fold sis. You have to give God something to work with as well. As long as you are going against His will, things will always go wrong. Confusion comes about when we deliberately go against the will of God. We constantly think we are smarter than God and can do things how we want to do them. Then we get into trouble and want to blame Him for not having our back."

"You are right. I know I definitely need to repent and get back to me. I was raised in the church and I feel a void sometimes because I don't pray or read the Word like I used to. I give thanks for meals, but I haven't sat down and really had a good prayer in a long time; one where I have a conversation and pour my heart out to God. I definitely need His help with relationships because I feel lost."

"Rose look, I don't have one answer for you because there are so many different dynamics to relationships. All I can tell you is to learn to set boundaries. Simply put if a man doesn't meet the criteria, move on. And please, if you don't hear anything else, don't revisit the past. Ex-boyfriends, ex-husbands, ex-whatever's are all ex for a reason. That was a season that passed so keep it in the past. Pray that God releases those spiritual ties and let the past stay where it was. Don't rehash the good times because you will end up falling into a trap and getting your feelings hurt all over again."

Rose nodded in agreement as Terry continued.

"Look at it like garbage. Every Monday you take all the garbage from your house, put it in the receptacle and walk it to the curb to await its disposal. When you get home later that evening, you walk the empty receptacle back to the garage and go about your business. Now when you throw items away, you don't wait till the garbage man takes it away then jump in your car, chase the truck to the dump and go searching for what you threw away, would you? Then why would you go back to the trash you got rid of when you put so much effort into letting it go? Nine times out of nine, when you end a relationship with a guy it was for good reason. There is a passage in Proverbs 26:11 which states - *As a dog returns to his vomit, so a fool returns to his folly.* Just think about that. It is so straightforward I don't even need to elaborate. Why would you return to a past that holds no future for you?"

Rose's cell phone vibrated and not a moment too soon. Whenever anyone talked about Troy it made her nauseous, so she welcomed the interruption. It was an important call she needed to take, so she excused herself from the conversation and walked into the kitchen. After a few minutes, she returned to the den.

"I am truly enjoying this conversation but duty calls. I have a little drama down at the office I have to take care of." Rose gathered her purse and keys. "Terry, thanks. I really enjoyed this. You always are so honest with me, and I appreciate it."

"No problem at all sis."

Rose gazed at her brother-in-law for a second. She knew it was wrong, but at that very moment his handsome appearance and caring spirit captivated her. The way he thought was attractive to her and without thinking she let her thoughts drip from her mouth.

"You know Terry, my sister got a good man in you. I wish I would have seen you through her eyes."

"Saw what through her eyes? What is that supposed to mean woman?"

"Just means Rochelle saw something in you pure. She saw the man you were going to become…the good devoted father and husband. My perception was so distorted because I was so busy in love with that jerk, I didn't see anything around me nor could I focus in on a good man. Maybe if I wasn't so wrapped up with him and cheering him from the stands during games, I would have seen you right next to me."

Rose placed her hand on Terry's shoulder for leverage and leaned in to kiss him on his cheek.

"Do you think you could have been happy with a girl like me? I know back in the day I was like the spokeswoman for the chubby chick, but I mean me as in right now. Say in a different lifetime with different circumstances?"

"Rose, what kind of question is that? I can't answer that."

Terry responded in a confident manner, yet still letting it be known that he was a man of character and had no intentions of acting inappropriately.

"I know, I know…I am sorry."

"No, don't take it like that. Rose, you are a very attractive woman and I have always thought that even since high school…no matter what your size was. You just need to understand that there is more to relationships than just physical attraction. The question you are asking me, I can't honestly answer. You are asking me to speculate what a relationship would have been like with my wife's sister. I can't disrespect my wife and even allow my mind to wander there."

Rose couldn't believe she allowed those words to come out. She had never crossed the line with any of her sisters' men before, and didn't know what was going on inside. *Dang, have I gotten that desperate that I am hitting on Terry? Edith Rose Hughes, what is wrong with you? That is so wrong. Why did that come out? Have I liked him all of these years, or is desperation just oozing out of my pores now? Maybe it was just having a confidante…someone who I could ask intimate questions about men and get honest responses. Well, I need to clean this up because I don't want a riff in my family…and definitely don't want to damage anything with my sister. I love that girl.*

"I understand. I apologize for putting you into that position. I didn't mean it like that. I was just asking from a standpoint of me as a person. Not like you and I physically…well, that came out wrong. You know what I mean. Like if there is something wrong with me in general. You know…well…never mind. This is not working," Rose said, now embarrassed and flustered. "Hey, thanks for the tea."

"Anytime."

Terry placed his hand on Rose's back and escorted her out his home. He placed his forearm on the inner frame of the door while grasping the crown molding as he watched his sister-in-law enter her vehicle. Still embarrassed, Rose waved as she put on her seat belt, slid on her sunglasses and drove off at incredible speed.

Chapter III

Girl Fight Club

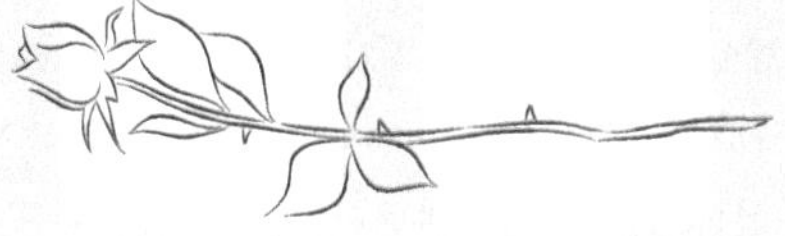

Two years ago Candice received financial aid to attend a cheerleading camp in Michigan. During her stay she befriended a spicy young lady named Camille. Upon introductions, Candice discovered Camille lived in West Pointe where her grandmother resided. During the camp the duo gravitated towards one another and a friendship was birthed. They stayed in touch after the camp and when Candice moved to West Pointe as a permanent resident, it made her transition to the area a bit easier with Camille in her corner.

"That concert is going to be bananas. I wish I could go, but I have to…"

"Come on Candy, you have to go with me. Remember how much fun we had at the concert the summer before last? That outfit you wore was too cute!"

"Yes, I remember how much fun we had laughing at those two simple chicks we went with. That fool tossed his shirt off the stage and they both caught it and held on to it like that shirt was a marriage proposal."

"Candy, why did I forget about that? That was comedy! Remember they went into the bathroom crying, while both of them were still clutching the shirt?"

"A dirty, sweaty, disgusting shirt at that! That was so stupid. He was cute, but not all that! Actually, he was a scrub if you want to be honest."

Camille grinned from ear to ear as she reminisced on the carefree incident.

"He? Funny how we never use his name anymore."

"*He* because I can't believe I used to think *he* was cute. *He* looks like *he* is on crack now. *He* is pretty dusty. Ugh! What were we thinking?"

Camille burst into laughter, then composed herself to speak.

"Off subject, but I forgot to tell you about this old head I met the other day."

"Oh Lord. Cam what is up with you and these old men? Where did you meet this one?"

"A few weeks back I got off work late. You know my car was in the shop and since my mom is so infatuated with her boy toy, she didn't care how I got home. This particular day I was pissed and didn't feel like waiting, so I decided to walk. So, I am walking right, and this shiny white car pulls up. I don't know what kind of car it was, but it was real nice."

"Girl please tell me you didn't get in the car with a fool you didn't know, did you?"

"Dang, can I finish my story? So he pulled up and told me he usually doesn't do this, but I looked like an intelligent girl…"

"Hold up, stop the freaken presses. What guy says that a girl looks like she is intelligent in the middle of the night? You get off work at 8pm. He was looking for a hooker! What did you have on? Weren't you wearing your work outfit? He had to know how young you were. My goodness, did he pull up playing Kells?"

"Real cute, but no he was playing some of that old school music from the 70s. And no, we don't have uniforms anymore. All that is irrelevant. Now will you hush and let me finish? So it was getting dark and he told me he just wanted to make sure I got home safe. I figured heck, why not? I am not stupid…I kept one hand in my purse on my blade. He was cool though. Real gentleman like, opening doors and stuff like that. He works at some government office or is a politician or something. I think he said he works with the mayor. I really was just paying attention to him talk because I was pressing buttons on his navigation system. He gave me his business card and told me to come by his office because he may have a possible internship available for me filing papers or something. It has to pay more than that ol' raggedy retail clothes shop I work for."

"Girl, you playing with fire!"

"Yeah, yeah, yeah. Anyways, I called him and he was cool. I respect his hustle. At least he doing something with his life, unlike these guys around here. I went to his office a couple times, but seemed like each time he'd get a bit bolder."

"Bolder how?" Candice responded disappointed, yet curious.

"I don't know. Just how he would come at me sideways. Like he'd ask me to come by his house and clean it up, or he would tell me to walk behind his desk and give him a massage. Stuff like that."

"Ok heifer, you left out a huge chunk of that story. Rewind and go back to the drive home. Why did you let some man know where you live? Cam, that was just plain stupid."

"Like I told you before, give me credit…I am not stupid. This guy has a position in the public eye. I have seen him on TV before and in the papers. He is about forty some years old and I think he is married. I was just trying not to get caught up in some scandal with my name all over the paper, so I cut it off. I'm not as dumb as you think! I was just trying to get some paper from him."

"Umm, hmm."

Candice was skeptical as she knew her flirtatious friend probably went further than she was admitting. *She probably crawled under the desk after that massage knowing her. That is so nasty. And what is wrong with that old perverted man? I should look him up and go tell his wife. No, that is none of my business. Just change the subject Candy.*

"So what is up with that new girl," Candice asked. "The one that transferred in from out of state. You hear the rumors about her?"

"The rumors that she is gay? Yes, it is true."

"How do you know?"

"Umm…I know because she hit on me."

"Hit on you? What in the world? Are you sure, or do you think you were misreading signals."

"Candy, trust me…I have been hit on quite a few times by women. I know when a girl is coming on to me or not."

"That is just crazy to me. What do they say? Like how do they approach you?"

"It is crazy because they come at you like a dude. I mean, maybe not so forward though. They hold back a little bit, but it is obvious that they are hitting on you. The first time it happened to me I was caught off guard. I was like, oh my God, did a girl just hit on me? But you know what…it is like normal now because it happens so frequent that I don't even notice it."

Candice did not respond. This was the first dealings she had with same sex attractions. Prior to this she only heard about it on television; now it was going on through her school. Feeling uncomfortable, she steered the discussion in another direction.

"What you getting into tonight Cammy?"

"I dunno. Man, my moms is trippin' right now. Cierra got in trouble again and mom actin' paranoid about everything. She got me on lockdown. I just hope she gets over these little issues before the turnabout dance."

"I completely forgot about that dance. I still need to get an outfit. Keep your job so I can use your discount. So what Cierra do?"

"Girl, plum lost her mind. Hold up, let me back up. A few months back she ran away with this older guy for a week or so. Before she left she told me about it, but I just kept quiet. I knew where she was, but I figured Momma was trying to be dramatic about it. Not to mention Cierra is quite annoying, so I knew it would be just a matter of time before he chewed her up and spit her back out."

"That ain't right girl. Why didn't you tell your moms? You know she was probably worried half to death. You wrong for that one."

"Trust me, she will be fine. What you need to understand about my mother is it is all about show. All she cares about is how we look as a family. She wasn't worried my sister left, but she was worried about how Cierra running away made us look bad as a family. That is why I didn't say nothing. She is more concerned about trying to keep that man of hers happy."

Candice shook her head.

"Little Cierra?"

"Yes, little sweet nice Cierra. Oh that is not all. Her latest stunt is the kicker. The one that made Momma put us all on lockdown. Ok, are you ready for this?"

"I guess," Candice responded as her voice tapered off. She was always fond of Cierra and it hurt her feelings to see her going down the wrong path. She began an internal crusade to exonerate Cierra's actions with rationale as she tuned in to hear Camille finish her story.

"This one actually caught me off guard. My baby sis got caught up with some fight club, or that's what they are calling it anyways. Probably over that same dude she ran off with. They made a big fuss about it because some boys videotaped it and put it on YouTube. I am surprised you didn't hear about it. Been all over the news."

"Yea, I did hear about it, but never would think it was someone I knew. Wow. Little Cierra?" Candice responded still in shock.

"Yes girl, little innocent cute Cierra. She claimed it was not a fight club and it was just a fight these guys happened to get on tape with her and this girl that disrespected her, but you can never believe a word out of her mouth. I always told y'all she was a lying little heifer ever since she was born. I don't know what is wrong with her, but at two years old she started lying and hasn't stopped since. That girl is nothing but trouble!"

"Those fight clubs are retarded. To fight because some stupid boy tells you to is just flat out dumb. I mean I do understand the urge sometimes…

believe me I do. There are some simple broads at our school, but that is ridiculous to get on camera and act a plum fool for these dudes attention."

"I think it may be deeper…like some issues at home or something. I dunno. You remember Johna that was in our school for a few weeks then all of a sudden disappeared? Well I heard she was cutting herself on her arms and whatnot. Come to find out her mom was a meth addict and she basically had to do everything on her own. Her aunt came down and snatched her up and moved her to Arizona."

"Whoa. Yea I remember speaking to her and she was real dark and distant, so I kept it moving and handled my business. I did wonder why she always wore long sleeve shirts. That is wild. You never really know what someone is going through. That is messed up."

"I know, right? That tripped me out too. Now we have issues at home but nothing like that. But heck, even with our issues and normal family drama, Cierra is so spoiled there is no reason for her to be acting out the way she does. She always gets her way and Mom gives her everything… well except for good home-cooked meals."

Candice knew her friend had serious issues with her mother, so oftentimes she would try to diffuse the conflict.

"Your mom seems cool, but I know it is completely different when you live with someone. And her food ain't that bad, is it? Stop clownin' that woman."

"Not that bad? Candy let me tell you the real. My mother has two sisters and she is the oldest, therefore she thinks she knows everything. Her sisters try to teach her how to cook by sneaking in helpful tips here and there, but she is just off in the head and content on being rebellious and doing things her way. She finds a way to destroy it one way or another. Her favorite response is – *I know already*. As my aunt says, my mother knows everything about nothing. It is sad actually because her food is so awful that we usually eat take out or fast food. God forbid if she actually cooks something. Her problem is she spends so much time trying to make it cute that it has no flavor and the meat is usually always pink…no matter what meat we have. I will say the good thing about her cooking is you will lose some serious weight. I don't know what she does while preparing forty-five minute meals in three hours, but you eat it and it feels like fish bones scratching the inside lining of your stomach. Her stuff will straight clear you out!"

"You stupid girl. Why don't you and your sisters help her out?"

"For one, she don't listen. Like I said, she thinks she knows everything and she straight butchers every meal she comes in contact with. I don't even know how she achieves it with some meals. For two, I live in a house with all chicks - my two biological sisters, then my evil, tattle-telling step-sister. Being in a house with all these women drives me nuts. We all get to grabbing for the Midol at the same time and this house is straight chaos. We mess around and be like the Tour De France up in this batch…all of us cycling together."

Candice laughed uncontrollably.

"Girl, shut up! You are making my side hurt!"

"What? I am not even trying to be funny. I am being serious. We send my step-dad to Costco's and he comes back with a big ol' bulk box of pads. That's what he gets for messin' with my momma. I know in retrospect if he knew what lay in store for him ahead, he would have ran full speed in the other direction. He gay anyways…my mom just too desperate to see it. She done got herself in knee deep and now she can't get out."

"Gay?"

"Yes, gay. This man is a straight up fruit cup. I don't know if he got touched when he was little or what, but something just ain't right with him. I swear sometimes he wears pads too cause he has some serious mood swings. I can't really explain it, you just have to be around him to see. Little things like how he has more skincare products than my mom, or how he just speaks with this sassy tone. Oh, I got a good one for you. Last Halloween, why did he dress up as a French maid? I mean fish net stockings, heels, spaghetti straps, feather duster and all. What make it so bad is he just did it to answer the door to give away candy. Big ol' grown man sitting on the couch with a little skirt, hairy legs and a duster in his hand watching the home shopping network…literally running to the door when the doorbell rings. What straight man you know does that?"

"Shut up!" Candice had laughed so hard her nose became runny. She took a tissue from her desk and violently blew. "Sorry about that. So you heard from your dad lately?"

Camille paused before responding.

"No, not in a while. He got some new family now, so he is not paying attention to us."

"I don't understand men Cammy. My daddy left us for my aunt. What was he thinking? My parents were married sixteen years and this chick, my momma's own blood, came in and destroyed our family. Part of me still hates him for that."

"Yea, that is jacked. My situation is a little different. I can't blame my dad too much because my mother is the one that cheated on him. The broad thinks we are stupid and don't know, but I did the math. My step-dad was in the picture way before there was any talk of a separation. My mother was wrong for that, but hey, my step-dad was just as wrong messing with a married woman at the time. What can I say? He was acting like a typical man, so sometimes I don't even feel sorry for him."

"I don't understand what goes through their heads."

"Blood…and it is not the head up top. That is all they think with."

"I am starting to believe that Cam. You know that seems to be the only thing Dre thinks or talks about now."

"You ain't gave that boy a taste yet?"

"No, I haven't. Hey, hold on for a second."

Candice put the phone down and shut her bedroom door for privacy. She sat in her desk chair and rolled over to the window to look at the stars in a telescope her father bought her; the last gift he gave her prior to departing. She watched as an airliner darted across the dark navy sky.

"Ok, I'm back. So, when you do it aren't you scared the condom could break?"

"No, I am not scared. If it happens, it happens. That's life. Sometimes I don't use condoms though because my body doesn't like how it feels. I think I am allergic to latex or something. Besides, men move so much better when it is off."

"But what about STDs…or babies?"

"Babies taken care of. Mom had me on birth control since I was twelve. And STDs…well, like I said it's life. You can get hit by a car crossing the street, but does that mean you stop walking?"

"Yea, but I look both ways before crossing fool. I take precautions!"

"What I am saying is accidents happen regardless of precautions. You can't live life in a bubble scared to experience stuff. The guy who took my virginity gave me HPV, but it is not that serious. Doctor said it is pretty common. Then I got Chlamydia from this one guy, but in his defense he didn't know. The girl he was messing with was a slut-bucket and pulled the rubber off. But you know what, God is good because it could have been worse. I could have gotten HIV or something, so at least it was something that was curable."

Candice couldn't believe what she was hearing. *She is playing Russian roulette with her life. I would scold her about being stupid, but not like it is going to change anything. I am still curious about this sex thing. I don't understand if there are so many things that can go wrong…STDs, babies, or a guy just outright leaving you and telling all his boys…why do people keep doing it? Maybe I just don't understand how it feels or something.*

"So what does it feel like? I mean does it actually feel good?"

"All depends. Some guys know what they doing and others…well, their effort is cute. It is hard to describe how it feels. There is this pressure when it goes inside, and it is real intense. I like how it feels when they look me in the eye and knowing I am pleasing them. That turns me on."

Candice knew her friend had a quite a few guys on her resume so she figured she'd ask some additional questions to satisfy her curiosity.

"Who was the best?"

"The best? Hmmm, let me think. I have to say hands down it was Nathan. That boy was a straight freak. I mean girl, before he came over, I had to jump in the shower and wash from head to toe. I literally had to scrub my scalp because I had no idea where he was going to put his mouth. He was one of those brothas that you can't invite over after you put a perm in or he will sweat it out. He just got out not too long ago and this man is… wow, he is just so dang sexy. I call him migraine because the first time we had sex my head was just throbbing!"

"What he do time for?"

"Girl, it don't really matter. He was so fine. He got tatt's all over and he just has this sexy swagger about him. I am getting excited just thinking about him."

"You are so nasty! What is it about you Cammy and these bad boys? And yes it does matter. One of these days if you keep messing with those type dudes, they are going to go upside your head."

"I dunno girl, but I need a thug to tame me. And if it did go down and we got in a heated debate and it got physical, I think I could handle it."

"If that makes sense to you, then ok. That is not cool letting some guy thump on you. I hope you aren't letting these guys hit you!"

There was an awkward silence on the phone.

"Camille Renee Simon, please tell me you aren't letting these guys abuse you!"

"Next topic."

Candice was disturbed with the thought of her friend putting herself in harm's way, but she knew once Camille had her mind made up, she was going to do whatever she wanted to do.

"So like I was saying before, I wish you would stop blocking that boy and join the rest of the world. It really ain't as serious as you making it out to be. Don't be scurred."

Candice was always the type to think of the consequences of her actions. She was not scared of the physical pain of sex, but she did fear the ramifications of giving in and how her boyfriend would treat her afterwards. Would he like it? Would he stay around or leave? Would he tell everybody? How would that affect her future if she became pregnant? These were the thoughts that consumed her mind and in contrast left her baffled at her Camille's nonchalant approach to sex.

"I have a question Miss Simon. Why did you decide to give it up the first time?"

"I dunno girl, I guess it was curiosity. You hear about it on TV all the time and in songs. Seemed like everyone was doing it…not to mention I wanted to know why my mother was always choosing men over us. She acts like a nympho or something. When a guy comes around she is like that old throwback flick Coming to America…*bark like a dog, a big dog, woof.* Anytime a guy tells my mom to jump she does. So hell, I learned from the best. Did I ever tell you about the time I caught her in the laundry room on top of the washing machine with another guy between her legs?"

"That is a little bit too much info. You can keep that story. I don't need the visual next time I see her."

"That image has been burned in my brain, so you have to sit and listen. Yea girl, she was in there having sex with this guy. I don't know if it was the spin or rinse cycle, but I wasn't supposed to be home and went to wash my cheerleading outfit. Washing machines are supposed to clean dirt, but apparently it had no affect on her! Safe to say I bleached the top of that washing machine the next time I used it. Anyways, this was right when she met my stepfather, and my dad and her had separated for a couple months. She just doesn't know how I could just completely destroy her world if I wanted to. She forgets I been by her side while she was running through all these men. There is so much dirt I have on her, but I just don't say anything. When your mother is hypocritical and a liar, that makes you pretty much develop an F-it attitude."

"I don't know what I would do if I saw my moms getting her groove back like that. That is too much for my brain to handle. Is that why you just decided to have sex?"

"Yea, pretty much. I figured hell, there must be something to it since my mother about kills herself to get a man, so let me see what all this hype is about."

"I don't even know what to say about that one Cam." Candice was still trying to shake the image of her friend's mother on the washing machine with another man. "So who was the first guy?"

"The first person I was with was this guy named Daniel. He lived around the way from my real dad's house in Florida. Met him when I went to visit my pops one summer."

"How did it go down? Did he pressure you and you gave in? Details."

"No, he didn't pressure me at all and he didn't use any pickup lines. I actually chose him. I was young at the time and mad at my father for something. Maybe I thought he didn't fight hard enough for my mother? Or maybe I was just mad because I knew if I were him I wouldn't fight either. In any case, my feelings were hurt and I was just acting out. Prior to that trip, I already had my mind made up that I was going to lose it that summer."

"How do you just choose a guy and say yeah, that is who I am going to give it up to?"

"What kind of question is that Candy? We choose them just like they choose us."

Camille was becoming upset at Candice's disposition. She felt Candice was unfairly judging her yet she continued her story.

"So like I was saying, my dad was taking me to the store to get some new clothes or something. On our way there I looked out the window and like a movie, things moved in slow motion. This man was outside washing his truck with his shirt off and I almost melted in the seat. His body was so sexy it was not even funny. When we got back home, I made sure that I changed into something cute and walked down the street past where I saw him. Once I got to his block, I walked past his house and pretended I accidentally got lost in the neighborhood so I could ask him for directions."

"You are a hot mess! Other than him being fine, why him? What made you want to give it up?"

"It is hard to explain, but I was just going through some things and Danny understood me. We were like good friends and just hung out. He was a really cool guy and was respectful. I guess that is why I chose him. Not to mention all the other girls on the block wanted him, so it kind of made me feel good that I had him all to myself. He gave me all his time and undivided attention...well, except for when he had his kids."

"Kids? Plural?"

"Yes girl, kids. He was older than I was and had two children."

"What if you would have gotten pregnant?"

"What if?"

"What do you mean what if Cammy?"

"Just what I said...what if? If it happened then I would have dealt with it."

Candice was troubled her friend mentioned abortion in such a callus way.

"Wow, just that simple to you huh?"

"Hey, don't judge me until you have walked in my shoes Candice Naomi Richards," Camille stated as she had been waiting for the opportunity to recycle the sarcastic rebuttal. "You don't know what you would do until you get put into that position."

"Ain't nobody judging you girl. Why you all sensitive? Hold up, my mom is calling me again. I swear I never get a break. I will be right back."

Candice ran downstairs to see what her mother wanted then came back to her room.

"Ok, I'm back. Do you know she made me come down there to pour her a glass of water? I mean she was only feet from the kitchen. I know she been at work and all, but grown folk act like we they slaves or something. Like we aren't tired too."

"I know that is the truth. My mom basically makes me raise my younger siblings. I sometimes wonder what my compensation would be if I got paid. The other day I sat there and looked at her and thought to myself – so if I take care of the kids, wash the clothes and clean the house, exactly what is your purpose? I mean aside from being a head doctor for my step dad...and I don't know how she manages to do that as big as his stomach is. Seems like she would suffocate!"

"Cam, shut up!" Candice began laughing and tried to ignore the disagreements between herself and Camille. "Back to this Daniel guy. Did it hurt?"

"Yes, it hurt! I actually wasn't expecting it to hurt that bad to be honest, so the first time it was over pretty quick because I couldn't take the pain. It helped that he was very considerate and gentle with me. Are you scared? There is nothing to be scared about. I mean true, it hurts like hell the first time, but eventually you get used to it."

"It is not so much the pain I am worried about...it just doesn't feel right. The way Dre comes at me, it makes me feel cheap. It is hard to explain, but it is like we get close then I just feel bad and stop. He doesn't make me feel any better whining and crying about blue-balls and how I am leaving him."

"Girl, you need to learn how to please that boy. Shoot, beat him off or something. This market is competitive now. You are a sophomore and you got the finest senior at our school. Half those senior broads mad at you because they want to be with him and trust me...I am quite sure they would be willing to use their mouth or do whatever else he wants. That is not an ordinary man you got there...that is some prime realty. Not to mention, he may go to the league one day. Suck it up, literally, and you never know...you may get lucky and get a couple kids out the deal. Then you'd be set for life!"

"Girl is you crazy? I am not even made like that. I couldn't get pregnant just because I think a guy may take me somewhere."

"Women do it all the time, so don't feel bad. Heck if I was in that position, I would. Why not? You get the Rover, the big house, the black card, the perks."

"Perks if you consider the financial side, but I want more than that. I want a man to love me for me. I don't care about those material things because they have no substance. All those things you obtain mean nothing if you going to bed at night to an empty bed wondering where your man is, or worse...him bringing home some STD you can't get rid of!"

"You sound so old sometimes. I guess you and I just approach life different. You my girl, but shoot I am looking for a baller. Call me a gold-digger or whatever. I plan on going to college to better myself, but I'd much rather marry into wealth. I am tired of working and I need someone to captain-save-this-ho from this house before I go crazy."

"I guess I am old. I'll be that. I just don't get some things. I am not a gold-digger, female hustler or whatever you want to call it. I don't get screwing guys just because some money or a house. Then again I guess I am just different because I also don't get chicks referring to one another as ho's and b's. Makes no sense to me, but whatever. I guess I am old-fashioned."

"Well old-fashioned ho, listen to me closely. You need to take care of that man before someone else does!"

Candice allowed Camille's words to permeate as she sat in silence. Her first reaction was retaliation with a verbal onslaught of Camille's character, but she remained quiet believing there was some truth in her words. If she didn't do something and do it fast, Andre would be gone forever. At this point Candice was tired of talking, but before she could make up an excuse to get off the phone Camille prepared one for her.

"Candy, my mom is home and I don't feel like hearing her mouth. I am going to text you later."

"Ok, later girl."

Chapter IV

Women Fight Club

Rose was often teased by her siblings for her lead foot. To their dismay she didn't let their witticism discourage her from purchasing the sports car she always wanted. Oftentimes she'd drop the top on her convertible regardless of the weather; this day was no different. A bit nippy for most, Rose's blood was still lukewarm from her daily morning three mile jog. Without utilizing her turning signals, she managed to become one with her convertible as she darted in and out of traffic in route to her office while reflecting back on her journey.

In college, Rose was a beauty consultant for a major cosmetic company. During this time she learned how to identify potential clients, prepare promotional materials and come up with creative marketing ideas. Part of her job was to learn how to create a professional portfolio and put together client presentations. Her employer also taught her how to apply makeup correctly, however she felt the products she sold could be improved so after a year she stepped away from the company. Utilizing her background in chemistry, she jotted down several ideas for creating makeup products that eliminated synthetic dyes, fragrances and preservatives. She drew inspiration from Ancient Egyptian women and continued to study and experiment with emulsions, surfactants, emollients, moisturizers, waxes, thickeners and various active ingredients. Rose became frustrated because she couldn't configure the formula to her liking, but she continued to get compliments on her radiant glow when she experimented on herself.

During her tenure at college, she auditioned for a walk-on role for an indy film shooting near campus. Overhearing a conversation on set she interjected and ended up filling in for a sick makeup artist, thus her resume began. Rose used this opportunity to land a part-time professional makeup artist position for a local television network. Throughout her remaining years of college, she also did freelance work for hair and beauty shows, fashion shows, as well as weddings and general consulting to family and friends. This period of time allowed her to learn another aspect of the cosmetic business, as well as develop the social skills she would need later in her career.

After graduation her dream was deferred due to life choices and obligations, however Rose cloaked it near her heart. She immersed her time reading books about millionaires and successful women entrepreneurs. Rose believed that money invested in her well-being was an invaluable return, so aside from researching cosmetic trends she purchased books that ministered to her health, mind, body and spirit. Now as an adult, if the opportunity presented itself again, she was determined to take full advantage. Tired of allowing life to dictate its course, she grew weary of waiting for something to fall into her lap and allowed ambition to pave her way.

Rose reinvented herself and became a risk-taker, yet savvy business woman. After consulting several dermatologists, she saw an early trend in mineral makeup and finalized her formula. Shortly thereafter she purchased a patent and grew her business from her home using a cheap Dell computer her ex-husband left and the garage as storage for her product. She dedicated a minimum of fourteen hours a day to her vision, operating around the clock until she worked a huge distribution deal with a major player. Due to her social networking skills and willingness to ask questions, she forged many business relationships. The assistance of a venture capitalist propelled the mineral makeup company forward, but Rose was never complacent. She continued to analyze and research the market and developed an at-home airbrush unit which gave women the ability to create the same soft even finish that professional makeup artists use in Hollywood. As products continued to be created, Rozi Cosmetics testimonials grew exponentially and developed a reputation for manufacturing makeup that makes your skin look flawless, youthful and radiant.

As business grew, Rose negotiated a deal with a small, yet reputable clothing company on the verge of filing bankruptcy to share their offsite warehouse in exchange for a lump sum amount. The deal was risky and ate a considerable chunk of Rose's capital, but she felt it would position her for success. She discerned their desperation and was elated when they took the deal; a deal that paid off as she was able to acquire their business within eight months.

The family that owned the company had been in the business for twenty years and the stress played a toll on their health. When Rose made an offer to purchase they accepted without any hesitation. The family took the money and retired in northern Texas while Rose added their clothing and accessories line to Rozi Cosmetics. The additional products complimented the current company portfolio of her popular mineral foundation products and fashionable accessories such as lipsticks, mascaras and lip glosses. There were also very favorable responses to her new line of skin care products which included facial cleaners, sun screens and acne treatments.

The Rozi brand was building momentum. Rose used various marketing channels for her products including wholesale customers, boutiques, spas and online shopping; a medium which allowed for international distribution. In addition to the warehouse and company acquisition, Rose was able to purchase an office building. Rozi Cosmetics headquarters consisted of a small group of individuals, therefore there was additional occupancy in the building. Rose decided to lease the additional office space to several tenants including a youth ministry, an insurance company and an advertising design firm.

With her fingers firmly gripping the wheel, Rose sharply turned into parking lot without spilling any of her soy protein infused fruit smoothie, which sat patiently in the cup holder. She pulled into her designated parking space two inches from the cement pillar, folded her sunglasses, and sighed as she anticipated the busy day ahead. Walking down the landscaped pathway, she reflected the success of the business she built and thanked God for where she was at that moment.

As she walked through the automatic sliding door approaching her opulently furnished office, she was acknowledged by a mixture of counterfeit and sincere salutations. Rose's employees were like family, but at times there was tension and drama in the office. Aside from these occasional fallouts, the staff at Rozi Cosmetics became an extremely close-knit, loyal team. They all had the utmost respect for Rose due to her relentless work ethic, diligence, and the generous benefits package she offered. Rose's investment into her employees showed in the value they placed in their work. As a result of their efficiency, last year this fifth-year company recorded revenue over $13.5 million, which was a huge accomplishment to Rose as it exceeded her expectations. Headquartered on the outskirts of her hometown, the main office consisted of forty-five employees with only seven of them being men.

Due to personal reasons Evelyn, one of Rose's favorite employees and best accountant, had to resign. Initially Rose didn't replace her position in hopes that she would return, but after a few mishaps and backed up work she decided to hire a temp. It worked out that Rose's old college roommate had started her own recruiting company. Over the years the two stayed in touch via e-mail and occasional calls.

"Premier Recruiting, this is Susan Meyers. How can I be of assistance to you?"

"Hey girl, look at you sounding all important. How have you been?"

"Rose, is that you? Hey, what a surprise. Glad to hear your voice. How have you been doing?"

"Not too bad Mrs. Meyers. Business is good, so I can't complain. So how have you been? How's your headhunter company coming along? How's your family?"

"Well you know the four kids keep me on my toes, but other than that life is good. The business is coming along. Like with any business, you have ups and downs…then there are so many trends, the economy… hey, boring stuff, right?"

"Wait, back up. Four? I thought you only had three children. Did you have another?"

"No, I include my husband on the list because he is like raising a child."

Rose smiled to express her amusement.

"To what do I owe the pleasure of this call Ms. Hughes?"

"I need a favor from you."

"Sure, anything. What do you need girl?" Susan inquired.

"Last month one of my best accountants left. Long story, but her teenage son got his little girlfriend pregnant and I guess her mother kicked her out. So Evelyn, my old accountant, basically moved the girl in and is helping to raise her granddaughter so the kids can finish high school. I offered her a position to work from home part time, but she had so much on her plate she just needed to step aside from the workplace to get her family in order."

"I could only imagine. Where do I fall into play? I assume you need a replacement?"

"Exactly. I have met some crazy candidates via Monster, and I just don't feel comfortable with Craig's List just yet. With the amount of things we have coming up, I don't have the time to waste. My HR lady who usually does the hiring has been out for three weeks due to back surgery, so I need someone to filter out people before they get to me. If I could just get a temp for now, that would help out tremendously. Then maybe if it works out after six months they could go perm. I won't have them necessarily digging into the financials, but I have a lot of other tasks for them. It is imperative that they are bright and have accounting experience."

"Rose, it is funny you say that. I have the perfect person. I know this girl personally. She comes from a good family that used to attend my church. Graduated about a year or two ago and she is very bright. Recently relocated to your area. Now this is just a suggestion, but if possible I'd hire her as an intern. Trust me, you don't want talent like this to get away from you."

"At this point, I will definitely consider it. Hey, I don't want to take too much more of your time, so I will have my assistant contact you with the posting, and then we can take it from there."

"Great! I will be looking for it. Hey, it was good hearing from you Rosie. We have to do lunch sometime and catch up."

"Sounds like a plan. Take care Susie!"

* * *

"Rose, we have Natalie Myles here to see you."

"Send her in."

Natalie entered and immediately gave Rose a good impression. She was well dressed in a two-piece cream suit skirt with Jimmy Choo heels and a matching handbag; accented by a Tag Heuer diamond encrusted watch and white gold crystal drop earrings. Rose really admired her style as she was sharp as a tack, yet very business professional.

"Hi, I'm Rose as you may already know. And you must be…"

"Natalie. Natalie Myles. Nice to finally meet you Miss Hughes. I have heard so many good things about you and the company."

"Nice to meet you too. And may I say, girl, those shoes are to die for. My goodness those are bad!"

"Thank you! Actually, my mother bought them for my birthday."

"Sometimes moms have to let us know they still have it, huh?"

Rose felt herself getting off track thinking about her late mother. Something about this girl made her feel comfortable. She tried to fight through her biases, but had a feeling she would hire Natalie. The job was hers to lose, as long as she didn't say anything stupid.

"So tell me a little about yourself. Susie speaks highly of you. I see here you graduated from the University of Southern California. My brother-in-law is a huge USC fan. What brought you east?"

Natalie sighed regretting her inability to tell a lie and allowed her response to be transparent and truthful.

"Sad to say, but it was a man. It ended between us, but I just fell in love with the area and couldn't go back. Plus the cost of living is so high in California."

"I can understand. Don't be hard on yourself. Been there done that before, regarding the man, and had the rug snatched right from under my feet."

"Amen girl." Natalie replied.

"With your background, why would you want to work here? I am quite sure most of these major corporations are chomping at the bit to get someone in their office like you. Why would you pass up possible internships with them to take a temp job with us?"

"Well Miss Hughes…"

"Please, call me Rose."

"Rose, before Susan ever told me about this opportunity I knew who you were. I have read your story numerous times before and have followed your company growth. I aspire to be like you and feel that if I work in an environment where I have such respect for my employer, I'd be prone to work harder. I also feel you would be a good mentor to siphon from, and possibly after a probation period, if I prove myself maybe there may be an opening in the company for me."

Rose continued to be impressed by Natalie. Interviews are usually filtered through Rozi's HR person, but she had called in sick. As fate would have it Natalie skipped a step in the interview process and was able to speak with Rose directly. She continued to ask a series of standard questions, along with specific ones about business operations. After a few minutes passed, Rose closed the folder she had open which contained Natalie's application and resume.

"Natalie, I am not going to beat around the bush. I like you and I think you would be a good fit here. Susie suggested I hire you as an intern versus a temp, but I feel there is no experience like just jumping in and getting your feet wet. When I tried to build this company, there were some investors willing to take a chance on me because they believed in me. I like your style and ambition, and this office could definitely use someone like you. I would like to offer you a position…pending your background investigation of course. However, there is one stipulation. I won't be hiring for an intern position…I would like to hire you as a perm."

"Oh my goodness. Are you serious?"

"Yes I am. You have something in you, and I see bright things in your future."

Natalie began to cry.

"I am sorry. This is so unprofessional. You probably think I am a looney toon for crying."

"No girl, you are fine. Everything ok?"

"Yes," Natalie replied as she blotted her eyes dry. "I don't want to lay all my problems on you. Let's just say I came out here looking for one thing and after that fell apart it has just been one bad thing after another. This has been the best news I've heard since I been here."

"I know you will like it here at Rozi Cosmetics. Of course there are formalities…background, forms to fill out, acceptance letter, etcetera, but if you want to become part of our family we welcome you with open arms."

After those words slipped from Rose's mouth, she thought about the term *family* and felt a retraction brewing.

"Let me rephrase and say a family with issues. You know how catty it can get in an office full of females, but when it is all said and done, we all have love for each other. I try to create a family atmosphere. We work hard and play harder…when we're not fighting," Rose stated in a cynical tone.

"I think I can hold my own Rose."

"I believe you can, otherwise I wouldn't have hired you."

"Thank you for this opportunity! I promise I won't disappoint."

Rose escorted Natalie out of her office and sat down at her desk fully content with her decision.

* * *

Natalie stepped right in, and within a few short weeks, helped the accounting team operate more efficiently. For the first time in months Evelyn's absence was not felt. Rose admired Natalie's perseverance, however there was a slight problem; the women in the office were giving her a hard time. Rose anticipated this may be a problem as Natalie was a foxy young lady who dressed everyday with a style most women would envy. Her clothing was not necessarily expensive, but she had a way of putting outfits together in a classy manner and carried herself well. Aside from her appearance, Natalie's ambition propelled her in being proactive with work and bringing new concepts and ideas to the table. Of course this was not popular with senior employees as they often were resistant to change.

One day Rose was on a call with one of her vendors when she heard two women screaming at one another. She politely asked if she could return the call and shuffled out her office to detect the turbulence.

"I have never done anything to you. Listen to me closely, I worked too hard to let someone take from me. On everything I love, you will make the Westside come out of me if you ever disrespect me like that again!" Natalie said while pointing her finger at her co-worker Angie.

"Well if you learn how to wear clothes that fit right, then you wouldn't have to worry about tripping over my purse!"

"You kicked your purse out in the aisle on purpose you old hag. I am not stupid. You have been acting foul towards me ever since I started working here, and I never did anything to you!"

"Look here you little young, two-bit trick…"

"Ladies!" Rose shouted. "This is a place of business. What is wrong with you?"

"Rose, you need to get this little girl. She had the nerve to…"

"Angie! I don't even want to hear it. We had this conversation before. Natalie…in my office right now!"

Rose stood and watched as Natalie put her shoes back on then walked into the office. She followed behind Natalie and then slammed the door.

"Needless to say I am very disappointed. What got into you?"

"Rose, I am so sorry, but she was asking for it. She has been provoking me ever since I started working here. She throws my pens away, disconnects my keyboard, swaps my chair…and that is just what I can remember off the top of my head. At first I let it slide, but that petty crap gets to you after a while. When you confront her, she just lies and denies she did anything. I don't know what her problem is, but as soon as she saw me, since day one, she made up in her mind that she didn't like me… and I never said anything to warrant her disdain."

"Nat, Angie is a nice person when you get to know her, but she just has some personal issues that she has been dealing with."

"That is no excuse for her acting like a fool. Just because you are bitter about something in your life doesn't give you the right to lash out at others. I know I am young, but there are certain things I will not stand for. I will not let anyone disrespect me!"

Rose looked at Natalie breathing hard trying to calm down, and burst into laughter.

"I am sorry, I shouldn't laugh. You say you were going to take it back to Cali, huh? How exactly are Westside beat-downs performed again? Do you pick up objects, or is it just fisticuffs?"

Natalie reluctantly cracked a grin.

"It's not funny. That woman is lucky she didn't get hurt. Lord knows if she would have stepped foot around that table, it would have been over. I had already took my earrings off, so I was ready."

"Nat, you are a spunky little thing. I like that in you because it reminds me of me at your age. Listen, don't let Angie get to you. She really is a good person once you get to know her, but it is just this wall she puts up. Don't worry about her. If you have a problem with her, just shoot me an e-mail and I will handle it without making a big commotion."

"Thanks Rose. Just let your girl know to watch herself!"

"You warmed the office up today so cool off and take the rest of the day off. I'm sure you could use the time and you have us way ahead of schedule."

Natalie was still upset, but accepted the offer and took the time off.

"Ok. I will see you tomorrow then."

"See ya Nat…I mean Westside."

Natalie smirked. As she walked out, Rose surveyed the office through her door to ensure there were no additional casualties. She made eye contact with Angie and gestured her hand to signal a request for her presence. Angie rolled her eyes as Natalie walked past her and entered the office.

"Shut the door behind you."

Angie shut the door, and immediately went into her spiel.

"Rose, that girl is out of control. You need to do something about her. I didn't even do anything. She tripped over my purse and thought that I…"

"Girl, don't sit here and lie to me. What is wrong with you? You almost have kids her age. Why you picking with her?"

"Rose, I am telling you she got issues!"

"Angie, how long have we known each other? What twelve years? I knew you before this business or anything…we go way back. Remember,

I know you girl. She reminds you of her, huh?"

"I don't have the faintest idea what you are talking about."

"I thought this may be a problem, but I figured you'd be grown up about this and able to handle it. Ang, it is me girl."

"Like I said, I don't know what you are talking about, honestly. I mean, if you mean that little young whore that Rodney picked up from high school, got pregnant and left me for…then yes she does favor her a little."

"Girl, you can't do that. Did you even think about the repercussions at all? Do you know what kind of mess I would have had on my hands if she actually tripped over that purse? It could have been a freak accident where she hit her head on the side of the desk. Or worse…you two could have gotten into a brawl and harmed others."

"Oh, you don't have to worry about that. That young broad better recognize. While she sitting there pulling out her earrings, I'd be whaling on her!"

"You are missing my entire point. What I am saying is you are too old to be acting like that. That is stuff females do in high school…pick fights with girls just because. You are supposed to be older…wiser. You have to think!"

Rose paused then attempted to take the edge off the conversation.

"Like the other Rodney…can't we all just get along?"

Angie wanted to stay upset, therefore she clinched her jaw in an attempt to conceal any impression of a smile which could sneak through.

"You always have jokes Rose, but the problem is…they usually aren't funny."

"Yea and it wouldn't have been funny if that young girl got a hold of that horrible weave that you have in right now."

Angie used her hand to pat her weave, self-conscious that her tracks were showing.

"Seriously Ang, listen to me. We go way back and I love you, but you have to stall that girl out. She has been the best thing since Evelyn left. Natalie is getting things together that, quite frankly, your team has been dropping the ball on. I understand you have a grasp on our corporate culture, but you are stuck in your ways and she is approaching this with fresh new technology and ideas. She is proactive with learning new software, and overall is good for this company."

"It is bigger than that…than just not liking her for her looks. These young girls think because they are pretty, they can get whatever they want. Men, jobs, they just get favor everywhere. I can't believe that you, my homegirl, promoted her over me!"

"First of all get your facts straight. I didn't promote her over you. You are still a senior. I hired her as an Accountant I but gave her a slight salary increase based on merit. Her title did not change, but she put in the effort and did more work in three short weeks than you did all year."

"Whatever girl. I guess so."

"As long as you've known me I have been a straight shooter, so listen to me good. This is my livelihood. I don't owe anything to anyone. There are no alliances here…everything is based on work performance. I love you like a sister, but I am not beyond firing anybody. I am not going to let something like this cause a divide in my company that I soiled so hard to build. I absolutely cannot have a liability working here. You can either get it together, or you will be walking out that door with a pink slip of paper. Do I make myself clear?"

"Is it like that?"

"Yes, it is like that! Angie, I love you, but you got to get your personal life in order. You need to let that hate go that you have towards him. It is bleeding into other areas of your life. Why do you let that man steal your joy? It has been how many years now? You need to be delivered from him."

Angie sniffed sloppily as she tried to swallow her tears and keep her composure. One look in her concerned friend's eyes and tears leapt from her face.

"It is so hard Rosie. You don't know how it feels to have a man break your heart like that."

"I don't know? Are you serious? Do you know how much…"

"I didn't mean it like that. I am just saying there is a lot more to the story than I let people know. I was told that I was not going to be able to have any more children. I love my two girls dearly, but I always wanted a son. When Rodney left me, earlier that morning I discovered I was pregnant. I was so elated because I thought God was answering my prayers for a son. After all, Rodney has all boys. I went to grab my phone to call him and realized I accidentally had his cellular because we purchased the same brand. I respected his privacy and didn't look in his call logs or anything…even though I wanted to. On my way home I felt it vibrate, and when I checked it, it was a text message from some chick saying all kinds of stuff she wanted to do with her mouth and whipped cream. How she was going to do this and that and how she liked how he treated her to dinner…in bed. I was so sick that things became hazy and I honestly don't remember how I got home, but what I do remember is I lost the baby. What made it so bad is I knew this girl Rodney left me for. My older sister used to baby-sit her. Small world, huh?"

Rose was taken back by her story and tried to show support for her friend, yet still keep it professional because of the setting. She had plenty of time to console her after work, and wanted to avoid a situation of favoritism. Rose just made her company attend a mandatory ethics training course where one of the points covered was conflict of interest, so she found it ironic she now sat trying to diffuse bickering between a long time friend and employee.

"Ang, that is rough. The girl was wrong, Rodney was wrong. Believe me, I am not taking up for them. All I am saying is Natalie is not her. I don't care if she makes faces like her, is built like her, or whatever the reason…there is no reason for you to mistreat her, or any other female for that matter. And this is not coming from her or your little spat today…I have been sitting back watching this with my own eyes."

Angie sat in silence.

"You have to get this under control. Here and beyond these walls. Natalie is not a threat to you and your life, relationships, or anything else so stop approaching her in that manner. That girl didn't do anything or say anything to you…all she did was breathe the same air and you formulated this hate campaign and started attacking her. No woman deserves to be treated bad just because she is cute, or reminds you of someone, or you feel she is a threat. That is ridiculous!"

"But what about when she…"

"Look, I am not going round and round on this issue. This is your verbal warning. Get it together girl. Please don't make me have to do this again, do you understand?"

"Understood."

Rose felt bad her friend was hurting, yet she had a business to operate. She opened her desk drawer and rummaged through it until she located a gift certificate to a local spa she didn't have time to use.

"Ang take the rest of the day off and get yourself together. I want you to leave here and use this card and go pamper yourself today. Get a nice lunch, a massage, and your nails done…my treat. The only thing I ask in return is for you to relax."

Angie nodded and mouthed the words "thank you" without audibly speaking a word. She cleaned the remaining fluids from her face with a coffee napkin, walked out and secured the door as she exited. Rose pulled her hair behind her head and sighed deeply. *Whew. I need to go workout or something. These heifers are driving me crazy today!*

She paged her admin assistant into the office who entered with pen and notepad in hand.

"I think there is too much tension in this office. We all need a little vacation. I want you to register us for The Show. This year I want to take the entire staff with me. I think it is important for us all to see innovative makeup techniques and stay on the edge of new trends. Airline, hotel, expense it all."

Her assistant wrote diligently while enthusiasm dominated her facial expression. The International Makeup Artist Trade Show, or "The Show" to those in the industry, was an event Rose looked forward to each year. This was the first time Rose decided to take the entire team.

As Rose walked towards the door, she stopped and turned back as a brief epiphany surfaced.

"While you are at it, throw in one additional ticket. I think I may take my niece this year. Make it two. Maybe I may just give a ticket away."

Rose slid her duffle bag over her shoulder.

"I am leaving to go to the gym. I need you to cancel and reschedule all my afternoon appointments. I also need you to be my eyes for me when I am gone. Can you handle all that?"

"Sure bet."

"I have my Blackberry on me. Things should settle down in the office for the rest of the day, but if anything happens give me a call. After I workout I will be working from my home office this evening, so keep me posted if anything comes up."

"Will do."

Rose walked to her car murmuring under her breath.

"I can't believe I am…well, my age, and women my age are still fighting. This is ridiculous! Sometimes it feels like we are still in high school."

Rose tossed her bag into the passenger side and plopped down on her butter cream leather seats. With one hand she recklessly slid her sunglasses on, popped the clutch on her sports car and peeled out the parking lot.

Chapter V

A Grown Up Love

A pearl white Infiniti Qx56 limousine pulled up in front of Candice's home and sat patiently awaiting her arrival.

"Candy, it's here."

"Ok Mommy, give me a second."

Lisa opened the front door and let Andre in.

"You look nice today Mr. Abbott."

"Thanks Miss Richards."

Andre stood in the foyer and watched as his date clutched her dress above her knees and slowly walked down the stairs. Candice wore a purple dress which coordinated with Andre's tie and cummerbund.

"Whoa!" Andre responded as his eyes surveyed his girlfriend.

Candice was happy Andre found her attractive. She began to blush as he looked into her eyes and slid her corsage on her wrist. Candice tried to be elegant while pinning on his boutonnière, but she pricked him twice. Frustrated, she relieved her mother from her picture taking responsibility and waved her over for assistance.

Shortly after the needle poking incident, a few photos were taken in and outside of the home, then it was time for the young couple to leave. Andre opened the door to the limo, and Candice crawled across the leather seats. She was greeted by two of Andre's friends along with their girlfriends. The girlfriends attempted to speak, but Candice could sense their insincerity. The couples had decided to eat dinner prior to the prom so they went to Rico Caffini's, a popular Italian restaurant right outside of town.

Dinner was delicious and the environment was relaxed, yet Candice felt uncomfortable. Her desire was to have an intimate dinner alone with Andre versus being across the table from girls with ill intentions. Most of the young women barely ate any food fearing they would spill something and ruin their dresses. In contrast, the young men all had their coats draped over the back of the seats while devouring their food and licking their fingers.

Eventually dinner was complete and the group of teens headed towards the prom. Candice laughed and danced, but in the back of her mind she wondered what the night held in store for her. She knew her boyfriend wanted to have sex, and wrestled back and forth with the idea to give into his demands. She rationalized submitting her virginity to him as prom night was the textbook romantic event for teens to hook-up. It was close to end of the school year, everyone was dressed up, many had hotels and most had extended curfews.

After a couple hours had crept by, the sweat-drenched couple sat at a table to drink some punch.

"Baby, I have something special planned for us. Let's get out of here. I have my car waiting outside."

Candice was reluctant, but nodded her head yes as she caught the gleam shooting from Andre's eyes. She sat in the car and looked out the window anticipating what was to come. Candice didn't want to disappoint him, so periodically she would give a faint smile to ensure she wouldn't back out this time. Andre held her hand with excitement as he maneuvered through traffic until he reached a popular hotel chain. Candice had a flashback because the last time she visited this hotel it was a family vacation and her parents were happily married, or so she thought.

The two pulled into the hotel and Andre turned the car off. He reached over and passionately kissed his girlfriend. Candice knew what was expected from her but still acted surprised.

"What's this about?"

"Well, you said you didn't feel comfortable in my pop's house, so I figured I'd get us a nice romantic room to set the mood."

Candice sat in the car while Andre checked in. She was still apprehensive but felt this was a better environment than his musty smelling bachelor-pad-esce home. Andre returned with the room key, grabbed her hand, and escorted her to the $55 suite with free HBO. She entered the room and sat on the edge of the bed awaiting instruction.

"Take your clothes off and get comfortable. I will be right back."

Candice went to the bathroom and removed her clothes. She stared at herself in the mirror while adjusting her hair. *What am I doing here? I don't want to do this. But if I don't then he will leave me.*

She stripped down to her sexy bra and panties, which she purchased for this occasion, and stared at her muscular abdomen as she sighed heavily. Time elapsed while Candice was standing in front of the mirror. Her daydream was halted when she heard the latch mechanism click as the hotel door opened.

"Baby, I am back. Come to daddy. You don't know how long I been waiting for this."

After a few seconds of hesitation, the door flung open. Candice stood with her bra, panties, and high heels on, highlighted by the illumination from the bathroom lights.

"My, my, my!" Andre began to bite his bottom lip. "I may let one go before I get to you looking like that."

She walked over to her boyfriend and lustfully kissed him like he was in the military leaving to go to war, as his hands roamed her body and delicately tried to seduce her. She loved the way his touch felt, and her body temperature began to rise.

"I got us some wine. Just lie down and let me set the mood."

Andre walked over to a bag sitting on the chair and pulled out some candles. He proceeded to light the candles, then poured Candice a glass of Zinfandel; the only cheap wine he could purchase without a fake ID. As he walked over to her, she sat upright in the bed with the blanket wrapped around her torso.

"Thank you baby!"

Candice took a sip as she watched her boyfriend strip tease until he was completely naked. She saw men naked before on television but never in person. *Ugh, is it supposed to look like that? Why is it two different colors? And why is he standing there all cocky?*

Andre crawled in the bed with Candice and lay on top of her. He began kissing her neck and continued down her body until he reached her panties again. He took both of his fingers, dug them under the elastic of her panties, and tugged to pull them off.

"Slow down baby. We have time. Don't rush."

"Sorry Candy. You are just so sexy, and I want you right now!"

"Come here and kiss me Dre."

Andre began to kiss Candice as his fingers ran down her body and snuck under her panties again. Candice knew what was happening and felt scared, yet curious at the same time. Andre took his fingers and rubbed them inside of her while letting out a moan to show his excitement. Candice arched her back as she felt uneasy, then grabbed his wrist.

"Hold up baby…chill for a second."

"Come on Candy. I will be gentle. I promise it won't hurt. How about I just put half of it in? You know, just until you get used to it."

"Andre, I said stop. This is just not right."

Andre became aggravated.

"Why did you let me take all my clothes off if you knew we weren't going to do anything? Huh? Tell me Candy! This is bull. I did all this for you, and this is how you repay me?"

"Oh, so I owe you now?" Candice's feelings were hurt so her defense mechanism kicked in.

"Candy, you know what I mean. I have been real patient with you. You can't do this to me. Not now," Andre aggressively pleaded.

"I'm not doing anything to you. I just don't want my first time to be like this."

"Look baby, you have to understand men. You can't do all this…get half naked, smell all good, kiss on me like this, then just stop. It physically hurts us."

Andre took Candice's hand and placed it on his genitals.

"We don't have to do it right now. I respect you wanting to keep your virginity, so why don't you just kiss it for me? I'll teach you what to do."

Candice was taken back by how forward Andre was. *I know girls at school talk about how fun it is and how guys reactions are, but that just seems so nasty to me. Look at that thing. He wants me to put my mouth on that? That is disgusting. And I am really not trying to have that stuff in my mouth.*

"Dre, take me home."

Andre pushed Candice away and aggressively put his clothes back on; ripping two buttons off his shirt in the process. In a fit of rage, Andre punched the nearby table hard enough for his keys, wine, and other items to fall onto the floor. Candice was scared at his reaction but glad she made the decision to stop and was not going to fold.

"Baby, don't be like that."

"You are trippin'! I go out of my way to try to please you. You never do the same! This relationship is one way. All I do is give, give, and give… and all you do is take. I get nothing in return. The hell with you Candice!"

"The hell with me? So if I don't jump and do everything you tell me to do, then you done with me, huh? Sorry, but I just don't throw tail around like that! I love you, but I told you that I am not ready. My mom is already stressed, and I want to go to college. I am not trying to get pregnant or catch some STD."

"STD? What are you trying to say?"

"I am trying to say that you have messed with some skanks in the past, and there is no telling what diseases are festering up inside you."

Candice did not mean to come across disrespectful, but she was upset with his ultimatum, and figured if she started an argument she could kill the mood and have Andre take her home immediately. Worst case scenario, her back up plan was to ask him to get something out of the car, then lock him out of the hotel and call her uncle to come pick her up.

"I can't believe you said that to me. If I am that much of a ho, then why are you with me Candice? Why even bother? I might as well just go out and screw everyone who throws themselves at me!"

"Well maybe you should. Just make sure you take me home first."

Andre was extremely upset, yet he had a respect for Candice that he never felt towards any other female, including his mother. He sat in the chair until Candice got dressed, then stormed out the hotel, slamming the door so hard the echo filled the hallway. Candice was quiet the entire ride home. Soon as she stepped out the car, Andre's disgust provoked him to accelerate and drive off with the door still open. The door almost hit Candice and his behavior induced her to cry. She stood there for a second in a daze astonished at how cold he treated her. Listening to his tires screech as he turned the corner, she attempted to gather her composure, then wiped her tears before walking into the house.

* * *

A few weeks had passed and the dispute between Candice and Andre blew over. A persistent string of *I'm sorry* letters and text messages, bad poetry read aloud in public and a variety of flowers eventually broke Candice's will and she forgave him.

Candice had nothing planned for the weekend, so she assumed she'd be spending it at home; that was until she received a call from her boyfriend. Seeing his name show up on the caller ID of her cell phone made her feel warm inside. She dedicated a custom ring tone in his honor and oftentimes found herself texting him random messages throughout the day.

"Hey Dre."

"Hey girl, what you doing?"

"Nothing. Just about to read a magazine and look at some new shoes. What you doing?"

"Just thinking about you. So what do you have planned today?"

"Nothing. Why, what's up?"

"I had something special planned for my Candy-cane."

Candice rarely grew tired of his shameless, on-the-fly nicknames.

"Special, huh? What is it?"

"I can't tell you right now. Just put on something really nice. I will come pick you up at two-thirty."

Candice was enthusiastic about her date and thought maybe Andre had truly prepared something romantic for her. She ransacked her closet until she found a cute sundress that her mother picked out during their last shopping outing. Candice wanted to look good for her man so she stood in front of the mirror holding her dress, rotating occasionally while matching various accessories. Once she found the right combination of jewelry and sandals, she took a shower, put on her "smell goods" as she referred to them, then went downstairs to await Andre's arrival. It made her feel grown-up going on dates.

Andre arrived and escorted his date to his powder blue 1968 Chevy Impala, a vehicle he inherited from his deceased grandfather. He frequently boasted of plans he had to trick out the classic vehicle. Everything was preordained from the fresh coat of matador red exterior paint, to the black leather custom bucket seats with his name embroidered in the headrest. His father pleaded for classic restoration, but Andre was determined to turn it into a lowrider and install 100-spoke custom painted wire wheels to match the interior.

Candice thought it was cute how he talked about his vehicle, but didn't know anything about muscle cars or the repairs and customizations he mentioned. She recognized the visible signs his ride was deteriorating such as the plethora of rust spots, and it was apparent immediate repair was needed due to the acoustics emitted from the engine, but that was irrelevant as Candice wasn't superficial by any means. Despite his automobile woes, she thoroughly relished in the attention she received and enjoyed getting away to spending time alone with Andre.

"So, where are you taking me?"

"Be patient baby. I promise you will like it."

The couple drove throughout the city until they arrived at the Blue Gill Lake.

"What's this all about?" Candice asked in her detective tone searching for clues.

Andre smirked, but didn't respond. He pulled into the parking space, opened the passenger door and extended his forearm to escort his girlfriend out of the car. As she adjusted her dress, he shut the door and went to his trunk to retrieve what appeared to be a small cooler and a picnic blanket. Andre grabbed Candice's hand and walked her over to a big oak tree next to the lake. He delicately laid the blanket on the ground and invited Candice to sit using hand gestures.

Candice's detective investigation came to a halt as she realized what was going on. She wished she didn't solve the case so promptly and prayed that she made a mistake in her analysis. Reluctant in her stance and holding on to a shimmer of hope this date would turn for the better, she eventually seated herself on the picnic blanket. As she inspected it, she noticed a few faded teddy bears and realized it was Andre's old baby blanket. Candice tried to digest her surroundings, but no matter what spin she put on the scenario, romance was not present. The day was hot and sticky even nestled in the shadow within a congregation of trees. The location of their picnic was damp and reeked of lake water and weeds. Candice could have enjoyed herself under different circumstances, but due to his instructions to dress up she didn't feel comfortable and was quite irritated. As Andre stared attempting to serenade his princess, he opened the cooler and pulled out two Lunchables and two sodas.

At this point, Candice's thoughts began to scamper faster than she runs the 200. *Aw hecks naw! I know he didn't have me dress up looking all cute to come down to this lake and eat some crackers. Be nice Candice…at least he tried. No… you know what, why be nice? This is ridiculous. Not that I mind coming to the lake, but don't tell me to dress up nice to come to this crap. And this lake is disgusting at that. Look at all the moss and mosquitoes swarming. Ugh!*

"I thought it would be nice if we had a little picnic. Here you go, this is for you."

Andre handed the cracker, cheese and meat container over to Candice, and as she reached to accept it, an ant fell from the tree on her arm. She frantically shook her arm until the ant was launched into the grass.

"Nut un. Baby, umm…I love you, but this ain't working. We need to go!"

"Go where Candy?"

"Umm, somewhere nice…like you promised. Let's just drive around. Heck, we can eat these in the car."

Andre's feelings were hurt that Candice didn't appreciate his gesture, but in the back of his mind he had an ulterior motive. He thought the lake scenery would be a better environment to convince his girlfriend into having sex versus his musty house or a cheap hotel. While he walked back to the car, he didn't assist Candice in. She stood there waiting for him and watched as he walked to the trunk, threw the cooler in, slammed the trunk, then entered the driver's seat. Candice paused to prevent from saying something stupid, then entered the vehicle.

"Look Hulk, we all know you strong and everything and have to show you are a manly man, but that is stupid to break your trunk lock because you mad. Stop throwing a tantrum!"

"It is bigger than that Candy. Here I am trying to plan a romantic day for you. Figured we'd watch the sun go down and make love by the moonlight which shimmers off the lake. It really is pretty, you just are so stubborn sometimes that you won't even give things a chance."

Candice looked at Andre, then burst into laughter.

"Oh, I am sorry. You were serious, huh? I am sorry, start over again. I will be serious."

Andre started the car, threw it into drive then peeled off. Halfway down the road, he thought about the events that just transpired and began chuckling. This snowballed into contagious laughter which seized Candice as well. They joked around and ended up going to an electronics store so Andre could look for a new car radio. After gawking at the new gadgets, Andre let the memory of his failed attempt at the lake slip his mind. They drove to a local pizza buffet, enjoyed each other's company, then he took Candice home.

When they arrived back home, the two hopped out of the car still stuffed from pizza. Candice sat on the hood, while Andre leaned against the garage door. She felt this was as good a time as any to engage in conversation.

"Tell me Dre, what do you want to do with your life?"

"I don't know really. Outside of school, probably try to make it in the NFL. If that doesn't work, I'd do what I have to do to make money, then take the loot I save and drop it into a laundromat or car wash. You know I've been watching those real estate infomercials and reading up on the real estate game. Take profits from my other businesses and get a few houses in rundown neighborhoods, do minor repairs, then flip 'em. Maybe keep a couple on the side as rental properties. Do that for a while until the money rolls in, then take that money and open a barbershop and rim shop. I got a ton of ideas, but at least if football don't pan out I have a backup plan, unlike most cats."

Andre shook his head in agreement with himself as he was pleased with how his master plan sounded. He continued, "I was thinking about partnering with Junior. We could put the barbershop and rim shop right next to one another. You know…it is like cars and haircuts…just a guy thing. I think business would be bangin'."

Andre clinched his fist and welded it to his chest to demonstrate.

"Thinking about calling it - One Heartbeat. You know, like how we do after we score touchdowns and whatnot. Since that is like my brother, I think the title fits."

Candice couldn't believe the words coming out of Andre's mouth. *That is a real jacked up goal. Naw dawg. Anyone that wants to be with me has to go to college. It is not going down like this at all. And what is up with that One Heartbeat crap? Maybe I just don't understand male bonding, but that sounds real gay to me when they do that. Junior always riding Dre's coat-tail. He is such a rider.*

Candice didn't want to explode and go off, but her thoughts were running rampant because she truly cared for Andre's well-being.

"That is stupid Dre! Plain dumb as hell. Do what you have to do? All the talent you have, and you want to throw it away on drugs? That has to be the most idiotic thing I've ever heard. Look, I know it is hard financially for your pops, but there are better ways to make money. The risk outweighs what little reward you see. You really are not thinking outside the box. Not to mention, that is not sexy at all."

Candice took her hands and rubbed them on Andre's chest in a seductive pattern.

"If you need help with the applications, I will do what I can. Besides, college men are sexy to me. Men with degrees turn me on. If you need help, let me know."

Andre took Candice and laid her on the hood of the car while kissing her. Even though she was pissed how the day started, she was happy to spend time alone with her man.

* * *

A few weeks passed and Candice wanted to sneak out to be with her boyfriend. His father was out of town on business, and his little brother was staying with some cousins. Candy went downstairs and was stopped by her mother.

"Where you going Candy?"

"We have this meeting for track tonight, then I have study hall at the library. I will probably be home around nine-ish."

"Make sure you don't stay out too late. A pretty girl like you doesn't need to be out all hours. Who is going to bring you home?"

"One of the girls on the team, and if not them, Dre."

"Candy, call me if they fall through. Don't go trying to be Miss Cross Country and walk home. And don't be hanging out with that boy either! You need to be home no later than ten, do you understand me?"

"Yes ma'am."

Miss Richards had been working double shifts, so she passed out on the couch before Candice even left the house. Candice felt bad for deceiving her mother, but she knew she wouldn't let her go out with Andre on a school night. Candice snuck around the corner, and Andre was waiting with his car barely running. She jogged to the car, anxiously jumped inside, then leaned over to kiss him on the cheek. He looked at Candice with a grin then pulled off.

After a fifteen minute drive, the couple arrived at his house. Andre grabbed Candice's arm and tugged her inside.

"Go pick out a movie and I will make some popcorn."

Candice walked to the wall of infinite movies and randomly grabbed one. She didn't care about the flick; just wanted to spend time with him. The movie started, and she snuggled under her boyfriend. With her head buried in his chest, she listened to his heartbeat as the explosions from the action movie rattled the photos on the wall.

Andre began stroking Candice's hair; a touch that drove her wild and often made her let down her guard. Eventually the two began kissing and Candice used her hands to rub on his body. In the heat of passion, his hands started exploring her body as well. He took her wrist and firmly placed her hand between his legs. *Wow, that thing is hard.*

Candice retracted her hand and Andre stop kissing her.

"Don't be scared of it. It won't bite. Do you want to see it?"

Candice nodded as she felt that was the response he wanted. Andre unzipped his pants and pulled it out.

Looking at her naked boyfriend, Candice's mind began to wander. *His body is so nice, but ugh, why does his stuff have to look like that? I thought maybe I was tipsy off the wine before and that made it look ugly, but that thing is just wrong because I am super sober now. He actually wants to put that inside me? He is going to have to cover that thing up or something. Now I see why they made condoms, if for nothing else than to cover it up.*

"Put a condom on."

Andre reached over on the coffee stand where he apparently pre-coordinated the night's events. He took his teeth and ripped open the wrapper.

With the skill of a seasoned vet, he took one hand and rolled the condom down the erect extension of himself. He wiped the lubricant from his hands on the couch and proceeded to kiss Candice while unbuttoning her shirt. His lips navigated down her chest to her navel, and he began to tug at her shorts. Candice was still uneasy, so she didn't move. A persistent, teenage-hormone-driven Andre grabbed her panties and attempted to move them over to the side.

"We need to slow down baby."

"Not again. Why are you teasing me like this?"

"Dre I am sorry, but I am just scared. This is not right. Not like this. Not on a couch with popcorn kernels stuck to my butt. That is not cute at all."

"How do you want it then? You want to go to my bedroom? You want me to light candles? I don't know what you want me to do to make you feel comfortable? I have tried everything. I spent money on hotels. I tried to prepare a romantic evening by the lake. Nothing is good enough for you. What do you want me to do?"

"I don't want you to do anything but be patient. This doesn't feel right, and I want my first time to be special. Not only that, but I just want to make sure that nothing changes with us. I don't want to be like those girls tossed to the side and rumors circulating around. Not that I care about what people think, but I just don't need that unnecessary drama."

"Baby, I am here for the long haul. I need you right now. You can't leave me like this…I would never do the same to you. I don't think you understand what you are doing to my body by teasing me like this."

Candice rolled her eyes.

"Ok, tell you what. We don't have to do anything, but why don't you do something for me. Say I take this condom off, and you just put it in your hand. Kiss me like you were before and just let the magic happen."

"No, I am not in the mood for beating you off right now. You are completely ruining this mood. Go in the bathroom, do what you need to handle yourself, then please take me home. It is getting late, and I am not trying to get into trouble."

"Come on Candy. The prom, now this? In some wicked twisted way, do you get off giving me blue balls or something?"

"Please Dre. Don't make this harder than it has to be. Go pour some water down your pants to calm down, and let's go."

"Arrrgh!"

Andre screamed with frustration and kicked over the coffee table, which was holding his car keys. He snatched the keys from the floor, then stormed out the house.

Chapter VI

The Ideal Man

The next day Candice had a visitor.

"Candy baby, come downstairs. Somebody is here for you," her mother stated. Candice took her time strolling down the stairs for fear it was Dre. When she walked around the staircase banister, her eyes lit up like a little kid.

"Uncle Lenny!"

"Well are you going to stand there or come give me a hug?"

Candice ran towards her uncle and jumped into his arms like a little girl. He was her favorite uncle for numerous reasons. He was very easy to talk to, down to earth, and liked to help Candice train for sports as he was a former track and field national champion.

"So what are you doing in town?"

"I hadn't heard from your mother since you guys moved, and since she does such a good job at not returning my calls, thought I'd stop in. Hey, enough talk. Get dressed…I am taking you two beautiful ladies out for dinner. And Lisa, no is not an option. You know you need to get out, and this is my treat."

Lisa agreed. The three went to dinner, laughed and had a good time. After dinner they arrived back at the house and Candice's uncle turned towards Lisa and instructed her to go inside.

"I want to take a walk with Candy if that is ok?"

She nodded, pleased that her daughter had a positive male role model.

The two began walking around the block while chasing the remaining daylight. Candice became quiet because she knew her uncle was about to probe and ask her direct questions about what she was doing. Candice forged a bond with her uncle realizing that he would never violate her trust and go back and tell her mother. Nonetheless, it still made her feel bad at times because she hated to disappoint him.

"So I assume you have been busy lately? Last time I heard from you was the thank you letter I received for those shoes I bought you. I was hoping everything was ok with you and your mom. I emailed you that last chess move, but haven't heard from you in months. Your middle game is getting so much better. It is crazy because I remember teaching you chess as a little girl, now look at you."

"I am sorry Uncle Lenny, I still want to finish our game, but I've just been real busy with track and life and everything. You know the situation with my dad leaving with auntie really messed mom up and just trying to be here with her, for her. I dunno, life is tough sometimes. I know I am still young, but I feel older. A lot of times I don't know how I should feel about stuff. Should I be mad at him? Should I be mad at my Auntie Lynn for taking my daddy? I don't know what to feel anymore."

Candice's uncle wanted to approach this topic with caution, but once he spoke he realized he too had a lot of pinned up emotions tied into this family fall out.

"I know baby, and he is a jerk for doing that to my baby sister. Lisa is such a sweetheart and doesn't deserve it. You know, it is perfectly ok to have those mixed emotions. At first I didn't know who I was more upset with either – him for messing with my twin sister Lynette, or her for messing with him. In any case, I still get livid just thinking about it. Lynette has always been jealous of your mother for one reason or another, and I just don't know what happened to her. We used to joke that she got dropped out the crib on her head or something, but to be honest, I think it is deeper than that."

"What do you think happened? Or is that adult only info?"

"It's hard to say. When Lynn was in high school, she always messed with the wrong guy. Athletes who would dog her, dealers, you name a bad guy, and she was on him. She progressed to older guys and even married men. I don't know what snapped in her head because we weren't raised like that, but she just mixed spirits with the wrong type of men, and it has escalated to this…her willingness to take her own flesh and blood's husband. I somewhat suspected something because of how your dad would stare at her during family functions, and then I noticed little things here and there."

"Little things like what?"

"I pay attention to body language, and some things you can just sense. If you would go into the kitchen and they were the only two in there, you could tell something had just transpired. Or when he would hug her, just the way their bodies reacted and how they would kiss each other on the cheek real close to the corner of their mouth. Lynette is foul and I can't do anything but pray for her…that is if I am doing one of those everything-must-go sales prayers and I pray for the people I usually don't have energy for. The blue moon prayer list. I catch 'em every blue moon."

Candice began to laugh and appreciated how her uncle understood her frustration and attempted to make light of the situation.

"Candy, I need you to do me a big favor."

"Sure, what you need?"

"We all know how stubborn your mother is. After Mom passed, no one really helped out with expenses. I was in the hospital at the time, otherwise I would have helped. In any case, I have this settlement check and I want to give some to your mom. I know she has been going through some tough times, and I really think this extra money would help."

"So you want me to hide the check until you leave so my mother will stop trying to put it back in your suitcase?"

"Actually, I had to approach this one like chess and think about it. Really it is a simple move and avoids all that hassle. When your mom is not paying attention, take a check from her checkbook and bring it to me. I will just go to her bank and deposit it directly. That way I don't have to deal with her not accepting it."

Candice agreed. There was an awkward silence as the uncle and niece thought about family issues and what went down, then after five minutes of silent reflections, her uncle spoke.

"Can I ask you a personal question Candy?"

"Yes you can, but the answer is no…I have not done anything with anyone."

"Good, keep it that way."

"I can't stay a virgin forever though. Eventually I will have to give it up."

"Eventually yes, but not now. Hopefully, prayfully, you will give yourself on your wedding night. And don't say it like *give it up*. That makes it sound cheap and like you have no reverence for what it really is. Have respect for the gift God gave you. Don't be in a rush to grow up. Trust me, you aren't missing out on anything. Besides, boys at your age don't really even know what they are doing. They think they are putting it down, but they have no clue."

"I can't tell. The way my friends talk about it, it must not be that bad."

"Tell me, how many partners has one of your friends had? Just pick one."

Candice immediately thought of her friend Camille.

"For one of my friends, it is eight…that I know of."

"Eight? Oh my Lord. Trust me if it was that good to her, she wouldn't have that many partners. It is apparent she is going around seeking fulfillment for a void in her life, and that is just not the right way to go about it. You girls are too young."

"Like I said, I am not doing anything, so don't include me in that *you* tally."

"*You* aren't, but *you* are thinking about it. And sometimes, left alone with our own thoughts, we rationalize and do stupid things. The things you constantly meditate upon will eventually manifest in your life. See one thing you need to understand about men and women is they think differently. Now keep in mind, I am giving you this from a male perspective. This is coming from a man who did things he is not proud of in his past, and I am trying to warn you about the type of guy I used to be. You need to realize that boys at that age, for the most part, only think about one thing. I know it is stereotypical to say that, but it is the truth. It is not talking down about them, but it is a scientific fact that their bodies are at a point where they feel these uncontrollable urges for sex."

"I can agree with that." Candice said trying to absorb wisdom from her uncle and apply it to her relationship with Andre.

"So tell me this. What do you want out of a relationship? You want a guy to take you to the movies? For a man to cook for you, or maybe take you out to dinner? To just hold your hand in public, or stroke your hair while watching TV? A man to be there to talk to? A man that is there for you to hold on to?"

"Yea, that sounds about right. I want all those things," Candice confidently responded.

"Now if you want all these things in a man, why would you settle for less?"

"What do you mean settle for less?"

"Let me make it plain for you. I used to be a high school guidance counselor. I have seen so many girls just throw their all into a guy who couldn't care less. It is so one-sided you wouldn't believe. I used to wonder if girls knew how boys truly felt about them, and the things they said to their friends afterwards, would women still throw themselves at men? Guys at that age want sex…period. Why would you give up your most valuable asset, your most precious gift, to a boy who is not giving you anything in return? That makes no sense to me. Relationships are about give and take. That is all take. They take, get off, then go on about their business while you are sitting there with a list of unfulfilled items you want in a relationship."

"Uncle Lenny, it is different with Andre and me. Don't get me wrong, we have our problems just like regular relationships. Some things we are together on…like fitness and sports and whatnot. Then other things we really don't see eye-to-eye on. There are some places I am just not ready to go."

"Sex?"

"Yes. I know that looks bad, but it is not that way. See, we bond so much when we are together. With both of us coming from homes where a parent left, it is like we have this connection. And I know that he loves me and just wants to be closer to me and…"

"Sorry to cut you off, but stop right there. You know what Peanut, I'll tell you straight how I see it. That is a crock of snot. I know this is not holy of me since I am saved now, but I know men. I was once a young boy. The best thing you can tell them is to go F off. Maybe not saying it literally, but have the disposition that if they walk away from you for you not giving into their demands, then you will be ok. Guys bank on you chasing after them once they throw tantrums!"

"You don't understand Uncle Lenny. I mean with us, we…"

"Why do women, young and old, always say you don't understand? As soon as someone says something about a female and her failed relationship she goes on a tangent – *you don't know him, he loves me, he's a great guy, he's nice to me, we do a lot of things together, he believes in God, he is good with kids, he really loves me, we have a connection.* You say all that aloud trying to convince yourself, but deep down within you know something in your spirit is telling you this isn't right. Within time, most guys let their intentions be known by their actions, and heck, nowadays guys flat out tell women what their intentions are. And you know what happens? Women take one kind act as a glimmer of hope and finagle the relationship to create something that doesn't exist. Females need to stop trying to think for men and start listening to their instincts."

Candice became quiet.

"The problem is you are stuck on an idea that doesn't exist. You are fabricating a fairytale ending, when it is not a fairytale that you are subscribed to. You need to dismiss the notion that he has minor faults, but you can work through it. The reality is if he were the one, he'd respect your decision to wait. Having sex is not going to bring you closer. If anything, it will just complicate matters. You are too young to understand all the emotions that go along with having sex."

Candice's uncle looked over at his distraught niece as she twirled a leaf in her hand by the stem trying to fight back her embarrassment.

"Look baby, I am not trying to fuss at you, I am just telling you this out of love. You have so much potential, and I don't want to see you get hurt."

"I understand Uncle Lenny, but I just feel stupid at times. Like, I know the stuff you are saying is about right, but it is just hard when you are on this end. You make this so cut and dry, but this relationship thing is difficult…especially for girls my age."

Candice's uncle wrapped his arm around her as they walked and kissed her on her forehead.

"I want you to try something."

"Sure."

"From now on until you enter college and beyond, I want you to approach dating like a job interview."

"A job interview?" she questioned.

"At my last job when our hiring manager posted for a position, she had certain criteria before they could get to the next level of interviewing. If they didn't meet those base requirements, she immediately discarded their application."

"Ok…what does that have to do with me?"

"When you have a young man who is interested in you, approach it like a job interview. We just listed qualities you want…holding hands, watching movies and whatnot. What you need to do is come up with a pre-screening list. You need to set guidelines like - *Does he reverence God? How does he treat his mother? Is he respectful to women? Does he have a job? Does he have ambition?* Set a long list and if a guy doesn't meet these, move on. Trust me, you are wasting your time, and life is too short to waste on a foolish, non-ambitious man."

"That is an awful lot."

"Well, it should be much longer to be honest. You need to set your standards high, otherwise you will be left with mediocrity. And trust me, when you don't put out, a man will let his true intentions be known. Time removes imitations of love! Lust is temporary, but love lasts a lifetime."

Candice's uncle picked up a rock and threw it down the sidewalk; somehow making it skip several times as he intended. As he tossed the second rock, he continued his point.

"Let me tell you what bothers me Candy. When I used to counsel those kids, there were numerous times I watched the transformation of a young, sweet innocent girl, to a young lady who has been exposed to more than she should at her age. There is so much peer pressure from the media on how young women are supposed to look and act. I flip through the television stations, and I see all these girls on these videos half-dressed, allowing these men to put them in sexual positions and make sexual innuendos and gestures. That is not even speaking on the lyrics these guys release into the atmosphere.

"I look at these girls and think to myself - That was once that cute little girl who dreamed of marrying her prince charming and having a nice family of her own. The little girl who liked playing house and combing her babydoll's hair. The little girl that would make ant soup in the backyard, or try to make cookies in her Easy Bake Oven. I know people mature with age, but what happened in her life to make her lose who she was? She was on the path of becoming a woman, and somewhere along the line she met a man and took a wrong turn and as a result became this promiscuous vixen. Who was the first little boy to approach her and introduce her to his sick, twisted perversions? The little boy who convinced her to participate in deviant sexual behavior? The little boy who exposed her to a lifestyle and emotions and feelings she was not ready for and sent her life down a spiraling path which also damaged her future relationships? Or even deeper, who was the first man who abused her before she even met that little boy? A father? A stepfather? An uncle? What man in her life violated her trust and deflowered this precious little girl?

"Candy, I look at these young girls, and with me having no children of my own, I immediately think of you. You are so pure and sweet and dear to me, and I just want to protect you. It would break my heart to see some boy get over on you. I don't want you to end up damaged emotionally because some guy, in his selfish, lustful state, convinced you to participate in his perverted fantasies."

"Uncle Lenny, I really don't have anything to say about that because I agree. I understand what you are saying, but why do you keep calling it perverted? I thought sex was supposed to be a beautiful thing? I don't think it is always a demented thing like the media portrays. Plus, I believe there really has been a push in my generation with safe sex. Most adults don't give us credit. I don't think kids are as irresponsible as they used to be."

"My dear Candice, that is the problem with your generation. The enemy has a stronghold on your mind and has tricked you into believing it is ok to have sex with whomever as long as you strap up, wrap up, or wear rubbers, as we called 'em in my day. Let me be clear…there is no such thing as safe sex. That is just a sick, twisted way society leads you to believe sex is just a casual act and there are no ramifications for participating. Condoms break, and even if they don't, they still have pores in them. My father had this saying - *it is like putting a screen door on a submarine hatch.* Your generation still has astronomical numbers regarding teenage pregnancies as well as STDs, so throw that safe sex jargon out the window. The only way to have safe sex is not to have sex at all!"

Candice continued to play with the leaf in her hand while listening to her uncle.

"Let's go back to this perversion thing. Babygirl, do you know what perversion is? To be perverted means to deviate from what is right. It is wicked, misguided and distorted. Sex was not meant to be perverted, but to be something enjoyable to married couples. Anything outside of that is perversion…plain and simple. Sex with animals is perverted. Sex with children is perverted. Threesomes, foursomes, orgies, women on women, all that is perverted. Sex outside of marriage is perverted.

"And trust me, I am not trying come across judgmental because I have made my fair share of mistakes in the past. I speak the truth to you out of love. I speak the truth from a young boy who took advantage of young girls when I was your age. I speak to you from an adult man who has used women in the past and have been used myself. I just want to keep you from going down an unnecessary path that will lead to heartache because trust me, the grass is not greener on the other side.

"The things I am telling you are not based on opinion, it is in the Bible. I am telling you Candy, that is what turned my life around. The Bible basically gives us the blueprint for living and warns against participating in perverse sexual activity. You need to understand that when you engage in sex, it makes it hard for you to interpret and analyze things correctly. It is almost like your discernment meter is broken, and you lose a bit of your common sense. In other words, it makes you stupid. So to answer your question, if you believe in God and in the Bible, then the Bible is *right*. If it doesn't align with the Word of God, then it is perverse. Make sense?"

Candice shook her head.

"I guess so. I never looked at it that way. The pressure is just tough sometimes. It seems like the people who are having sex know something

I don't. It almost appears that they act different afterwards. I think that is part of my curiosity. It is almost like I am missing out on something. Everyone is growing up and I am still little young, inexperienced Candy."

"If I were you, I'd be happy you haven't given into the pressures of society. All those people that you try to impress in high school are going to be worn out, tired, busted and disgusted after you graduate. You can't worry about what people think about you or you will never go anywhere in life. Trust me when I say sex is a lot more than just physical gratification. There is a spiritual side to it. Pick up your Bible and read it sometimes. Read the first eight verses of Genesis 34 where it talks about Shechem laying with Dinah and how his soul meshed with hers. Or in I Corinthians 6:16 where it says if you join with a harlot the two become one flesh. It is imperative that you read the Bible and develop an understanding for yourself because the world will try to talk you into some nonsense. They will tell you sex is ok, and that the church just tells you can't have sex to scare you and control you. There are so many foolish people out there, and if you let them, they will speak nonsense until you start to believe them. And heck, even if that were true, why is it such a big deal to abstain from sex? Why do people want to persecute you for saving your body? The *why* is because they are unhappy with themselves, and it is a destructive force within them causing them to be disruptive and bring chaos to others. Like my grandmother used to say – *misery loves company*."

"I hear what you are saying Uncle Lenny."

Candice appreciated how her uncle cared about her well-being, and his words carried a lot of weight and often influenced her in a positive way. She always felt she could be straight forward because he never judged her and told her straight how it was.

"So, when you use that term *spiritual tie*, do you mean just bonding on another level? Is that like another level of love-making or something?"

"There is definitely a connection Candy, but it is one that was created to be enjoyed during marriage. You see, when you let a man enter your body, there is a join that happens. Basically, a bonding, or fusing of spirits. That is why you notice a change in your friends. I can't tell you how many times I have seen a good girl sleep with a brotha from the streets, and in a matter of time her entire demeanor changes. If you sleep with a person who is a liar, cheat, thief, or whatever, then eventually you will start to inherit some of those same characteristics. And that works both ways because women can have influence over men as well. When old folks say that you young people aren't ready for all the emotions that go along with sex...that is what we are talking about.

"Let me give you a visual. I am going to approach sex like a checking account. Let's just look at two basic functions – deposits and withdrawals. If there are larger withdrawals than there are deposits, then you could incur overdraft fees and possibly deplete your account. Follow me so far?

"Sure," Candice replied.

"Well sex involves deposits and withdrawals too. When a man penetrates you, he leaves a deposit. Not just a seminal deposit, but a spiritual deposit as well. When he withdraws, he takes a piece of your spirit with him. If you keep letting men inside you, those deposits and withdrawals accumulate and cause structural damage to your soul...thus preventing you from being whole, or balanced. It is like it messes up your checking account. In other words, it makes it hard for you later on down the line to sustain a healthy relationship when a good man comes along.

"Why do you think you see so many people struggling with relationships? They have so much spiritual baggage that they can't sustain a healthy, long-lasting relationship anymore. They have allowed so many people come along that they can't keep track of the deposits and withdrawals, and their spirit is in an overdraft state. Then the new person you meet has to rummage through your past bank statements, if you are honest enough to reveal it to them, and try to figure out when your account became negative. That is the best case scenario. In most cases, people hide their past because they fear what their partner would say and enter into the relationship already in spiritual debt. These people have no hope at debt relief because they won't take advantage of the spiritual debt counseling that comes from open communication with your spouse. They'd rather use all of their energy attempting to keep their past hidden.

"Candy, don't get me wrong, being married is a beautiful thing and the best way to keep your spiritual checkbook balanced...as God intended. What I am saying is when you do things to deplete your spiritual account, you create problems later on down the road. What may seem harmless now will put you in a situation where you incur unnecessary fees that sometimes take years to recover from. Am I making any sense to you?

Candice was overwhelmed by the conversation. Some of the things her uncle said hit close to home and hurt her feelings. As she gauged her relationship to his advice, she responded, "Yes. I hear what you are saying."

"I don't mean to talk your head off baby, but I have seen a lot. I want the best for your life, so I am adamant about you preserving yourself. Yes, you can be forgiven for mistakes you have made, but why even make those mistakes to begin with? Why put yourself in a position where you will have to live with the consequences of your actions…especially for actions you didn't even want to participate in the first place and were pressured into?"

As the two approached this point in the conversation, they were close to home. Candice allowed his words to permeate her thoughts. She went up to her room while her uncle and mother talked in the living room until late hours of the night. Candice's uncle was the only male role model in her life since her dad left; a father who never wrote, nor called. She knew that whatever her uncle told her, he spoke it out of love.

Candice sat on the edge of her bed and thought about the conversation she just had with her uncle about relationships. As she ingested his words, she thought about the love she had for him, and reminisced on her last e-mail chess match with him.

You know, uncle is right. I have so much potential, and I shouldn't just throw it away just because of someone else's wants. I need to start thinking about me and what I am going to do to get out this house. I have been approaching life like checkers…being spontaneous jumping from here to there. Maybe he was right? Maybe I need to sit back and approach this like chess and pay attention to my next steps because I don't want to end up in a situation like my mom, or some of these other women I know. The problem is, what do I do about Dre? I truly love him and don't want to let him go.

Candice was reluctant at first, but took out a sheet of paper, and like her Uncle Lenny instructed, started jotting down traits she would like in her ideal man. Exhausted from the long day, after listing a few traits Candice fell asleep with pencil in hand.

Chapter VII

A Teenage Love

As a little girl, Rose was enthusiastic when she had the opportunity to visit her grandparents. Oftentimes she'd bring a bag of dolls over and play quietly on the floor in the den as her grandfather read from his extensive collection of books. The ambience would forever be etched in her memory as it titillated her senses. The smell of fresh yeast as her grandmother prepared rolls from scratch, her grandfather's books absorbing the oils from her fingertips leaving her hands dry, and the sound of the grandfather clock which sat adjacent to her grandfather's desk. The antique grandfather clock would chime every hour and had a calming effect on Rose, while simultaneously dampening the mood reminding her one less hour she had to spend with her grandparents. There was a level of warmth and comfort that Rose received which was induced by the love between her grandparents; a nostalgic feeling she cherished well into adulthood.

In Rose's teen years, a malfunction within an old clothes dryer led to a house fire which damaged the majority of her grandparents home. There was extensive structure damage, but her grandfather was determined to rebuild as the land was invaluable to him. As Rose rummaged through the collapsed wooden frames which once held the home together, the surrealistic backdrop became overwhelming. The aged photos of the grandchildren aligned on the mantle and collectable figurines her grandmother acquired over the years were now a somber memory. It was hard for Rose to comprehend years of her grandparents sweat equity now gone in a matter of hours. Money saved in vintage Sanka coffee tins served as emergency funds and means to buy necessary items for the household. As far as Rose knew, her grandparents were never in lack and always had nice things. Now expensive China and dishes lay broken while parts of the furniture, with the plastic covering Rose grew up despising, were saturated in soot and ash.

The smell of smoke was undeniable as Rose walked through the remains shaking her head in utter disbelief. This was her second home, but there were no walls and a gaping hole in the roof. In the heap of incinerated books and drywall, Rose observed the grandfather clock which was now charred and reduced to mere firewood. A tear outlined her cheek, but halted shortly thereafter with reassurance from her grandfather's firm touch on her shoulder. He took Rose's hand and walked her to the front porch, which surprisingly was in tact. Rose was hurt, and she couldn't understand why her grandfather was so adamant about rebuilding something so broken. She wanted him to just take the insurance money and move someplace different. Rose felt it would be impossible to recreate the same home, and the thought of starting from nothing was painful.

As the two sat on the bottom of the porch, Rose buried her face into her hands. Her grandfather pointed to the possessions scattered across the lawn and stated, "Babygirl, all these material possessions we can accumulate again. The important thing is no one was hurt. As long as I have your grandmother and a strong foundation, we can do anything we put our minds to. Make no mistake about it, we will rebuild!"

Rose's grandfather took his toothpick out of mouth and placed it in the top pocket of his worn denim overalls. He leaned over the side of the porch and rooted his fingers into the earth. With a handful of dirt he sat upright.

"This soil has been in my family for four generations now."

In 1862 his great-grandfather escaped from the south in search of acquiring land using the Homestead Act. He was determined to make a new way for his wife and unborn daughter. Despite not knowing the first thing about farming, he understood this opportunity and the importance in acquiring good land with fertile soil. Story has it he prayed and visited several plots of land until God told him to stop at this plot. This was a man who couldn't read nor write, and didn't know the first thing about agriculture, and within five years of hard work, determination and resilience was able to meet the requirements of the act and acquire the deed. His great-grandfather eventually learned how to read and write. His stress on education was invaluable and positively affected the next four generations of their bloodline.

"My great-grandfather toiled over this land until he had something to leave my grandfather. At age 62, my grandfather died and passed it to my father, and at age 38 my father died and passed it to me. Yes this may look bad right now, but we must have faith and see what is not there. My lineage has shed too much sweat, blood and tears for me to give up and walk away. This land is a part of our family legacy. We just have to chip away and build slowly until our house is put back together. All it takes is a little persistence!"

After listening to her grandfather, Rose began to understand the historical significance and his will to rebuild. She realized that some things were worth fighting for and vowed if she ever had the opportunity to be in a better place financially that she would keep the property in their family for generations to come.

* * *

For a feel of comfort and security, one of the first purchases Rose made for her home office was a grandfather clock. Rather than complimenting the contemporary theme of her home, she opted to recreate the atmosphere of her grandfather's den and purchased a traditional limited edition heirloom quality grandfather clock with the distinct Westminster chime she became accustom to at her grandparents home.

It was 9pm on a Friday night, and Rose had no immediate plans. Her clock chimed to alert the empty home a new hour had arrived, which also reminded Rose of a hunger pain that needed to be addressed. Not feeling up for the task of cooking so late, she contemplated several food choices until sushi became the forerunner. Wearing jogging pants and an old over-sized sweatshirt which used to belong to her ex-husband, she slid on a ball cap and headed down to her favorite hibachi and sushi restaurant. After a brief stint in traffic she arrived and walked towards the counter to place an order.

"Welcome Rose."

"Hey Dat."

"What can I get for you this evening?"

"This is going to be for take-out. I think that I will have the Sashimi & Sushi combo, but instead of the tuna can I get…"

"Smoked salmon?"

The harmonious deep voice interrupted Rose's sentence and immediately paralyzed her speech. The bass crawled over her shoulder and sent a chill down her spine. Her heart thumped so hard it detached and plopped into her abdomen. *Oh my Lord…Troy!*

Slowly turning around and trying to hold her composure, Rose responded, "What are you doing here?"

"Last I checked this is a free country. Are you going to stand there or give me a hug? It has been almost a year since I saw you last. I would like to think it is all water under the bridge now."

Rose stood firm, reluctant to hug her ex-husband and revisit past feelings, but before she could react he extended his large arms and wrapped them around her. It had been a long time since she felt the touch of a man, so she rested her head on his chest and hugged him back. It felt good… that was until memories of the pain he caused resurfaced and kicked her off her temporary cloud back into reality. She abruptly ended the hug.

"Ok, that is enough. So what are you doing in town?"

"Actually I have moved back. Things didn't work out in California, so I decided to come back. I've only been back for about four months and just had this craving for some sushi tonight. We must still be linked spiritually. Remember how we used to wake up in the middle of the night and eat leftover sushi while laughing at infomercials? "

"Don't remind me."

"I don't think us meeting here was a coincidence. You don't believe in fate? I mean look, you are even wearing my sweatshirt. What do you say we get our table? I have a craving for some hibachi, and we can eat your sushi as an appetizer."

"Fool, do you see what I have on? I just planned on running in real quick. Does it look like I want to eat dinner someplace?"

"It never stopped you before. Come on Rose. No one of importance is here."

Rose was leery regarding his intentions given his past, but it had been so long since she had male company that she fell victim to his soft brown eyes and conceded to his request. An emotional uncertainty plagued Rose. She was frustrated that she built up a surplus of resentment, yet still found him attractive.

Troy's business attire showed signs of a fatigue, yet he was still clean and had the slightest hint of refreshing masculine cologne. He stood six-foot-four with a short freshly lined haircut, shaved face with groomed goatee, and perfect white teeth. This former second team All-American collegiate lacrosse player was definitely easy on the eyes and caught the interest of a table of women off at a distance. Aside from his exterior presentation, Troy was an educated man who obtained a MBA from Northwestern and spoke Spanish, French and German fluently. Troy worked with his father's company utilizing his skill set to specialize in international business. Rose didn't realize it at the time, but her exposure to his business world later served as a blueprint to build her cosmetics company.

The estranged couple walked to the secluded area and placed their order. As they waited, Troy ordered raspberry Sake for the two.

"So you trying to get me drunk off this rice wine to take advantage of me?"

"Would that be such a bad thing?"

"I see some people haven't changed. So why did you *really* move back here? You have a child here or something? I know there has to be some motive."

Troy smirked.

"I tell you Rose, I just missed this place. I thought I would be happy in a big city, but I guess at heart I am just a small town guy. Not to mention, the cost of living is extremely high so financially it made more sense to move back. I caught an incredible deal on a loft right outside of town. All I have to really do is paint it."

Rose struggled to keep her thoughts inside. She didn't care about his loft or anything going on with him. She kept reliving their ordeal, and before she knew it she dove into her unanswered questions.

"So…how's my cousin doing? You seen her since you been back?"

"Oh, here we go."

"Here we go? I am not the one that tried to turn that whore into a housewife!"

"You know what Rose, I just wanted us to have a friendly dinner. Do we really have to get into it?"

Rose grabbed her purse.

"This was a bad idea. I see you are sensitive, and just like usual, trying to turn this thing around like it was my fault. I loved you unconditionally and supported you and your career. You are the one that left, remember? You have some nerve! I'm gone…"

Troy stood up and utilized his muscular frame to block Rose from exiting.

"Please sit down. I am sorry."

Rose rolled her eyes.

"For what Troy? Stay for what? This is not going anywhere."

"I don't want to end things like this baby. Look, let's get this all on the table. Sit down, and ask me anything you want to know and I will tell you the truth."

As much as Rose wanted to leave, she couldn't pass up this opportunity to release some questions which remained in queue at the back of her throat.

"Ok, I just want to know why? I mean, cheating was one thing, but with my cousin Felicia? I was so close to her. Why did you do it?"

"I didn't mean for it to happen."

"Why do men always say that? That makes no sense. And you know, maybe I could have handled it better if you slept with her and moved on to the next. But you? Man, you are a handiwork. You and her moved in together Troy. Do you know how that felt? Do you know how low I was? Do you even care how bad that hurts when your spouse cheats on you with family? It took everything in me not to kill her."

"It is not what it looked like."

"Well paint the picture for me bruh."

Troy took a shot of Sake and gently dropped it on the table.

"Let's just get this out, then never speak on it again. You want the truth, well here is the truth. To be honest, your cousin has always been attractive to me, but I would never cross that line. Well you remember when I put her on with my homeboy Arthur? I didn't think anything of it and figured they were gelling. So one day out the blue she called me at work and…"

"At work? What was this ho doing with your work number in the first place?"

"Let me finish woman. First of all, don't read more into this. It was what it was. She got it from his cell phone apparently. Anyways, she called me at work and wanted to plan a surprise for Arthur. With his birthday being a week before Christmas, she asked for some suggestions. You remember that surprise birthday party that we had for him?"

"Yes, I remember. I remember I didn't go because I had food poisoning, and instead of staying home to take care of me, you went to the party," Rose responded sarcastically. "But like you said, all water under the bridge, huh? Continue."

"We talked off and on for a couple months trying to plan it. We kept a Christmas theme and…"

"We? Ouch! Ok, I am cool. Go ahead."

Troy shook his head and continued with his story.

"We planned it with a Christmas theme. I thought she was flirting at times, but I didn't want to read more into it. A day or so before the party, she was driving his truck and dropped her lipstick. When she did so, she found some panties stuffed under the seat. Now I knew he was cheating, but that wasn't my place to say anything. She had suspicions for some time, so she asked me what to do. I told her I didn't know anything, of course. She wanted to call the party off, and I begged with her to reconsider. I mean, we invited all these people including his mother…so I told her to just suck it up until after the party, then handle the panty situation later.

"So we get to the party, and it is pretty nice. She had one too many drinks. I was in the kitchen playing with her son, and she stood in the doorway watching. She told him to go upstairs to get ready for bed and waved me over. I didn't realize at the time that she was standing under a mistletoe. She kissed me…and I kissed her back."

Rose's leg began to furiously twitch under the table.

"I guess you forgot you were married, huh? Aw, that was so cute. She finally found a daddy for her kid who wasn't incarcerated. Whatever! That boy doesn't look anything like the alleged father. And then her baby daughter? I won't even go there on how many men she had paternity tests on and they came back negative. You have no idea what you were messing with. How could you see anything in her?"

"Honestly babe, I was confused. I loved you…still do. I was just going through things at the time. I don't know if it was midlife crisis or what, but my body was changing, and I just didn't understand what was going on. In retrospect it was just lust, but I couldn't see clearly at the time."

"How long before you slept with her? And more importantly, why didn't you just end it with me? Why did you keep going back and forth between us? That is nasty!"

"We slept with each other that night."

"Oh my God. You slept with her that night?" Rose felt vomit slowly creep up the back of her throat. She tried to handle her emotions, but was hurt and wished she never evoked the conversation.

"I need to understand this. I am sitting at home curled up in a ball from pain, and you are twisting this ho like a pretzel getting your rocks off? Where? How? Like did you suggest you guys get a room, or what?"

"She asked me to come back later on, so…baby, it is really irrelevant. The fact is I did it. I did it, and I was dirty and wrong. Rose, I should have ended it but I was just scared. I didn't know what to do."

"Scared? Scared is wondering where your man is, then going to his office and see your cousin on the table knocking over papers as your husband's face is between her legs. Do you have any idea how that felt? Do you know how that image is permanently burned into my head? Do you understand how this has affected me and my trust for men? Do you even care?"

"Yes I care."

"No you don't. You narcissistic bastard! You don't care about anyone but yourself. You have no idea how humiliating that was for me. Heck, you don't know how humiliating it was for your father. A man of his stature who built his wealth off principles of honesty and integrity. A man who knew what fidelity meant and stayed with the same woman for thirty years. All that your father worked to build, and his son turns around and wants to be a philanderer? You hurt him Troy because he didn't raise you to be like that. I promise the only reason I kept your last name was out of respect for your father. You brought such shame to the Hughes name that I wanted to cast it back in a positive light."

"Cast it back in a positive light, huh?" Troy's cynicism penetrated his tone. "Rose, please stop being dramatic. I understand you were attached to my father and respected him, but believe me there were things you didn't know about him. Yes my dad loved you, and I know about him being a silent financial partner when you started your company, but let's not make this more than it is. What happened was between you and I and had nothing to do with my father and how he felt. Baby look, I didn't mean to…"

"Stop calling be Baby you punk a…"

"Hey…we are in public so calm down! Yes, I cared. I cared and do care. I was just confused."

"Confused about what? What is there to be confused about?"

"It was just complicated. I had your cousin feeding me info on you, and I just didn't know who to trust."

"Feeding you info? What did that broad say?"

"It is pointless Rose. That was in the past. I don't want you to start anything with her. Just let it go."

"Stop protecting her and just tell me what she said. Trust me, if I haven't killed her thus far, I probably won't. What did she tell you?"

Troy's sigh was dense with frustration.

"I suppose you aren't going to let this go. I can't remember specifically. Just things about you flirting with other men and how she thought you were sleeping with your personal trainer. Said you were going out to lunch with him and how she knows you wanted to sleep with him…and that you basically told her in not so many words."

"Oh my goodness. I feel like punching that chick with a phone book.

This is a trip. My own blood. Wow!"

"Leave her alone."

"Leave her alone? Did you actually believe that crap she was feeding you? This coming from a woman who planned a party for her man and kissed *another*...a married *another* at that...in the kitchen. You actually believed her? I can't believe this."

"I didn't know what to believe."

"Troy...I don't owe you any explanation at this point to be perfectly honest with you, but I want to set the record straight. I had a personal trainer, and yes he was attractive and I told her that. However, I never once crossed the lines...not once! I actually called him to end our sessions and the front desk receptionist at the gym told me he was in the cafe across the street having lunch. Yes, I went to the café to meet him there, but I didn't even sit down to eat. I told him being a married woman, out of respect for my husband, I thought it be best if I replaced him with a female trainer. Nothing happened Troy. I am not even constructed like that. I can't believe Felicia said that. After all the dirt she has told me...all the guys she let run through her...and she has the nerve. I can't believe this."

Rose shook her head overwhelmed by the lying and betrayal of her cousin. Tired of her character being attacked and without thinking she blurted out, "You do know she had a thing for you frat boys, right? She was a *Sweetheart*. Do your research...I am sure some of your boys know about her."

Troy was dumbfounded.

"I am sorry Rose. I should have believed you."

Rose still tried to cope with the pain and Troy's answers weren't helping her to heal. There were still answers she wanted to know, but feared the responses if she dared to ask. Already hurt from resurfacing her past, Rose figured she might as well get all her questions out on the table.

"I know I shouldn't ask this, but why her? She cuter than me? Her body better? Sex better? Be real with me Troy. We aren't married anymore, and we are just two adults having conversation. What did she have over me?"

"I can't really even explain it. It is like when you are married, there are just certain things, sexually, you don't do with your wife. Then you have that one freak that you just can do any and everything to. I was selfish and caught in the moment I suppose."

"That is bull Troy. True I am not a prostitute like her, but I was always willing to do whatever you wanted, wherever you wanted. Positions, toys, food…you name it, I was game. Hell, I'd even took stripping lessons just to please you and fulfill your fantasy, so I don't buy that excuse. You just liked something about her."

"It was deeper than just sex. I fell in love with her little boy, and as far as her…it was just this pull she had on me."

"Yea, it was a pull alright…she is a demon!"

Troy knew the situation was sensitive but couldn't help but burst into laughter.

"I am not laughing at all boy, I am dead serious. That woman is evil. I hope you got a HIV test too. Felicia has been known to pull a condom off in the heat of passion and play the pregnancy card. She has caught numerous guys doing that and collected alleged abortion money."

"Don't worry, I am taken care of."

Rose thought back to the events that transpired. The infidelity caused a plethora of emotions ranging from hate and heartache to stupidity and embarrassment. She was disrespected and deep inside felt Troy treated her like a whore. Knowing the information about her cousin's sexual history, she couldn't help but think about him compromising her health. Rose recalled her bouts of temporary depression where she created pictures in her mind wondering if Troy touched Felicia the same way. The cycle of emotions made her feel as if she were going insane.

Rose sat staring at Troy through two lenses simultaneously. On one hand he utterly repulsed her because of what he did, but on the other hand she so longed for him to say the right words so that she could forgive him. She figured her forgiveness would be based on the answers he provided to her final question.

"Last question, and I will let this topic go. What happened? Why did it end? Felicia burn you?"

Troy took his second shot of Sake the waiter poured mid conversation.

"No, nothing like that. I told you, I am clean. I don't know what happened. Just differences I suppose."

"Differences? Like what? You are leaving part of the story out Troy."

"Like I thought we were monogamous, but she felt the need to straddle the neighbor's 19 year old son differences."

Rose snickered. In a vindictive way, she was glad he experienced the same pain she felt.

"Doesn't feel good, does it? I told you when you were packing to leave that she wasn't crap. Did you listen? No!"

"You made your point Rose. There is one thing I don't understand.

What makes me not listening to you any different from you not listening to me?"

Rose knew where this conversation was headed but attempted to play dumb.

"What do you mean?"

"Don't try to get quiet now. You know what I mean woman."

"Nobody is trying to get quiet, and who are you getting funky with? If you have something to say, say it."

"When I continued to tell you that Chad wasn't about anything, that is what I mean. I was in love with you, and you kept playing me over that fool. He was going around doing all kinds of dirt and you just kept jumping back into his arms. I pursued you for years while you were in love with another man. You have no idea how that felt!"

"It was not like that Troy…not like that at all."

"Explain to me how it was then because obviously I must have missed that memo."

"I loved you Troy, you just have to understand that situation. I grew up with this guy. Ever since junior high, I basically spent all my time with him. I didn't know anything outside of him nor our stupid little town. By the time you moved to West Pointe, I had already vested four years into Chad. When I found out you went to my college and we started talking and hanging out, I fell deeply for you…but I guess my fear of the unknown took over. I can't really explain it, but what I can say is what you and I had was completely different from what Chad and I experienced."

"If you say so," Troy responded standoffishly now redirecting the mood of the conversation. "So did I answer all your questions? Can we end this conversation? Can we just agree that we both hurt each other and move on?"

Rose wanted to keep going, but she was emotionally spent.

"I am done. Let's just enjoy dinner."

"One last thing baby. I am sorry. I truly am. I am not sorry because things didn't work out with her or anything of the sort. I really do love you, and I made a big mistake…and for breaking your heart I sincerely apologize."

Rose had been waiting years for Troy to sincerely say he was sorry, and it caught her off guard. Even though she was still hurt, his apology warmed her heart. Well…either his words or the Sake.

"Thank you baby. I appreciate it. I am also sorry for Chad. I never meant to hurt you."

Rose realized she slipped and called him baby, but at that point it was too late. *I hope he didn't hear that. Oh what the hell. I might as well enjoy myself.*

Rose and Troy reminisced about dating in college and their good years of their marriage. The two joked about the hibachi chef, who had a habit of dropping his spatula at least once during his routine. Rose felt a youthful vigor she hadn't experienced in a long time.

"Rose, baby, I got one for you. Do you remember when we were in high school and used to go down to the Krush Roller Rink? Remember…"

"Don't even say it. When T-Shirt Teddy fell down and got his afro stuck in that girls' skates?"

Troy burst into laughter.

"I will never forget that. T-Shirt Teddy…who used to wear those super tight Run DMC t-shirts and the black rimmed glasses with tape on the nose part. That was one funny looking dude. I tell you what else I remember. I remember how cute you looked that night."

"Cute? Boy you don't remember. You were too busy with that little hot Latin hoochie-moma you brought. What was her name again?"

"Don't go there Rose. You know I had eyes for you even then. You were just in love with Chad."

"Whatever. You were like Richie Rich back in the day. There were a lot of girls who thought you were fine and wanted you, but you always had girlfriends at other schools. I remember when there was all this talk about the new kid. I always thought you were cute."

"Whatever nothing girl. I wanted you so bad. People thought because we had a little bit of money that…well, I don't know what they really thought. I used to tell people I had girlfriends at other schools because in actuality, I was really shy. I had a couple aggressive girls come at me and we fooled around a bit, but I never had the one girl who captured my heart. That one girl was you."

"Boy, get out of here. That is like those same lines you tried to use to get me naked when we were dating. "

"Rose, I am serious."

"Ok Troy, if you say so. Mr. Serious if you were so infatuated, then what did I have on at the rink that day?" Rose posed this question not expecting a response.

"I remember you had that pink outfit on, with that little cute scarf. You looked like an angel to me the way you moved around that rink so effortlessly. You had no idea of the thoughts going through my mind when you were skating backwards."

"Given we were married, I think we reenacted out a few of those fantasies."

The two became giddy, while easing into each other's company again. Rose was impressed Troy remembered and the flattery slowly thawed a piece of her heart, thus making her more receptive and vulnerable.

"No, I have one for you Rose. Do you remember your first year in college when you had that one roommate? What was her name again?"

"Scary Cherry?"

"Yes! How could I forget Scary Cherry…the girl whose grandmother used to make her eat Vicks."

Rose chuckled as she recalled the events from her college dorm days.

"Poor baby. I will never forget her telling me that. We were talking about having colds and how our grandmothers took care of us. I told her how mine used to rub Vicks on my feet and put on some socks and layer me with blankets. This chick turned around and told me her grandmother used to feed it to them on a teaspoon. I was at a loss for words."

"That would explain why she was so off."

The two continued to talk and reminisce about high school, college, family and old events. It didn't take long before they forgot they were divorced. There was a sense of familiarity that came back, and they became very comfortable.

After dinner, Troy walked Rose to her car. Both feeling content from dinner and alcohol, they hugged each other. There was that awkward moment where the two froze in each other's eyes, and before they knew it they embraced and kissed impulsively. Rose bit her lip and jumped in her car while her eyes squinted with her sexual seduction look.

"I miss the smell of your hair baby. I miss tugging on it, and how you nibble my ear."

Rose tried hard not to fall victim to Troy. He had a physical magnetism which she was unable to escape from in the past. She felt a rush of heat flow through her body as she envisioned him embracing her after a night of love making. In an attempt to cancel the thought, Rose chose to ignore his comment, thank him, then leave.

"Thank you for dinner Troy."

"Thank me," Troy replied with sexual innuendo in mind.

Rose looked over Troy and without a second thought she ignored her better judgment and whispered, "Come home baby."

Troy obliged and followed Rose home. Soon as they hit the door, the divorced couple rekindled their flame and went at it with the vigor and recklessness of teenagers. His hands ran through her hair and with the appropriate amount of pressure and intensity, guided her body as he desired. After a few minutes of foreplay, the once estranged couple ended up making love in the foyer, kitchen, and bedroom.

Morning rolled around, and the sunlight gently smacked Rose in the face. Her head was pounding from a night of Sake and sex, and her hair was all over the place. She looked at Troy still sleeping on his stomach and kissed him on his shoulder. Her kiss woke the sleeping giant.

"Man, what time is it?" Troy asked with eyes partially glued shut.

"It is 7. You want some breakfast baby?"

"Sure. Give me a kiss first."

Rose leaned over and kissed her ex-husband.

"I love how you look after sex. Come crawl back on top of me."

"Boy stop. If you want some breakfast let me get started. I can jump on you afterwards."

Rose went downstairs and prepared Troy's favorite breakfast; a Spanish omelet with mushrooms, tomatoes, red peppers, onion, jalapeño and cheddar with four slices of crispy bacon and a little bit of ketchup on the side. Motivated by the aroma, Troy half-dressed and proceeded down the spiraling stairs. He stood there in the kitchen with his dress shirt unbuttoned, designer fitted-t revealed, untied tie draped around his neck, slacks, no socks nor shoes.

"Baby, what's all this?"

"Breakfast for you sexy. I made your favorite."

"Man, you went out the way. Thank you."

Troy kissed Rose on her cheek, and pinched her butt.

"You should have put that on the plate."

"Boy, you are bad. Maybe later. We have all day."

Troy took four bites of his omelet and recklessly dunked each one into a pool of ketchup on the side of his plate before speaking a word.

"Actually not today, I have some business to attend to."

"That is ok. Maybe tomorrow then? Whatever works for you."

"Look Rose, I had a blast, but I don't want you to misunderstand last night."

"Misunderstand? What do you mean?"

"What I mean is I love you…but I don't want you to think that me putting this magic stick on you is a sign we are getting back together."

Rose's feelings were hurt by his arrogance and the way he talked to her, but she tried to maintain and not snap. She rationalized his behavior thinking she was reading too much into it, and tried her hardest to convince herself it was only sex. She could detach herself if need be, or so she thought.

"No, not at all. I wasn't thinking that. I just enjoyed the time with you, that's all."

Troy took a bite of bacon then murmured, "Good. Glad we understand. So tell me, when can I see you next?"

Troy's words triggered irrational thoughts in Rose. *See, he does still love me. He just needs his space, but in time I can see things working out with us…especially after last night. The way he looked into my eyes and told me he loved me? Things look on the up and up. I truly feel like we can move forward from our past since he acknowledged he hurt me.*

"I don't know baby. Maybe we can make it a painting date. Didn't you say you needed some help painting your new loft?"

Troy stopped chewing and hesitated before responding.

"Yes, but I don't need help with it. Everything is cool."

"Oh, that is fine. You already hire painters?"

"Not exactly."

"Baby, that is too big of a job for one man to do. If you need my help, I am more than willing."

"Rose…I don't need your help. My fiancé has already started painting it."

Rose dropped her glass. Shards of glass hit her foot, but she stood numb to any physical pain as her spirit took a direct shot.

"Fiancé?"

"Yes Rose, fiancé. That is why I moved back. She is four months pregnant."

Rose felt the same vomit from last night nice resurface up the back of her throat. She couldn't believe she fell for him again.

"I can't believe you."

"Believe what? I told you upfront what I am about Rose. Don't try to act like you didn't know."

"I am such an idiot. Why would I think you would change? Like sex would dilute who you are. Get the hell out of my house!"

"Oh, it's like that? You wasn't saying that when you were clawing my back asking me for more last night."

"Troy, please…there is no need for us to get ugly at this point. You have done enough damage. Don't make me tear my place up to get you out of here. You used me then and used me again. I am so stupid to think you were sincere. You are trash…get out!"

Troy grabbed one more piece of bacon as he walked towards the foyer. Barefoot with shoes in hand and a mouthful of pork, he yelled out, "If you need some more plumbing work, you know where I am and how to reach me."

Rose laid her head on the counter and cried profusely. She took his plate and threw it into her stainless steel Sub-Zero refrigeration unit. Standing in a kitchen now partially covered with glass and food, Rose fell to the floor and curled into a ball. She clutched her knees, and buried her head in her lap while allowing tears to temporarily release some of the pain she was experiencing. After a few minutes, Rose got herself up and walked to her back patio; deferring picking up the glass for her house cleaners. As she stepped foot out on her wood deck, she looked over the scenery. Her view showcased mountains and a plethora of trees. Often times she'd go outside to pray because it was so beautiful and serene, she felt she was closer to God.

"Lord, why do I have so much, but it feels like so little? I know I am blessed, but why are my choices in men so bad? Are all men just dogs, or is it me? I already have limited contact with men because they are intimidated by my position. Then I fall into a situation where I look at life through an optimistic lens and think maybe my ex changed. I was so wrong about that. I don't understand anything anymore, and I am so confused and frustrated and tired of being lonely. Now I know I don't read my Bible as much as I should, but isn't there something in there about praying, and You blessing us with the desires of our hearts? Well my heart desires a good man, so if You haven't heard me ask the past four million times, let me say it again. Lord, I really I need a good man to come along to restore my faith in men because right now, I don't know what to think. Sometimes I think it is just not in Your will for me to have someone. Did You create a man for me, or was it meant for me to live alone for eternity?"

Chapter VIII

The Rec Center

In her teenage years, Rose received numerous compliments regarding her wardrobe, cute hairstyles and dimples, but she still felt insecure due to her weight. As she began to develop guys referred to her as *thick*, but Rose found it slightly offensive and it made her more self-conscious about her appearance. She participated in drill team, but had emotional eating habits and limited physical activity. When she left for college she determined that she would return home a transformed woman. Utilizing the university fitness facility and taking classes on exercise and nutrition, Rose decided to make a lifestyle change. As the years passed, she altered her diet and developed a rigorous fitness routine which allowed her to stay physically fit and keep the weight off.

The same perseverance that propelled Rose to redefine her physique carried over into her work. As the company grew, Rose developed a stringent, yet systematic approach to her CEO duties at Rozi Cosmetics. Exhibiting professional pride, once her routine was initiated it was near impossible to pry Rose from her work. Some of the tenured employees felt their fearless leader was on the verge of a premature breakdown if she didn't slow down her ferocious tempo. Rose overheard the water cooler confidentials regarding her unrelenting pace and need to schedule a vacation, but ignored their banter as she knew it was unrealistic to relax and ignore obligations with a company to run. She could just picture it now - on the sun kissed beach in Maldives with her PDA lightly dusted in sand, laptop closed yet blinking while faintly receiving a signal, text messages regarding logistics disputes, disagreements with the upcoming marketing campaign, upset board members for one reason or another. Sure a vacation sounded good, but how could one unwind with so much work to be done? Rose understood ultimately her decisions impacted whether or not her co-workers would maintain employment. Her tyrannous hustle kept food in their mouths. Never one to back down from a challenge, Rose welcomed the responsibility and used it as motivation to keep her drive churning.

Rose was not only committed to her office family, but to the education, physical and emotional well-being of youth in West Pointe and surrounding cities. An avid philanthropist, she sowed her money aggressively in the local recreational facility to provide the children an outlet to reach their full potential physically and mentally. Rose felt it was important to invest in the youth as these were the future citizens who would propel our society forward.

A common occurrence, this particular day Rose worked through lunch, occasionally swiveling in her chair to gaze out the window while munching on a lukewarm Sante Fe chicken wrap she ordered during the office run. She required temporary brain inactivity between reps of work to recuperate, however like her exercise routine, the rest period was shortened in anticipation of completing the set. Rose's pet peeve was procrastination and leaving work undone, so she pounded away fearlessly until 3pm when she summoned her assistant into her office.

"I am about to leave for the day. I need to head down to the recreational center and check on this after-school program. Call me if anything arises."

Rose snatched the keys to her black on black BMW 7 Series convertible from the edge of her desk and proceeded to leave the office. Driving down the winding road, Rose said a brief prayer asking for God to bless her life and reveal her purpose. How she enjoyed her work and adhered to the pace, she felt drained and overwhelmed with life as a whole. Although she created this successful company, many people did not know about the pain she dealt with inside. An unwavering feeling that people were only around her because of her success and not for who she was as a person, Rose desired to feel needed in a greater capacity. As much as she loved her work relationship, there were times she wanted to file for a divorce and walk away from everything she worked to build in an attempt to find herself.

Rose finally arrived at the recreational facility. Linden Center was a staple building in the community for many years, but due to the economic downturn interest was focused on survival versus restoration of this historic dilapidated facility. Being in a position to bless others, Rose spearheaded the rebuild and expansion of the recreational center to include a computer lab, tutoring area, library, café, rooms capable of holding gymnastics & martial classes, an Olympic size pool, new clay basketball & tennis courts, two new playgrounds, and a football field with a gravel track for jogging. It became a hub for the youth in West Pointe and kept many out of trouble.

As an active contributor, Rose also helped to create a diverse blend of activities and programs for the children. She periodically did checks to see how her programs were coming along, but more importantly to validate how her money was spent. With a fine tooth comb, Rose ensured they purchased new equipment, implemented the new proposed programs, and that the staff was knowledgeable and friendly. Going through her normal routine of checklists, she stopped at the front desk to gather some paperwork. While reviewing the program itinerary, she clumsily knocked a cluster of papers off the desk. As she squatted under the desk to organize the scattered papers, she overheard a young teen couple in the foyer arguing.

"Candice, if you love me you will do this for me."

"Dre, why now? What is wrong with waiting?"

"Wait? I have been more than patient with you and I am tired of waiting! Do you know who I am? All-State football. All-State basketball. Do you know how many women throw it to me, but I save myself out of respect for you? Do you know how many women would kill to be in your shoes? I am just trying to express my love to you, and you want to be selfish? I must not mean anything to you?"

"Baby, don't be like that."

"Look, this is how it is. Real talk, I am a man, and I have needs that have to be met. If you won't meet them, then someone else will. I am tired of playing games with you, so you have till tomorrow. If you don't show up, then consider us done!"

Rose couldn't believe what she just heard. Biting her lip to keep from jumping over the counter to strangle and scold the young boy, she sat in the crouched position with her rear resting on the back of her heels trying to remain motionless so she wouldn't appear to be eavesdropping. Even though she was a big whig CEO, Rose was still considerate and this conversation took her back to an uncomfortable place she had no intentions on revisiting. After the foyer cleared out, Rose stood up just in time to catch a glimpse of the young girl crying. Something inside told her to reach out to this girl, but she didn't. She proceeded to place the papers back on the counter, and left a note for the staff that she would return tomorrow to inspect the gym.

* * *

The sun rose and spoke its inaugural address to welcome the new day.

Rose slowly opened her eyes with this young girl still on her mind. A quick flip to the local news channel displayed a ticker alerting the West Pointe school cancellation due to a water main break. *I wonder if I will see her at the center today?* - Rose thought. A sense of conviction was so overwhelming Rose bypassed her routine AM workout to head towards the faculty. Rose couldn't explain why she was drawn to this girl, but she felt a strong desire to reach out to her.

As Rose patrolled the center, she was elated to locate the young lady in one of the side gymnasiums solo executing back handsprings, aerials and various somersaults. Rose walked in and initiated a conversation.

"Pretty good. How long have you been in gymnastics?"

"Since I was seven. Turn sixteen in a couple weeks, so I am sure you can do the math."

"Wow. Spunky. I was like that when I was your age."

"I am sorry, I didn't mean to come foul. I am just going through some thangs."

"Want to talk about it?" Rose responded.

"Just issues with my mom, boyfriend, school. Normal high school stuff. Hey, I know who you are. You are that CEO of that makeup company, Miss. Edith Hughes."

"Yes, I am she, but please call me Rose. All my friends call me Rose. Besides I never really liked Edith. It sounds so old, and I am not ancient yet. It was my grandmother's name. So what is your name?"

"Candice Richards."

Candice felt bad about being standoffish and checked herself for acting funky towards Rose. After her attitude readjustment, she realized that Rose could possibly assist her with a school assignment.

"Hey, I have a report coming up soon where we are supposed to write about entrepreneurship. I figured what better person to ask than you? Do you think I could call your office one day and ask a few questions? I promise I won't waste too much of your time."

"How about we go to brunch instead? It is much more intimate than talking on the phone."

Rose extracted her Blackberry from her purse and looked through the day's appointments.

"My next meeting is not until noon, so I actually have some time available right now."

"That would be nice. I'm game."

Candice finally let a grin surface as she gathered her belongings.

* * *

Rose and Candice went around the corner to Granny Red's; a local mom-and-pop diner, that aside from an all-day breakfast menu, also served soul food. Native Georgians, the owners were known to "stick their feet" in the food, among other rave reviews from locals and visitors alike. Rose stuck to a strict diet, but would allocate two days per month to eat whatever she liked. On these free days, sometimes she would come to the diner and enjoy her signature meal - a gluttonous portion of seasoned fried chicken, grits with cheese swimming in butter, collard greens with a tinge of hot sauce, macaroni-n-cheese and waffles topped with strawberries and drowning in blueberry syrup. With an understanding she'd have to put in extra gym hours, Rose shamefully scrapped a heap of room temperature butter on her waffles prior to addressing them, then devoured her food while discussing her a typical day at Rozi Cosmetics. She wanted to bring up the situation with Candice and her boyfriend, but didn't feel it was the right time.

After a short brunch, Rose left a generous cash tip under the plate of half eaten food, then drove Candice home. As they pulled up, Candice's mom was retrieving the mail, sorting through bills like an overhand card shuffle. Her eyes grew apprehensive as she watched the unknown black BMW slowly pull into her driveway. Rose stepped out and waved Candice goodbye as she jogged into the house. She walked closer to Candice's mom to engage her in conversation.

"Miss Richards, I am sorry to take your daughter to brunch without your permission. I had a conversation with her today and she mentioned she had a report due for school. I was just trying to help her out because she reminds me so much of me at her age. Candice is very smart and articulate for her age. All we did was eat brunch and talk. I hope that was ok."

Candice's mother looked disturbed, but tried to subdue her emotions.

"That is fine. I am just happy she is speaking with someone. Candice and I have not been getting along. I don't know what to do to get through to that girl. She doesn't communicate with me at all. Candy is like a completely different person since we moved back."

Rose knew couldn't resist the temptation to see how much information she could extract.

"This is not my business so forgive me if I cross any boundaries, but may I ask what the problem is? When did it start? She seemed to be a pretty well-rounded girl."

"Candy used to be an A student and has always been athletic. When she was seven years old, she competed in the USATF. She won the 200 and came in second in the 100 and hurdles…which was good given most of the kids who won first place were ten years old. She got a little older and won the youth division 200 meters at the AAU Junior Olympics for 12 year olds, and also won the youth 100 and 400 races at the USA Youth Outdoor Track and Field Championships.

"Once she became a junior high student, that is where it seemed like she began losing interest. She was state champion in the 200, but her passion for track seemed to diminish when she found out her father and I were breaking up. She has so much potential, but lately she has been into this new boy and her grades have been dropping. She lies to me all the time and doesn't think I know it, so I can't really trust her. I don't know what to do with her anymore. It is already enough stress just trying to be a single mom and hold our family together, then add in a child that blatantly lies in your face? I just don't understand what is going on with Candy right now."

"Well Miss. Richards…"

"Call me Lisa."

"Lisa, if you don't mind, I would like to spend a day with Candice and show her my world. I think exposing her to how I conduct business would be good for her. I also have some connections with professional athletes. The Olympic trials are coming up in Indianapolis this June. I have a good friend, a former track and field Olympian, that I'd love to introduce her to."

Lisa felt insulted and took it as her parental methods were in question.

"Why do you care so much? Do you have a daughter? Do you know what I am going through? I find it funny people with no kids always have a solution for what us single moms should be doing. *Show her my world.* Hell, I'd like to see you work a day in mine. See how my world is!"

"Lisa, I didn't mean it that way. I am sorry if I offended you. I just wanted to help. She just reminds me so much of me when I was younger and…"

"Leave my property. I don't care how much money you have. Get out now!"

Rose did not say one word. She threw her hands up while walking backwards, and as she started her car she saw Candice in the upstairs window allowing the curtain to wrap around her youthful frame. Candice waved with a distraught look on her face as Rose backed out the driveway.

Candice ran down the stairs to confront her mom as she entered the living room.

"What did you say to her? Why are you trying to ruin my life?"

"Ruin your life? Girl you are only fifteen. Do you know what life is?"

Lisa went to the coffee table, grabbed a stack of utility bills, and tossed them recklessly like a Frisbee with no intention on flying further than three feet.

"This is life. Taking care of your responsibilities. Not just throwing your life away on some silly boy, or whatever it is that you are doing!"

"Throwing my life away? You have no clue what I am going through. You are so busy being bitter about Daddy leaving with Auntie Lynn…"

In a split second without thinking, Lisa smacked Candice flush across her face. She was embarrassed, but more importantly her feelings were hurt because Candice rarely, if ever, got into any type of trouble which warranted a strike. Her eyes rapidly filled with tears as Candice ran up the stairs.

"Baby, I am sorry. I didn't mean to…"

Bam! Candice slammed the old wooden door shut so hard it rattled the items on her wall.

A few hours passed and Lisa knocked on the door, and in a soft motherly tone asked, "Candy, can I come in baby?"

"Sure, why not. It is your house, and you pay the bills."

She went into Candice's room and sat on the corner of the bed.

"So, are you going to eat dinner? I made your favorite."

Lisa prepared fried orange roughy, French-style green-beans, twice-baked potatoes and homemade corn bread in Grandma's cast iron skillet.

"Mom, I am not trying to argue anymore, I am just not in the mood to eat."

"Ok. I will put your plate in the fridge."

Lisa began to walk towards the door, then stopped.

"Candy, I am sorry. I just want you to know that you are not a burden to me. I didn't mean it that way. Mommy is just frustrated. Your father left me with all these bills and no money, and I am trying to make it the best I can. I get so upset because on top of all I deal with, I don't know how to help you. I want to be there, but I also don't want you to make the same mistakes I made and I just don't know how to convey that."

"I understand Mom. I just need space to work some things out."

"Well baby, just work with me. I am going through menopause so my life is changing the same time yours is. I don't want us to be distant. You are all I have." Lisa paused as she tried to figure a way to rectify the situation she destroyed. "And next time you see that makeup lady, please offer her my deepest apologies. She wanted to take you out, and I was rude with her. Tell her that I don't mind at all."

"Thanks Mommy."

As Lisa shut the door, Candice jumped off her bed and scurried through her gym bag. She pulled out the notepad she used to copy down notes from her interview of Rose. Along with her notes, she also had product brochures from Rose, as well as her personal business card. Candice grabbed the business card and called her cell phone number.

"Miss Edith, this is Candice…Yes…Oh, I am sorry, Rose…Yes, I would like that very much…Ok, see you then."

Candice hung up the phone excited about the opportunity to shadow Rose for the day.

* * *

Rose introduced Candice to everyone in the office, then gave her the rundown of operations from sitting in on a conference call to explaining daily operations. Absorbing this foreign environment, Candice started to open her mind to new ways of thinking. She always knew she had a God-given ability in track, but didn't know what else she wanted to do with her life. Hearing Rose's story and seeing the manifestation of her dream made Candice begin to think outside the box about her own life, dream and goals. *You know, I have always loved animals. Maybe I will go into veterinarian medicine. Then maybe in my spare time I can be an assistant coach for track or something. Or maybe, I can start up my own program for little girls and teach them ballet, and manners, and how to be a lady. I think that would be so cool.*

The day ended quicker than Candice would have liked. During the drive home Rose picked her brain.

"How did you like today? Was it an overkill?"

"Actually, no. I really enjoyed myself. Seeing you build all this from nothing really inspired me. I hope to have half your success."

"Well I am glad you enjoyed yourself. I am sure you will have more success than I ever dreamed…as long as you put your mind to it. Anytime you want drop in, my doors are always open for you. Call me anytime… you have my numbers."

"I appreciate that."

"I also have something else for you. Here take this card. This is a good friend of mine from college. She ran track and was a state champion. I am telling you, this girl was bad! She is a former Olympian and now she is a well sought after personal trainer. Maybe she can give you some insight on life as a collegiate athlete, career goals, and what to expect. I was thinking that we could go to the upcoming Olympic trials in Indy and I can introduce you two. If not, at least you have her contact info."

"I don't know what to say. You have been so nice to me. Thank you!"

Candice thought back to how she met Rose at the recreational center and felt bad that she was rude to her.

"You know Rose, I need to give you an apology. I am sorry for how I acted when we first met at the rec center. I was just going through some things at the time. It was nothing personal, I was just stressed."

"Anything you want to talk about?"

"No, not really. Just high school stuff."

Rose realized that she could not seize the opportunity to speak to Candice about the incident she overheard with her boyfriend without it sounding like she was eavesdropping. As she tried to figure out a polite way to bring it up, her niece came to mind and sparked an idea.

"Candy, I want to throw something at you."

"Sure, what's up?"

"I was thinking, you've seen how a CEO works, why not see how a CEO plays?"

"That sounds cool. What did you have in mind?"

"How about a good old-fashioned sleep over?"

Candice didn't know how to respond. She was overwhelmed with Rose's kindness, but the apprehensive about her intentions. *Why would an adult want a sleep over?* - Candice thought. After going back and forth, she decided it would be interesting to see Rose's home and how she lived outside the office.

"You know what Rose, that sounds fun."

"Cool," Rose responded as she took a swig of mineral water. *Lord I hope I am doing what's right. I just don't want her to go down the same path I did.*

Chapter IX

The Sleepover

Candice tossed the last few items into her girlish duffel bag. While straightening the cranberry comforter on her bed, she heard a car pull into the driveway. A quick glimpse out the window confirmed her ride had arrived so she promptly jammed two additional items in her bag then trotted down the steps. Lisa waved in approval of the prearranged sleepover as her daughter walked towards Rose's vehicle.

"Thank you so much for inviting me over. I needed to get away from here."

"Not a problem at all. I am glad your mother let you come."

"I am too. She actually seemed happy that I was leaving. Maybe she has a date or something?" Candice responded jokingly.

"Would that be a bad thing?"

"I guess not. I want my mom to be happy."

Rose smiled and continued to accelerate through town. She raised her forearm slightly to check the declining gas gauge.

"I usually always keep a full tank of gas, but I have been so busy lately."

"You know you just passed two gas stations, right?"

"Yes," Rose responded with a smirk. "Guess you can call it a pet peeve. I only get gas from stations that look clean. Given the options here, I usually just wait until I get on the outskirts of town."

Rose eventually cruised into her favorite gas station, fed her hungry sports car, then continued the trek home. Conversation was light during the drive, but enough to make the trip seem shorter than it was.

After a few minutes they arrived at Rose's posh abode in the hills. Candice closed the car door and paused to admire how the landscaping accented the stucco three-story home. There was a balanced decor of leafy plants, manicured shrubs and colorful fragrant flowers guarded by young palm trees; a definite contrast for a mid-western home but a welcomed change.

Rose guided Candice down a short flagstone path that led to the entrance of the home. After routinely disabling the alarm, one flick of the switch woke up the chandelier which dangled like expensive earrings and illuminated the foyer to reveal two bowed stairways that hugged the adjacent walls.

"This is *really* nice!"

"Thank you. I am glad you like it. You can put your bag down here. Come on…let me show you around."

Rose walked Candice through the foyer which opened to an even larger room. The living space had a huge plasma screen mounted above the fireplace, and three rows of stacking windows which provided a scenic view from the hills. The tour continued throughout the home and ended back in the living space.

Candice was overwhelmed by the environment. She really enjoyed seeing a woman obtain such nice things because it revived her optimism towards life and future goals. As the night winded down, the two relaxed in the living area while munching on an assortment of snacks and watching television. Flipping through the stations, they stumbled upon a reality show where several young, semi-attractive women fought for the attention and affection of one homely man. As the melee escalated, Rose shook her head in astonishment.

"So Candy, is this how the girls your age act? I know we were bad when I was younger, but your generation is on a completely different level."

"You would be surprised," Candice whimpered under her breath.

"I am sure you couldn't say too much that would shock me. What do kids your age get into?"

Even though Candice felt comfortable talking to Rose, she was apprehensive about speaking to an adult.

"Nothing really."

"Nothing? You guys act like drugs and sex didn't happen in our day? You can trust whatever you talk about will stay between us. Since I have a young niece, I try to keep my ear to the street and not be as detached as others my age. I want to know honestly what she is going to have to deal with."

Candice was still reluctant to respond, however Rose's genuine disposition made her trustworthy. She slowly began to open up.

"Kids smoke weed, drink, and there are some kids who do X."

"We had a lot of weed heads in my day. Sad thing is most of them became so immune they began progressing to stronger drugs. So you said I would be shocked. What else? If I could be in high school for one week, what would shock me?"

"Hard to say. Of course you have the nasty dances at parties and school dances. Then you have kids foolin' around at school…but I am sure *way back* when you were in school there were probably kids having sex in the custodial closet as well."

"Way back? Watch it!"

Both the ladies laughed.

"What do the teachers say?"

"Some of the kids at my school are real disrespectful. They sit there and curse right in front of the teachers and nothing is done about it. Heck, sometimes the teachers curse right back."

Rose empathized with the teachers as she knew it was a daunting task. From being active in the community and surrounding cities, Rose realized that in a lot of these cases teachers were put into situations where their hands were tied with funding and lack of support from the parents and community.

Candice completed her thought.

"Things are just different here. Can't really skip school because everyone is in your business. Somebody's parent is likely to see you. At my old school, they rarely kept attendance correct, so kids would skip all the time to hang out at other schools. It was really stupid because of the potential for fights to erupt."

"I remember in my teenage years if you had a dispute, you handled it and it was over. Watching the news, things are just so different now."

"Kids are crazy these days. My girlfriend's older sister told me they used to carry razors under their tongue or blades with them. Heck, nowadays chicks don't cut, they shoot. It is so easy to get a piece these days, and it is like if you know you are going to fight, why bring a knife to a gunfight? Not trying to be funny, but that is how it is and how people think. Folks just don't scrap anymore like they did in your day."

"That is awful! I am not trying to come across like one of those opinionated folks with no kids, but where are the parents? These kids needs some discipline."

"It is crazy how much you can actually get away with. I love my mom and she be on it…but I have some friends, and it is like their mothers be on some other stuff. I have this one in particular, who mind you, is still in high school, and has a boyfriend who is 20. The mother lets the boyfriend spend the night and everything. She even lets her daughter walk around in her underwear around the boy."

"Wow. My mom wouldn't even let my sisters have company over at all, and if someone came over, you best believe we wouldn't be walking around in some panties, or anything skimpy. It wasn't going down in my household like that."

"Yea, these girls nowadays are skanks. They do pretty much anything a guy tells them to. I have heard of several girls in my class that have done a threesome. Girls in my grade are just nasty. They actually will go down on a guy before they kiss him. I guess they think kissing is more intimate."

"What?" Rose took a second to process what she just heard. She knew these teens were sexually active, but she just never imagined it was as bad as Candice described. How she initiated the conversation, it started to become overwhelming once Candice opened up.

"I am sorry, but I am still trying to get over these little orgies. Threesomes? That is just so sad. How do they even accomplish talking young women into doing that?"

"I don't know personally, but I have had some girlfriends tell me about guys approaching them. They pretty much just ask outright. They walk up to the girl and tell them something like – *You know, I wouldn't be opposed to a threesome if you wanted to.*"

"And they actually fall for that?"

"Apparently so."

Rose shook her head, disappointed she couldn't do anything to influence these decisions made by young women. She felt guilty, but didn't know what she could do. Her curiosity got the best of her, and she continued to ask questions.

"I can't imagine how things will be once my niece is your age. We had promiscuous females in our school, but it was nothing like it is now. Out of curiosity, how many partners would you say girls your age have? Or better yet, how many would you estimate they would have by the time they graduate?"

"Wow. I think I would run out of fingers. I would say the average, if they are honest, is about twelve."

"Twelve?"

"Yes, and probably more if they are being honest. Most will probably say between four and eight. Being a virgin in my era is hard because *everyone* is doing it. They look at me like I am a leper or something because I have not yet."

"Trust me Candy, there is nothing wrong with being a virgin. I wish I could take back some of my experiences."

"Everyone says that, but sometimes the pressure is just so heavy. I don't know…it is just hard sometimes."

Candice's words struck a chord. Rose understood there were pressures she couldn't understand. In her day talking to an adult about sex brought about a scolding, thus the unwritten rule you don't do it, don't talk about it. As a young lady she vowed to never be that way. Now time has passed she found herself in mentor's shoes. Rose realized why adults were that way when she was younger, but felt there had to be common ground. Too often women her age looked down at younger women with a judgmental eye, instead of being real and telling them they have been there, done that. Rose wished someone would have shared their life stories with her when she was younger and possibly plant a seed which would have helped her make better decisions.

"Young girls in this current time experience things that I could not imagine. I agree that sometimes we adults forget how to relate to you. It's hard because we just see the end result and get frustrated because we just want you to get it. We don't think about how we felt at that age. Life throws so many things in your direction, trust me when you get to be my age, the things you think are serious in high school will be a distant memory."

"Sometimes I feel like life is passing me by. I run track, and it is like everyone is running while I am standing still and I feel like an outcast."

Candice paused.

"So did your mother talk to you about sex? How did you learn?"

"First of all, don't let them make you feel ostracized. People will do and say things to get you into trouble because they are jealous of you. Most of the time people are envious because you have the courage to have principles and go against the grain. And as far as how I learned - my mother? Are you kidding me? You must not know how things were done in my day. My mother's generation acted like they had mild heart attacks if you even mentioned sex. I, unfortunately, had to learn from a friend of mine named Autumn."

Silence interrupted the conversation as Rose flashed back to her now distant childhood. She advised Candice she would return shortly, and slid on some house slippers before entering the garage. Organized with crates from the container store, Rose rummage through totes until she located her high school keepsakes. A few minutes later she returned to the living room with a 7x5 inch journal. It was red leather embossed with a rose on the cover and a matching rose shaped key. The key dangled from a leather string attached to the diary and fit the lock which was affected by oxidation and displayed a tinge of rust.

"When I was younger, I felt I had no one to turn to. My sisters were vain, self-absorbed in themselves and getting boys, and I felt adults would just scold me. My grandfather purchased this diary for me when I was twelve. I was reluctant to incriminate myself in fear someone would find it, that was until my heart was broken. This diary affirmed my trust and was a safe haven for my emotions. During my high school years I used it as my basement, or a place to store all the things I didn't want to see nor necessarily think about. The things I couldn't talk to anyone about."

Rose ran her fingertips across the embossed cover tracing the thorns on the rose and exhaled through her nose. She used the key to carefully open the diary and began to skim through the contents. Turning the pages feeling the indent left by her penmanship, memories began to slowly resurface.

"I haven't looked at this book for ages."

Rose began to read silently while slightly smiling. She broke the silence and began to read aloud.

Hey diary, it's been a while. I was at the mall today and ran into my old childhood friend Autumn. She was the friend that introduced me to the world of sex.

I will never forget that conversation. It was a typical mid-summer day with absolutely nothing to do so I decided to ride my bike over to Autumn's to hang out. We were sitting on her blacktop driveway playing her brother's labyrinth game, and Autumn let out the loudest fart. I tell you, that girl was something special. I fell back under the shade of a huge tree in her front yard grasping my stomach trying to catch my next breath. Usually we would stay out there for hours just playing, eating popsicles and acting up. This particular day when we finally grew tired of playing games and laughing, our conversation took a detour into grown folks stuff. She turned to me and asked me if I had messed around with a guy before and of course I said no. I assumed that messing around meant more than kissing, although I truly did not have personal insight about what more than that really meant. She began to tell me that she had and about how much fun she had when she did and how I should try it.

I didn't want to look stupid asking questions, yet I found myself curious. Besides, it is not like I can go to my mom and ask her anything. She'd probably put me in private school for the question alone. I figured Autumn would be the closest thing to a resource, so I asked her what she meant regarding messing around. Sensing my inexperience, she gave a full description of what she had done with one of her male friends. The guy that she was referring to was not her boyfriend to my knowledge, but it was someone who would stop by when her parents were not home.

As I sat there, I couldn't believe how she made what they were doing sound so simple. She talked of him fingering her as if it was just normal and something all girls were doing. I tried my best to keep my composure so I would not let on that I was clueless about this new world she was introducing me to, but I have never been one that is good at hiding my facial expressions. I absolutely could not believe the things that my ears and mind were trying to take in and process. Even after her detailed description of what happened, I was still a little confused about what went where in her sexual encounters, but I was too embarrassed to ask. I had seen kissing scenes on television, but the things that she was talking about captivated my attention and was way more information than I had been given by any source in the past. Seeing as how I was only in the fifth grade and she was a grade above me, I could not understand how she became so experienced so quickly. I knew I should not be listening to all of this and we would get into deep trouble if anyone overheard, but I was taking everything she was saying in because up to this point she was my only source of knowledge concerning sexual matters.

Candice snickered.

"Yea, seems like you always have that one friend that introduces you to things you had no clue about and usually they are misinformed and tell you all wrong."

"Candice, I couldn't have spoken that better myself. That is what I was trying to tell you earlier about people trying to pull you down because they are jealous. They try to lead you to a path of straight destruction so you can be miserable right along with them. I like the way you speak. You talk as if you are a woman with years of experience behind your words. I know this is cliché to say this to you, but you truly are mature beyond your age. Your mannerisms, how you carry yourself, your aura. I wish I could go back and be like you. So many choices I would have changed."

"Choices like what?"

"Choices in the men I gave my time and energy to. Choices in the education route I took. Choices in the activities I wanted to participate in and never did. If I could go back, I would live life to the fullest and never let a man, or scornful hating woman, ruin my joy and keep me from doing what I want. I'd keep trucking forward and doing my thing until God sent the man he had for me."

Candice nodded her head in agreement.

"So what ever happened to that Autumn girl?"

"As we grew older, she developed physically before anyone else our age and became more experienced. There was a list of new guys who were added to the stories that she would reveal to me over time. And let me tell you, Autumn had a way of telling stories. She was a great orator… pun intended. The way she could draw a picture with words describing her encounters with these men always kept my attention. I felt like her verbal memoirs, which should probably have been unveiled only in a diary and then burned, were teaching me about things I would need in my future encounters with men…way into the future of course. I knew if I just kept listening, by the time my first interaction with a guy came, I would be well-informed and ready. From what I was hearing, she was not portraying any consequences for her actions other than getting a thrill out of it. Although I knew inside that there was more to it than that, her confessions to me about what went on in her home were like a magnetic force pulling me in and leading to a strong desire to know firsthand about the things she was speaking of."

Candice became quiet as she found the parallel in Camille and Autumn. She recalled the same curiosity from the stories her friend Camille told her. It was apparent to Rose that Candice had something on her mind, so she attempted to get her to open up.

"What's up Candy? You falling asleep on me?"

"No. I was just thinking."

"Thinking about what baby?"

"Just life. Life, relationships, men, everything really."

"You know Candy, if there is anything you want to talk about, or ask me, I am here. I want you to know I won't judge you, and I am just here to talk if you need me. Just look at me like a big sister."

Candice hesitated, but her curiosity got the best of her.

"What does sex feel like?"

"Whoa," Rose said as she wasn't expecting that response. "That is a loaded question."

"I was just curious. I can't really listen to the girls around me because I don't believe they know what they are talking about. I can't ask my mother because she would try to put me on birth control or something. I just don't understand what it feels like. Does it really feel good to women, or do women just say that to keep a man?"

"Well Candy, yes and no. Sex can be enjoyable, but it has to be with the right person. When I say the right person, I don't mean a boyfriend…I mean a *husband*. I am reluctant to paint you this fairy tale image that getting married will be bliss and sex will just be wonderful, because as you see I am divorced myself, and I am usually not one to give advice. I will say there were times that I truly enjoyed myself, and it was beautiful and magical almost. That agape love. Well, that is what I thought it was anyways."

"I wonder what it feels like for guys. They act like they are just going to die if they don't get any." Candice said as she reminisced about Dre and his multiple attempts to join with her.

"Girl, let me tell you firsthand, don't let some guy talk you into doing something you don't feel comfortable with. And in most cases, it feels way better for men than it does for women. Many women do it and don't even have orgasms. Trust me, the first time you have sex, confetti is not going to pop out of the ceiling and streamers won't fly. That is your body, and you need to reverence it. There is nothing more selfish than a high school boy. The only thing they think about is sex. I am not trying to be a feminist or anti-men because trust me, if anyone loves and respects men, it is me. But what you need to understand is in high school, they are not men yet. Carrying a pistol or fighting doesn't make you a man. Getting into trouble or playing sports doesn't make you a man. They are still trying to find their identity at that point. Not only are they boys emotionally, but physically as well. There are studies out there about the development of teen brains and how the frontal lobe, or the section where reasoning comes from, has not fully developed yet."

"I believe that to be true for boys, but girls are more mature," Candice replied in defense of her gender.

"Sugar, that study was for boys and girls. I don't want to discount you in any way because you are very intelligent, and trust me, when I was your age I thought I was more mature than others around me and had the answers, but just hear me out. From experience, when you are a teenager you just do stupid stuff. The problem is from some of the stupid things you do there is no turning back from. There are repercussions for your actions, and some of your actions as a teen can affect you well into your adult life, believe me. What you need to do is set goals and boundaries for yourself. Make sure if things don't line up, you are strict about adhering to them. If you want to go to college, then make sure everything you do right now is a building block to achieve your goal. If spending time with a no good boyfriend is not going to help you get into school, then maybe you need to eliminate him from your life."

"Rose, no disrespect, but that is easier said than done. I know my boyfriend has faults, but I truly love him. It is like with us both having a parent that left the household, we connect on a different level. I feel bad because all he wants in return is sex, and I am just scared."

Rose began to chuckle.

"Feel bad? Candy, I want you to think about something. I want you to visualize everything that your boyfriend does for you. Create a list in your head. Not a list of what you want him to do or imagine him doing…what he actually does. Now I want you to think about what you want out of a relationship. List everything. Now take both of those lists, and match them up."

Candice tried to defend the honor of her boyfriend so that she would not feel embarrassed about her decision to be with him, but the look of disappointment on her face was apparent.

"Candy, I understand the need for affection. My dad wasn't there, so I get it. The thing is, you have to protect yourself. How selfish is that for him to ask you to give up your body and you get nothing back from him in return? It makes no sense. Just think about that. He wants you to allow him to penetrate you and take your innocence…but on the flip side, he has not done one thing on the list of things you want and need out of a relationship. Like I said, boys that age can be very selfish. It is biological."

"What am I supposed to do then? If I don't give him some and try to satisfy him, then someone else will."

"Girl, when you get to my age you will learn that if they will leave that easy, then let them. Don't sit there stressing over who some man wants. I know this first hand. My husband left me for my cousin. Yes, it hurt like hell and cut me deeply, but you know what? I recovered and it made me stronger. He was not the one God had for me, but I tried to make something exist that didn't."

"Wow, your cousin? That sounds like some talk show stuff."

"Oh yea girl, it was something serious. I am calm now, but best believe when it happened it took several family members to restrain me."

"Are they still together? Seems like that would be hard to see them at family functions."

"My ex acts as if they ended it, but to be honest who knows what really happened? Maybe they are still sleeping with each other on the side. I don't know and don't really care at this point. I can't sit there day in and day out wondering what they are doing. And as far as her, she hides from me. I am not going to do anything to that woman, but it is funny that she is scared to run into me. I actually like it this way."

Candice was tickled with Rose's demeanor when speaking about her ex-husband and cousin.

"My boyfriend is this big time athlete at our school. You probably have seen him in the papers – Andre Abbott."

"My brother-in-law is into sports, and I think I may have overheard him speaking about that kid."

"He is an excellent athlete and has so much potential. When I transferred to this school, I basically kept to myself. I saw him but never paid him any attention. I tried out for track, and he saw me there stretching. He was actually the first guy to speak to me, and he was so polite…so much so that it took me off guard and I was extremely flattered. I don't know Rose. This environment is just different. People all in your business when you are dating and just the drama of living here. Even though we visited my grandmother and I was somewhat familiar with this town, it is completely different to relocate here and be an actual resident."

"Yea, this place does take some getting used to. It drains you."

"I was having a hard time adjusting here. Dre and I began to talk a lot more on the phone, then one thing led to another and we started to become intimate. We haven't had sex but have had some sessions get pretty heavy to the point he has had an accident a few times."

Rose began to laugh.

"Isn't that pathetic? Horny little devils."

"I know, right? But you know, in some weird way it made me feel good that I could please Dre. Not like I am having sex with him or anything, but just to know he wants me that bad that he climaxes. I can't explain it, but in a freaky sort of way, that turned me on. But as far as going through with the actual act, it just doesn't feel right. He has suggested I go down, play with it…all kinds of things he comes up with, but I am just not ready."

"Guys will say all that stuff to you. *Don't leave me like this girl. Just touch it a few times so it will go down. Just kiss it one time. Just let me put the head in.* They come up with some of the dumbest lines in a fit of desperation. Trust me they did it my era, my grandmother's era, and will continue to do it going forward."

"I just feel bad because he acts like it hurts him so bad, but from what I hear it hurts like heck the first time women do it too."

"Don't pay any attention to him Candy, he will be fine. It is not like he will die or anything. All he has to do is take a cold shower and sleep on his stomach all night."

Both Candice and Rose laughed thinking about previous encounters with men in heat.

"I don't know. Maybe I am stuck in a fairytale, but even if I were to give in to him, he always wants it in the worst places. In the back of his truck, on the couch when his dad is gone, or in his funky room. Maybe I am a hopeless romantic, but I just want my first time to be special…to be right. When he pressures me, it just doesn't seem right at all."

"Candy, don't let him make you do anything you will regret. Believe me I am…well, my age is not important. Point is, I still think about how bad my first experience was, and I didn't even see that fool but a few times after high school."

"What happened? If you don't mind me asking?"

"Do you want anything to drink?"

"No thank you."

"I am not avoiding your question. Let me go use the restroom then make myself some tea. This may be a long night."

Chapter X

The Basement

Rose took a second and gently flipped through the crisp journal pages as if she were reading a sacred document.

"When I was in college I wrote one of my last entries, then sealed this diary never to be opened again until today. I was in a place of self-reflection and spent a lot of time looking back at the mistakes I made. I wrote this about my childhood sweetheart."

> *At the age of 12, I began seeing a young man named Chad. I believed that he cared about me from what I knew about relationships at that age. I enjoyed his company and the attention he seemed to give to me. His physical affection by means of holding hands, kissing and hugging were so enticing to me. Spending all the time that I could with him became a priority for me. I did not know much, but I knew that I wanted him to keep coming around. My need for his embraces and amorous glances was actually more than I could totally comprehend at the time. All that I knew for sure was that I did not want those courting actions to end. Our relationship began by him asking me, through my friend Autumn, to be his date for the homecoming dance. It was my first one and I was really elated to be an eighth grader asked to a high school dance by a sophomore. This dance was the reason we began seeing each other. I did not know him well, but Autumn spoke highly of him and so I was happy to oblige when given the opportunity. When I begged for my mother's permission to go to the dance, she eventually, or I should say reluctantly, said yes.*

"At least your mother said yes. Mine probably would have thrown a fit."

"Candy, that is not necessarily a bad thing. I was glad she trusted me enough to let me go, but wish she wouldn't have. It would have saved me a lot of heartache later on in life, but at the time I was just so elated. Anywho…"

Planning for what I considered to be such a big event at the time was exciting for me. Deciding who was going with whom, how we would get there, where we would go for dinner, and what we would wear became the most important topics every day. My mom and I shopping for a dress was a pleasurable bonding moment for us. Her suggestions, I mean requirements, for what I would wear were not always appreciated at the time but I knew that she was looking out for my best interest.

So the big day finally arrived. I had such a good time just getting ready for the event, and the dress that my mother picked out for me was actually beautiful. It was a little black and white fitted, but not too short number. I went to get my hair done with my friends and was allowed to dabble on a little lipstick. We ventured out of my little boring hometown to dinner at the Olive Garden which alone made us feel grown…then off to the homecoming dance we went. It was a mediocre event, definitely not what I had pumped up in my head, but all in all I was glad that I had gone.

"Hold up, back up for a second. They had Olive Garden when you were in school?" Candice stated in a humorous tone.

"Oh, so you have jokes now?" Rose was amused.

"Ok, I am sorry. Continue your story. What ended up happening with that boy?"

Rose continued to read.

After that night we continued to see each other for a few months. We became boyfriend and girlfriend at some point during that period, and spending time together became a priority for both of us. We met mainly at my house because of the restrictions that my mother had in place for me, but there were a few visits that I was allowed to make to his house. As he became an important part of my everyday life, I began to care deeply for him. When he would kiss me and hug me and hold my hand I felt warm inside. I did not really know what love or in love meant, but I sort of felt a little pull in the secret and inmost recesses of my heart when we were around one another or when we would have to be away from each other, therefore I began to think it was love. All that I knew for sure was that I wanted whatever was going on between us to last.

There were several occasions when we were spending time together that the kissing and hugging and touching became intense. I had not had those feelings before with anyone because up to that point, nothing had gone past a peck or holding hands. It felt good while it was happening, but even then I was questioning myself. I knew that it was going too far too fast, but I did not want his affection toward me to come to a complete stop. I knew that what was happening I did not want my parents to see or know about. I knew that I should definitely not let this relationship and what we were doing actually cross the line into actually having sex. I can't remember where I heard it, but someone must have said that it was bad. It was in the Bible somewhere that you should not do it, but I did not know exactly why…just that it was bad. I kept my thoughts at bay because what was happening up to this point felt good. The closer we grew, the more intense our make out sessions became. I could tell he was growing frustrated with me when I would back away or move his hand.

One day, the phone rang. I heard my sister call my name, so I went to grab the phone. Was it him? It was my desire for it to be his voice on the other end of the line instead of one of my other friends. I picked up and the fact that it was him brought a smile to my face. He asked if I was going to come over, and I agreed. He told me that his mother was at a convention or something, and would not be home. He took advantage of her absence, and asked me if I would finally give him what he wanted. I told him that I did not think that I was ready for that, and then out came the ultimatum.

He said that I had a choice…I could give myself to him when I came over or I could stay home and end our relationship. I sat in silence. Where was this coming from? I knew he wanted to take our physical relationship further than it had gone in the past, but I did not see that blunt statement coming at all…and I certainly did not know what to say to him. I also knew that he felt I was a bit of a tease. I desperately wanted to continue the relationship, but I did not want to start having sex. At that moment, I could not give him an answer so he just left me with the option of showing up or not showing up at his house.

Rose took a break from her story to sip her tea. As Candice rearranged her leg which fell asleep, she noticed Rose's body mannerisms. The tone changed as she began to recall details from that day she buried deep in her memory bank to protect her heart.

Holding the phone to my ear, I just sat there. He had hung up, but I was just sitting there still holding the receiver in astonishment. What was I going to do? Did I really want to give my virginity to him? I sat there in unbelief that I was being forced to make this decision. Anxiety and a tad bit of anger began to well up inside of me. I wanted to cry, but could not for the fear that someone would ask me what was wrong, then I would have to tell what was happening, or either sit and bold face lie. Going to my room to attempt to find a little bit of privacy seemed to be my only option so I hung up the phone, turned to go down the hall, and tried to pretend that everything was normal just in case I bumped into anyone on my way. As I pushed open the door to my little yellow room, I knew that no solitude would be granted to me when I saw my annoying, know-it-all sibling.

I came to my room, and my sister was lying down, so I did the only thing that I could do...flop on my bed and pretend that I was asleep in an attempt to sort this mess out. What in the world was I going to do? I felt completely lost and abandoned by him and I had not even said no yet. Because we had been spending so much time together, I just knew that if I did not do what he wanted I would lose him, his companionship, his kiss, his touch, his affection, his attention, and what I foolishly thought was his love for me. I needed his affirmation, acknowledgment, or assurance that I was not insane for not wanting to go through with this. I needed someone to tell me that I was not crazy, but I could not tell anyone or seek out any advice. Doing so would probably result in the end of my social life until I was forty years old. Why was Chad forcing me to make this decision? I thought.

"I don't think I will ever understand guys. Where do these ultimatums come from? Dre had the nerve to give me one too. They act like the world is revolving around them, and if you don't do what they say then you are just this terrible person. I don't know sometimes. I mean, I love him, but he has issues. Part of me wants to leave, but then I feel like it is better to wait for him to change, versus starting all over. Dating is crazy these days."

"Well girl, I am speaking from the other end…the end that gave into the ultimatum. That is why I speak to you with so much passion. You are so young, and have so much life left to live. I see so much potential in you, and I don't want you to throw it away for some man who doesn't appreciate you or your gifts. You were created by God to do good things on this earth. You are not a terrible person for wanting to respect your body and wait. Ultimatums by their very nature are usually selfish. They are uncompromising demands. In most cases, people use ultimatums to make another person do something that they ordinarily wouldn't do. I have a simple theory on this. If a person doesn't want to do whatever it is you are trying to coerce them to do by free will, then why would you place this demand on them knowing that is not where their heart truly is? Now if someone has a drinking or drug problem, that is one thing. Those are necessary ultimatums that are tied into the health and well-being of another individual. But what I am talking about is these selfish relationship ultimatums. The ones where men pressure women into these sexual situations, or women pressure men into marriage or some sort of commitment. That is plum stupid to me. The end result is usually never good when someone is forced to do something they initially didn't want to do in the first place. In my opinion, ultimatums are only good when they are non-verbal or non-communicated…they are called standards."

"I hear you." Candice knew Rose was telling her the truth, she just needed some way to apply what she was hearing to her life. "So, what did you end up doing with Chad? How did you handle that?"

Rose lost her place. She used her finger to trace her pages until she found a reference point where she left off.

Getting up off of my bed and walking slowly toward my mother's room, still undecided, I felt something in my gut telling me not to go. For some reason I was not listening to that something. I knocked on the door, and she answered. "Can I go over Chad's house to watch a movie?" I asked. "Are his parent's going to be home?" she questioned. "Yes." I responded without any hesitation.

I thought to myself Rose, what are you doing? You know you should not have just stood there and lied to your mother. But then again…it is the only way you will be able to prevent losing your boyfriend. My mother paused for a moment and then hesitantly said that I could go. She went looking for her keys while I grabbed my coat, and I met her at the car. Though I was still feeling that twinge in my conscience, I continued on this path to save my relationship.

"You were on a mission, huh Rose? A mission to save your man."

Rose was slightly offended by her youthful sarcasm, but tried to use her story as a way to help Candice.

"I know I was stupid at the time. In retrospect, I have no clue what I was thinking. I am telling you this to illustrate the point I made earlier. Remember when I said you think things are so important at that age. I thought if I let him leave, my life would be over. I truly was foolish, but it didn't feel that way at the time. I was too young to cope with the introduction of these new feelings."

"I get what you are saying. I don't claim to have all the answers, and I know we young people can be dumb at times. Life is just hard. And with each generation, there are new sets of issues that the previous generation didn't have to deal with. No disrespect, but some of the things we are going through, your generation didn't. Things are just different."

"I can agree with that Candy. I couldn't imagine being a young lady your age right now."

"Back to your story. You were in the car with your mother."

We were in route to his house. The car ride over was devoid of communication, which left way too much room for my mind to journey off into an abyss of fear. I was having an overwhelming moment of crisis and I wanted to scream for help, advice, encouragement, discouragement, anything at all from anyone at this moment would have helped, but I just stayed completely silent. One of the most critical decisions I would ever make was right here in front of me and I had no one to talk to. As we pulled up in front of his house I grudgingly, and with an extremely heavy heart unbuckled my seat belt, reached for the door handle and got out. That had to be the longest walk up a driveway that I had ever made in my entire life. I was still questioning my decision and wondering how I could get out if it, but it seemed to be too late. My mother had driven off and he was already standing behind the screen door of his house waiting for me.

The grin that was permanently affixed to his face did not warm my heart on this day. I was so anxious about what he was asking or demanding of me that I felt queasy. The doubt about my decision that I felt way down in the pit of my stomach should have been enough for me to turn around and run for my life, but I did not listen to my conscience…I just continued moving toward him. He opened the door and seemed to be thrilled at my presence, but I no longer felt the same. His wants and what he claimed to be his needs were causing me to go against everything that I have ever been taught and what I felt was appropriate behavior for myself, but I wanted his presence in my life at that moment…more than I wanted to continue on a path that I knew in my heart of hearts was right.

He led me down the stairs into his basement which was filled with darkness and a faint, moldy smell. In an eerie way, it reminded me of a scene from one of those thriller movies (like Silence of the Lambs) when they discovered something heinous in the basement hiding within the cloak of darkness. It was so black I couldn't tell if my eyes were open or closed, so I squeezed his hand while he guided me. As we walked around the corner, a plaid reclining chair sat in the middle of basement floor. There was a dim light shining in from a small window near the corner of the basement's ceiling which allowed me to see as he led me by my hand to the chair. He pulled the string on the solitaire light bulb that dangled from the rafters to illuminate our path. As the light sway back and forth, I saw glimpses of old damp cardboard boxes and toys in storage from Chad's siblings reveal themselves, then hide back in the shadows of lost light. As he turned to give me a kiss, I leaned in to kiss him back. I was accustomed to the feeling of his kiss and his touch, so this interaction was not unusual for us. Grabbing my hand again he fell back into the cushioned chair, pulled me on top of him, and the kissing continued. His hands were roaming across my back down to my rear and back up my shirt.

Down in that basement, in a room almost completely void of light, I remember wanting to feel his love and affection but just not in this way. I wanted him to continue to kiss me but deep inside I did not want it to go any further. All of that was just wishful thinking though. Gently nudging me back out of the way, he reached to pull a condom out of his pocket and proceeded to put it on. He unbuckled my pants and instructed me to take one leg off. I hesitantly did as he told me to

At this point, I just wanted it to be over so that I could go home, but of course I could not allow him to know that for fear of his reaction. I tried to moan as I had seen on television, but my mind was completely somewhere else. I allowed him to finish and I got up, put my pant leg back on, sat back down slowly on his lap and waited there watching television until my mother came to pick me back up. I saw movement on the television, but couldn't hear anything because of the volume of my thoughts. Was that what sex was? No, it couldn't be. This is not what I imagined. It is not what I had seen on television and in the movies. I must still be a virgin because that could not be sex."

When my mom picked me up she asked me what we watched, and I made up a movie to satisfy her interrogation. Dead silence filled the car until we reached home, where I immediately went to the bathroom. Feeling the stinging sensation of relieving myself caused me to tense up to stop the pain. What has this thing called sex done to my body? Why am I hurting from what was supposed to feel good? I just wanted to cry over the disappointment of the experience. Realizing in that moment, in that second, that I had given myself, my power, over to him caused tears to stream down my face.

My response to his inflexible demands had now forever changed the path of my life. Everything in my life seemed so well-defined before that point, right/wrong, black/white, true/false. Now I was totally confused. How could I have done such a horrible thing? The young lady that my parents had raised me to be, the youth choir instructor, the Sunday school student, the regular church attendee, the Christian, the church girl that the guys in my neighborhood had referred to me as had now become something so opposite of that…and I could tell no one. I had accepted Jesus as my personal Lord and Savior at the age of twelve, and I was serious about my decision, but a few months later at the age of thirteen, I had sinned against God and done something I knew I would be ashamed for my parents to know about.

I retired to the solitude of our bathroom and stared at myself in the mirror for five minutes while questioning my decision. What do I do now? Where do we go from here? What will happen to this relationship? Will he even stay now that I had given my virginity to him? Do I look older? Will I give off any signs to alert my mother?

"That was a tough period of time for me. Now that I had crossed that line, I just felt completely and utterly lost. So when you say that Andre tries to take your virginity in places you don't feel comfortable, I can relate. I was deflowered in a dingy, dirty, moldy basement on a plaid recliner."

Chapter XI

Boyfriends

Candice sat in silence thinking about all she heard.

"What did you do after that? Did you break it off with him, or continue to see him?"

Rose shook her head from side to side.

"I am embarrassed to say that I continued to see that fool for quite some time. Oh, but that is not the end of the story. I will be right back…"

Rose became slightly nauseous reliving the events from her past. An alarm from a dying cell phone gave her an excuse to walk away for a brief second and get some fresh air.

While Rose was away, Candice stared at the television thinking about Rose's story. She found it intriguing that even though they had a difference in age, and experienced these trials during different eras, some things still seemed to be the same. When Rose returned to the room, Candice dove right in.

"Do you feel different afterwards? I mean what do you do after that? After you let a guy take your virginity?"

"I can't speak for others Candy because I don't know what other females went through. All I can talk about is what happened with me."

Rose used her thumb and ruffled through the remaining pages of the journal before returning to the section she previously read.

"I never used all the pages of this journal. Here are the last entries."

The following Monday I got up out of bed, as if nothing had changed to prepare for a normal school day. I took my shower, brushed my teeth, and got dressed. Before exiting the bathroom, I just stood there looking at my reflection wondering what this day would bring. Will he call me today? What is he going to say when we talk? What am I going to say?

Will he pretend that I did not even exist or would we interact as we always had? Concentrating in class was extremely difficult because my mind kept flipping back to what had transpired over the weekend. I wanted everything to just go back to the way it was before the weekend had begun. Back to kissing, hugging, holding hands, being friends and just talking…but unfortunately I would not get my wish. Because I had allowed Chad to penetrate me, nothing could ever go back to the way it was. My virginity was really gone.

School came to an end, the bell rang, and we all exited the building to get on our buses. As customary for the cool kids then, I headed toward the back to sit with a group of my friends. We were all just laughing and joking, but a conversation between Autumn and another girl that I knew named Shonda seemed to be serious and not coinciding with anything that was going on around them. Autumn was speaking, and Shonda seemed to be especially upset. Focusing in on their conversation, I heard Autumn say that Dion, who was Shonda's boyfriend, and Chad were over at a girl's house named Tina this weekend and that Dion had cheated. Without any personal control, I jumped into their conversation and immediately blurted out, "Chad who?" Autumn was facing sideways with her back towards the window, and with a smirk on her face she replied, "Your Chad! I thought I taught you better than that girl? How you going to let your man go over some other chicks house? You were supposed to piss on your tree and mark your territory."

My heart stopped. He had not told me anything about going over to any Tina's house this weekend. Even though I was upset he was over there, I rationalized the situation, and thought to myself - Well at least he didn't cheat on me like Dion did to Shonda. My thought didn't get a chance to take root before Autumn began to inform me that Shonda was not the only one whose trust was broken, and that she heard Chad had cheated on me also with a girl named Gennafer, who was also over there. I felt like I could not breathe. No, this could not be happening. What I was hearing come out of her mouth had to be a lie. There is no way. I had just given myself to him this weekend. How could he have had sex with another girl named Gennafer all in the same weekend? How could you mess with a girl who can't even spell her own name right. Jennifer spelled G-E-N-N-A-F-E-R. How retarded is that? Not only that, but she is a big, fat nasty slob. Does he know how that makes me feel?

According to Autumn's timeline, Chad cheated on me the day before I gave my virginity to him. This absolutely is not happening. I refused to believe it, but Autumn insisted that it was true and that she saw Chad with her earlier that day. I did not say another word the entire trip home. Staring out the window of that yellow bus was all that I could do. The mouths of my friends around me were moving, but I was not hearing a solitary word. That school bus could not arrive at my stop soon enough that day. I desperately needed to get to a phone so that I could ask Chad for myself. I needed to hear it from him or I would not be able to believe what Autumn had told me.

The brakes screeched and I stepped off and started down the street toward my little ranch style home. I looked at the ground, noticing every crack and weed and ant hill all the way home, trying not to think about or believe what I had just heard... but it was not working. I opened the door, threw my back pack off to the side on the floor, and went straight for the phone. My nerves were on edge as I dialed the wrong number a couple of times because of the trembling of my fingers and my slight loss of memory. The line on the other end began ringing and Chad picked up. After telling Chad what Autumn had told me, I asked in a gentle tone if she was telling the truth. There was a slight pause and then I heard him say – yes. For a second my brain could not even grasp that he had said yes, but once the sound of his voice finally clicked in my head, I just hung up. It felt like someone had taken a sledge hammer and swung it as hard as they could into my midsection. What? Did he just say yes to me asking him about sleeping with another girl the same weekend that I had given him my virginity? The same weekend I had given him my virginity? No, no, no, no, no! This could not be happening. How could he do this to me? How did this happen? How was it even possible? I was trying my hardest to make sense of it all, but it was not working. This had to be a nightmare that I was going to wake up from any minute. I wanted to pinch myself, but it would not help. All of this was really happening in my life. There was no dream for me to wake up from.

Walking back down the hall toward my room, I felt like I was going to throw up everything and anything that I had eaten that day. My brain did not know what to think, what to do, and so my body just kept moving until I arrived at my bed. I climbed in, pulled the covers over my head, and began to just sob…almost silently, but still uncontrollably. I cried until my abdominal muscles were tense, the whites of my eyes were bright red, and I had no more tears left to cry. After mustering up enough energy to pull myself off the bed, I walked across the hall into the bathroom and just stared at my reflection. Who was this person that I was staring at and how had her life come to this? Before this day, I did not even know that this kind of emotional pain was possible. I was so angry at him. I was hurt and irate at myself for allowing someone to hurt me like this. How could I be so stupid? If I had only said no, I would not be at this place in my life feeling this gnawing, burning, excruciating pain.

Rose closed the journal with her thumb secured between the pages.

"This was an emotional scar that I did not know if I would or if I could ever recover from. This happened so long ago, but I still feel the pain"

"Rose, I don't know what I would have done. It is easy to say what you would do in that situation, but until you are actually in it you don't know how you would react. I would probably feel straight rage. Heck, I feel mad now with you just telling me this story. How did you bounce back from it? Did he try to call you again to apologize?"

"Yes, he did."

A couple of days later, the phone calls from Chad began to pour in. I did not want to talk to him or really anybody for that matter. If I had my wish, I would just stay isolated and alone with my pain. Telling anyone that could provide any tad bit of wisdom, once again, just felt out of the question and I could not bring myself to do it. Who could help me that would not immediately, upon hearing what had happened, take it upon themselves to punish me or tell someone who could punish me? I felt trapped, all alone, and so desperately needed help. Because of fearing the consequences of asking for help, I just absolutely would not reach out to anyone. Left to my own devices, I went further into a pit of foolish decisions.

When I finally decided to take a call from Chad, he began pleading with me and telling me how sorry he was and if I would just give him another chance, he would not hurt me again. I felt that he may be a tad bit sorry for his actions, and it seemed like he really did not want to lose me, but that was nowhere near what motivated my next decision. My only goal at this point was to do whatever I could to keep my mother from finding out what I had done. To keep her from the knowledge that her little girl had started having sex, I decided I had to stay with him. If I did not, someone would begin wondering and asking about what had happened...and I just could not let that happen at this point. Not to mention the fear of what he would tell his friends if I did end it. Being from a small town, telling one person anything meant that everyone would know. Totally believing that I was making an intelligent decision, I set out on the path or the mission to keep what I had done a secret.

Seeing him at this point really just made me irate. I felt sick at the thought that I had given my virginity to someone who did not even care about me enough to let me know that he had slept with another girl the day before because he was tired of waiting on me to surrender to his requests. I never knew how precious my virginity was until I gave it to someone so undeserving of it. I did not want him to kiss me, hold me, hug me, touch me or even look at me. The truth of the matter is I only let enough of that occur so no one, including him, would question my sincerity in the relationship. Deep inside, I really hated him. I never knew at that age that another human being could cause such pain in the life of another. I had seen a dark side to life that forever changed who I was inside and eliminated my ability to trust anyone. I tried to keep up the illusion that I was this nice girl who could still see the best in people, but that girl was long gone. It was like something had snapped inside of me. My heart was shattered and it felt as if there was nothing that could ever put it back together again. I felt like I had no choice in the matter but to settle for this relationship and pitiful existence in this stupid little town from which I thought at the moment that I would never get out of.

Days turned into weeks and weeks turned into months. During this time he and I continued to spend time with each other and as we did, we resumed physical contact. Spending almost every day with him after school afforded him the chance for me to grow close to him again. I still never forgot what happened, but I thought that I had forgiven him. I rationalized because there was not much where I was from to choose to move on to. No other guy there seemed like a better option, so I stayed with the guy I had already connected sexually with. At least in my own mind, I was not out being with a bunch of different men and so remaining with him made me somehow feel better about what I had done and what I was back continuing to do. There were times that we had conversations about ceasing to have sex with one another because we were both raised in the church and knew that it was wrong, but we would last for an extremely short period of time and then be around each other again and that deal would be off. It was a continuing cycle of those conversations about us feeling bad, but then going right ahead and doing it again anyway.

"Rose, that is what I fear. I am scared that once I start, that we'd be doing it all the time. I really don't want to get pregnant right now. I want to go to school and make my family proud. It is just so frustrating because if you don't, you are like the outcast and guys run away."

"If I knew then what I know now, I would have told them to run. They are a waste of time. You can be doing something so much more productive. Now don't get me wrong…I am not saying it is wrong to have a boy you are interested in. That is completely healthy. What I am saying is when it crosses that line of sex, you are charting on dangerous waters. Not only pregnancy, but STDs, and emotional as well as spiritual ties to someone."

"You are absolutely right. Even if I wanted to though, I don't know how to end the relationship with Andre at this point. I mean, we have been through so much. How did it end with Chad?"

"It took a while because I was foolish in my repeated attempt to salvage something which was never there. True, we had fun hanging out, but we were never meant to be together. To answer your question, we continued to date. It seemed that the couple of years that we had now been a couple had flown by, and it was now time for him to go off to college. I understood that it would be hard on our relationship, but I figured since I had taken him back and we had stuck together this long that we would stay together through this. He had a completely different idea about things though.

"One visit he made to see me at my mother's house let me know that we were not on the same page. He came at me with this idea of how we should separate, but just not sleep with other people…so we can experience life. In other words, he wanted to get to know other females and see if there was something better for him than me. I did not argue, I just told him that was fine. Trying to hold on to someone who did not want to be kept was just foolish to me even at my young age, but I was connected to him, and still was emotionally attached. We verbally separated and I let him follow the path he wanted to take, but he still possessed a portion of me.

"I understand that attachment you feel. I was so lonely without him in our little town. I had spent all my time while he was in high school with him. Neglecting my previous friends, avoiding social events that would not include him, I became secluded from the entire rest of the world so that I could spend my time receiving attention from him…and he just up and left me. Once again I was left feeling hurt, abandoned, and completely alone. Why had I let him do this to me again? Different situation, same guy, years later, same results. I tried to hide the way that I felt from everyone, but I was tired of pretending. Wanting to seem like I was at least ok was such a task. Just the smiling and trying to get through everyday, and being forced back into socializing with the world I had left behind when I was with him was all so tiring. I just wanted to sleep my life away. Adventures out of town with one of my girlfriends Keyla was the only thing that kept me feeling sane. She could always make me laugh, so those road trips became my therapy."

Candice was glad her mother allowed her to spend the night with Rose. She found a lot of similarities in Rose's past and her current situation. She planned on using it to guide her in her relationship with Andre.

"So you just cut it off with Chad? You haven't spoken with him since?"

"Not necessarily," Rose chuckled. "I was a naïve girl. Phone conversations between Chad and I happened frequently when he went off to college. Although I was curious as to what his life on campus was like, usually in the past I kept those questions to myself so that it would not seem as if I was being a nag. He wanted his freedom and I was completely verbally willing, but mentally and emotionally reluctant to give that to him. Sharing information with me came on his timing…and I am sure there was an abundant amount of information that he chose to leave out. The funniest thing to me is if I disclosed everything that was going on with me, he wouldn't have been able to handle it because you know how men are."

"Oh my gosh, do I? They feel they can do anything, but God forbid you do anything at all they want to go off, and call you all kinds of names, and cry and whine about it. Dre acts like a big baby sometimes, I swear. It is ok for him to flirt with women, but oh my, he will lose his mind if any man talks to me. Such a double-standard."

"That is men for you. They think they own us like property." Rose pulled a bobby pin out her hair, and scratched her scalp. "Man, I think I am about due for a relaxer. Anyways, this is the last page.

Winter of my senior year in high school. It was a cold evening and my time was consumed with working my usual evening shift at this small clothing store on the main strip in town. Folding shirts had become such a familiar task to me that I could use that time for daydreaming. As my mind floated off into events that had occurred at school I failed to notice that someone was standing across the aisle staring at me. When I finally snapped out of the slideshow my mind had drifted off to, my heart slammed down onto my diaphragm and I physically jumped back into the clothing rack behind me. It was him, Chad, standing there with a smile as big as the entire state of Texas spread across his face.

I do not know exactly what he was thinking, but I was wondering what in the heck he was doing there? He was supposed to still be away at college. And why was he smiling? Did he really think that it was ok for him to just come in and out of my life whenever he felt like it? Was I sending off that signal? I did not want to be rude and unkind. The feelings that had developed within me up to that point still would not allow me to do so even if I wanted to, but was I supposed to interact with him now? He does not even know me or what all is truly going on with me and I obviously did not ever know him. My interactions with him showed him to have two different personalities. The one that showed me so much love and care and affection when we were in each others faces, and the other one that could stomp all over my feelings when we were apart. What was I to do with that?

Because I fell into a place of familiarity with him, and he was only in town for a couple days, I allowed him to drive me home from work. We sat and talked in the driveway that night. That next day he came back over and we watched a movie. The following morning marked the end of his winter break, so he returned to school while I remained in boring West Pointe. He gave me a call one evening that following spring. I recall my sister handing me the phone, and how I sat out on the back porch talking to him while swatting away at the country mosquitoes. I asked about school and his study habits. Even though we were not together, I still cared about him and wanted him to do well. In the middle of our conversation, he asked if I had met or messed around with anyone. The answer to his question about meeting people was yes, but the answer about messing with them was no. I had not been sexually active with anyone as I honored our agreement, and I was quite offended that he asked.

At the moment, logic set in and my mind began racing, so I bounced that question right back at him. Silence once again fell over the phone. I knew deep down in my gut what was coming next, and before I knew it he said – yes. This was the second time he betrayed me. Even though we weren't technically together, he gave me his word he would be faithful and he reneged again. This time I did not hang up. I asked him who it was and he did not give me any details. All he would say is that he had had sex with another girl. What was it with this idiot, did he just enjoy hurting me? I did appreciate his honesty for some reason, but what was really going on with him?

Even though he had crushed my world in the past, I still could not wrap my mind around this because I foolishly trusted him. He said he would not do this to me again! Here I am, with the opportunity to hook up with the new male friends that I had acquired, and although at times I wanted to because of my loneliness I did not do it because I stuck by my word to him. I have no idea why I even tried, but I did. And what did he do? He went right ahead and took my existence in his life for granted and did it with another girl. How could this idiot do this to me again? I thought. All the reasons why I hated him before came flooding back, so I informed him that I did not want to talk anymore and got off of the phone.

The path back to my bed to cry was so blurry. Tears welled up in my eyes before I could even reach my room. How could I have been so gullible and stupid again? Why did I even open my heart and body back up to him? He continues to take my heart, body, and feelings for him and trash them like they are absolutely nothing and I let him. Again! What is wrong with me?

My mind recalled the conversation that I had with his mothern which she told me that I had to be patient with him because she went with through the same issues with his father. I couldn't believe she said that to me. She was not the one going through this, I was. And furthermore, she was no longer even with his father so what kind of advice was that? Why should I have ever tried to stay when she did not stay with his father? Why did I ever even consider taking her advice? Had I become that desperate that I was taking advice from miserable women who weren't successful in their own relationships? I wanted to punch through the wall of my bedroom so badly, but that would lead my mother and everyone else to asking what had happened and I did not want to talk about it now, or ever. I decided at that point to cut him off, and focus on me entering college that fall. Now I am here in college, and that is a closed chapter in my life.

Rose closed the journal and tossed it on the coffee table.

"That guy was a jerk, and I was a fool for putting up with his crap for so long. That is why I am telling you all this. I hope something in my story sticks. There is no reason for a young lady to go through that nonsense. Crap like that pollutes relationships for years to come."

"I hear that. Well, there is some good to come out. At least you cut him off before you went to college."

"Well…sort of."

"Rose! Come on now, you still messed with him? Dang, that boy must have put something terrible on you in the bed. Why couldn't you let him go?"

"It was not sex that kept me going back to him. I was just emotionally connected to him because we basically grew up and spent so much time together. The sex was actually awful to be honest. I mean I would get horny enough to do it, but when we actually started, it just didn't feel good at all. I just orchestrated a string of moans and learned how to say the right things to please him. If he ever knew how I truly felt, his ego couldn't take it. Chad thought he was putting it down in the bed. Men have no clue how good we can fake."

"You are something else Miss Hughes. Ok, tell me how this finally ended. What happened in college?"

"When I got to college, I immediately received attention from a couple guys. One of the guys seemed nice, and since I was so used to being in a relationship, I felt being with him would keep some of the drama out of my life from guys approaching me. This guy was pretty popular, but the problem was I really wasn't feeling him. One time Chad came to campus for Homecoming, and throughout the entire dance he stood there trying to start a fight with my new man. It was so much drama, and ridiculous to be honest."

"Look at you, having men fight over you." Candice teased.

"It was not flattering. It was more stress than anything. Chad came up to spend the weekend there. Just so happened his boy toy Calvin attended my university. They acted like they were brothers since their names both started with "C" which is just stupid to me. I guess Calvin called himself keeping tabs on me, and no telling what kind of info he was feeding Chad. He had to say something though because that entire weekend Chad was acting a plum fool. He kept calling my room threatening to come over, and I my new man was scared of him. We had a party outside our dorm the day after homecoming, and Chad walked up to me and started talking crazy."

"Crazy like how?"

"I can't even explain it. It was like something came over him. I don't know if it was jealousy, or his little punk friend Calvin pumping him up."

Candice interjected. "What is up with these guys and their friends all up their butts like that? I don't get that male bonding thing at all. Dre has this friend named Junior, and he rides him so hard I wonder why Dre even wants to take my virginity when he has a piece right there."

Rose burst into laughter.

"I don't get it either. What I can say is Chad's friend Calvin is an extreme instigator. I don't know what Calvin said to him, but Chad walked behind me and started whispering things in my ear like *I know your man ain't putting it on you like I did*...and...*you know you miss what I can do to your body*. He started bringing up old sexual encounters where he felt he was doing something, and reciting them like it was going to make me horny or something. I guess he thought he was so good my panties were immediately supposed to get soaked and I would whisk him away to my room and let him ravage my body."

"Wow. I don't even know what to say about that one. I haven't had sex yet, but even if I had, doesn't sound like that would put me in the mood... especially given all he put you through."

"I know. That should have been enough, but I was stupid. My boyfriend was acting out at the time, so the next time Chad called, I met him at the food court. We sat and ate, and just had friendly conversation. I knew it was wrong but my boyfriend and I were on the rocks and I had no intention on doing anything with Chad. I had on a cute little tennis skirt but had to go back to my room to change because I had a part time job to go to.

"Chad walked me back to my room, and sat on my bed. As I changed clothes, we continued to talk about our hometown, school, and our family.

I was so accustom to being around him, I felt safe in his presence. We began kissing one another and Chad laid me down. I hadn't had time to put another top on, but I still had on my tennis skirt. While on top, his breathing became heavy, and we both became excited. Before I realize what was happening, Chad pulled himself out and was working his way inside of me. I felt this unwanted force and wanted him to stop. I told him to stop but he kept forcing himself inside of me. I never saw this look in his eyes before. I tried to wedge my arms and use my legs as leverage to stop him, but he was too strong to move. He forced himself inside of me several times before he stopped.

Rose stared at the coffee table with a glaze over her face remembering the incident.

"I was an emotional basket case as you can imagine because Chad had never violated me in this manner before. My thoughts streaked across my brain like shooting stars from rational to anger to fear. *What had he done? What had I done? Why did I keep inviting him back into my life?*"

Candice couldn't believe what Rose was telling her.

"I am sorry. If I knew that is how it ended, I wouldn't have ever asked. It is messed up that it took a situation like rape to make you two part ways."

"Umm…sad to say, but that wasn't the last time I saw him."

"What?"

"Candy listen to me baby. I have never told anyone this story before. I could sit here and lie to you, and fabricate and piece together parts of my past, but I want to be transparent with you and let you know the truth. Many women keep putting themselves into situations where they make foolish decisions for years, and I want to be real with you. Yes I was stupid, but maybe if you hear my story, you can recognize signs in your future relationships, and stop from making the same mistakes."

"I hear what you are saying, but I just don't understand. Did you not see all the signs before? How did you get caught up with him again after all that? All the cheating, and the lies, and then rape? After a man rapes you, why would you keep going back to him?"

"Believe me Candy, it is easy once you get tied up with a man. There are so many emotions that are wrapped into sex…feelings that no one wants to talk about because society wants to make it look like we can have casual sex with no attachment. I am not a super Christian, nor do I profess to know the entire Bible, but what I can tell you is I don't believe God constructed us to just have casual sex, or sex outside the confines of marriage. It is not right Candy. You will have a lot more regrets giving in to a man than you ever will waiting. That is why I am so adamant about you holding out and not letting any man pressure you. Too often we listen to men and find ourselves in positions where we convince ourselves that is what we really want. I don't want you to get put in a situation where you make bad decisions like I did."

"I hear you, and I am sorry…I don't want to come across as disrespectful, but I am just trying to figure all this stuff out. How did you fall back into his arms again?"

"I was really upset with my boyfriend at the time once again for being all dramatic trying to get attention from all these girls at school. Not only that, but he had told me his ex-girlfriend was back in town, so over spring break he planned on going over to see how her and her family was doing. I felt this was disrespectful, so I had a nonchalant disposition. Chad just so happened to call me during that funk I was in, so he caught me at the right time. He told me he would buy my airline tickets if I came to visit him in Florida. I asked my mother's permission, and with her ok immediately jumped on the opportunity. My main goal was to get my navel pierced by a salon my friend referred me to, but it did feel good to be in his presence again.

"When I arrived at his apartment, he instructed each one of his friends and football teammates to come by and give me a solitary rose. I thought it was cute at the time…definitely the most romantic thing he had done to date. We had sex that weekend, and because of the emotions wrapped up in the act, we thought maybe we were older now and could rekindle something. After all, this was my place of familiarity, and my resume of men would look better reverting back to my high school sweetheart, versus adding new men to the list. By the time the weekend ended, the only good thing that came about was my navel being pierced. I ended up burning the lasagna I prepared for him, and we argued the entire time until I left. We both realized that we were two completely different people and had grown apart. I was no longer the little naïve girl that waited for him to call and he was becoming something unfamiliar to me. Besides his physical appearance which was altered by Creatine and HGH, I had no idea who Chad was anymore. That was the last time I was with him."

"I don't even know what to say to all that. That was just…"

"Stupid, I know. But like I said, I told you all this for a reason. See how one choice you can make in high school can affect your life for years to come. I spent years, literally, dedicating myself to a man who I was no where near going to marry."

"That is wild. So I never asked, was he cute?"

Rose began to chuckle.

"He wasn't ugly, but wasn't the finest thing either. Let's just say he grew on me. Remember, I grew up in small West Pointe, so there was not much to choose from. The guys were either country bumpkins or no ambition drug heads with several children. Chad was a football athlete with a hard work ethic. I guess I found that attractive. I don't think he was as good as I hear Andre is but he played with a lot of heart. Chad was chubby like me, tall like his mom, and had a likable personality that made people gravitate towards him. Everyone thought he was a real standup guy…everyone who wasn't in a relationship with him."

"So, what did your mom think of him? My mother really doesn't care for Dre at all."

"I have to say my mom was the same. She thought he was nice, but overstayed his welcome when he came over, and ate too much food. My mother was well known in our neighborhood because she could cook so well. Momma definitely knew her way around the kitchen."

"Sounds good. I would love to have some of her food."

Rose's grin appeared to conceal the pain behind her words.

"I wish that I could too Candy, boy I wish that I could."

Chapter XII

Dear Momma

The conversation continued until midnight was behind them. When Candice brought up Rose's mom, she began rubbing her temples to alleviate stress.

"Is everything ok?"

"Yes, I am fine Candy."

"I was just checking. Is your mother ok?"

Rose's disposition created an incredible silence before answering.

"Well since I am telling you everything, I might as well not leave anything out. I have to back up to high school. Chad was a punk for what he did to me, but the issue of my boyfriend being unfaithful was not the only trial I had on my plate at time. My mother had been diagnosed with breast cancer and I was trying to ignore the entire situation. When I heard the news, I can't even describe what I felt. Unbelief and denial had to be the frontrunners however. *Cancer? Did I just hear them right? No, this must be a mistake. Not my mother. There is no way possible that this could be happening in our lives. Not to her. She is the rock of this family. She is always here for the rest of us. I rarely remember her being sick or even having colds. I must be misunderstanding what is being said to me.*

"My little brother was so small at the time, just a toddler when they broke the news to me. That alone led me to believe that she would be alright and be here many more years with us because I could not see how God could allow her to leave this earth without him being grown. Whenever the topic came up in our house about my mother's health my brain shut down. Blocking out issues in my life just by simply zoning out became part of who I was as a person. I had no one I could really express myself to anyway. The raging anger that was inside of me because of life dragging me down this pathway was more than I could bear to think about, so I just pretended that this problem did not exist either. I knew that I should not resort to doing drugs and alcohol, and I did not take that route. In the absence of my arrogant boyfriend, spending time with my couple of true female friends and with the new male friends I was encountering seemed to help a little."

Candice thought about the time when her mother had surgery to remove a cyst.

"I can't say that I know what you went through, but I know about trying to conceal the pain. I was going through a patch with my mom where we argued every single day. It was like I couldn't catch a break for anything. Nothing I did was good enough. During that time, my mother found out she had a benign ovarian cyst. My mind just wondered what I would do if was malignant? I think that is why I like spending so much time with Dre. It is like time with him takes my mind away from my mother and worrying about if her cyst will return or of anything else may happen to her."

"Candy that is what I did. These newly developing relationships distracted me from what was going on under the roof of our little brick home. The music blaring in the car and the laughter during road trips with my friend helped take a tad bit of the sting out of the turmoil I was feeling inside. I was learning over time that life could definitely hand you situations that you never imagined or ever thought you would encounter.

"I believed that I would be able to grow old with my mother there as my friend, and guide, and source of wisdom in the same way that she had with hers. My grandmother was still alive and I never expected that something would or could come along and take away the possibility of having the same experience that they shared. I wanted my mother to see me graduate from college. I wanted my mother to be in the delivery room with me when I birthed my children. I wanted my children to be able to remember her, to have the joyful experience of having a loving grandmother plain period. And yes, my wants were selfish, but I wanted her to continue to be a part of my life. Why this, why now, why her? None of my friends had any type of problem like this to deal with. Why me?"

Candice wanted to console Rose, but she had questions herself.

"Can I ask you a personal question? How did you end up dealing with it? I know that I am young, and sometimes I just don't know how to handle certain things emotionally. I mean, there is not like there is a manuscript for tragedy and pain you can pick up from the local library."

"Everyone handles it different Candy. After the news about my mother having cancer was presented to me, I heard it, but it was like I was just numb from it. Numb from every bad experience that I was forced to go through. Every time a commercial came on talking about cancer, or a television show mentioned a *survivor* or *someone who beat the disease*, I felt rage going through my body…but what could I do? What other choice did I have but to keep going everyday? I was angry, frustrated and hurt. Getting up, taking a shower, getting dressed, attempting to look half way decent, going to school, sitting through class, going to whatever activity I had practice for after school, coming home, eating, doing homework, watching a little television, going to bed, and getting back up to do it all over again became the dreaded cycle of my life.

"I was miserable and struggling to hide it. I wished so badly that something or someone could come and take me to a whole new world and that I could start my life all over again. Maybe I would not make so many stupid decisions the next time? Maybe my life would be better? Maybe I could be the most perfect child ever and never cause my mother any stress so that she would not be facing cancer right now? Part of it had to be my fault. The foolish arguing with my siblings, her constantly having to ask me to do simple chores, arguing and wanting to throw temper tantrums when she would not let me do what I wanted to with my friends and not letting me always see my *great and wonderful* now ex-boyfriend when I wanted. I did do well academically and I did well in my extra-curricular school activities but I just wanted an immediate do-over for all the things I failed at like being a daughter…but that opportunity never came. I started to write my mother a letter apologizing for everything I did, but I didn't get an opportunity to give it to her. I began early that morning before school and wrote two words on the paper – *Dear Momma*, assuming I'd have time to finish it when I got home. That evening my mother was taken from me."

Rose's story touched Candice and convicted her to check her attitude towards her mother.

"I don't know what to say about that. I mean it really puts things into perspective. I complain about my mother a lot, but looking at the big picture, I guess I have been disrespectful."

"Enjoy these moments. I wish I had my mother here to argue with. There is something to be said about a mother's love. Even though my marriage failed, my mother was not there to even see me get married. I can't tell you how bad that hurts. She was supposed to help me put on make-up and tell me she loved me. She was supposed to be the one sitting on the front row blotting her eyes to prevent the tears from ruining her makeup. I looked over to the seat where she should be, and there was no one there. That is not how I pictured getting married at all, and I will be honest, I had some pretty irate discussions with the Lord. I almost feel like God owes me something for taking my mom. I know that sounds crazy, but that is just being honest and how I feel."

"I can't imagine what you went through."

"Losing your mother is something else. I remember my teacher took me into this empty room and gave me a hug. She told me her mother died when she was 17 as well, and she was now 55, and that you never truly get over your mom passing away. I can't tell you how true that is. Just make sure you take my advice and live every day like it is the last. You never know what tomorrow brings, and instead of stressing about tomorrow, live in the moment. Enjoy these times with your mother. These are the times you build memories on. These are times you learn from your mother so you can pass her traditions down to your children. Learn as much from her as you can…about her, her past, your family, everything."

Candice nodded her head in agreement. She felt bad that her mother was still here and she mistreated her. Candice took a mental note of behavior she needed to address. She decided to pose a question to lighten the load.

"Ok, I know this is off subject, but how did you start Rozi Cosmetics? Like where did the idea come from? I think I read somewhere that it was a childhood dream of yours?"

"Yea, it was somewhat of a childhood dream. More so a teenage dream to be honest. Came to me one night when I was in high school. I think it was because of my mother having cancer."

"I'm sorry."

"Sorry about what?"

"Sorry about your mother. I am not trying to pry or be in your business or anything. If I knew, I wouldn't have asked."

"Candy, it is ok. After the things I told you tonight, I don't mind sharing at all. This is actually cleansing for me as I haven't shared these thoughts and feelings with anyone before. Something about you just reminds me so much of me when I was your age."

Rose took the cover from the couch, and tucked it under her feet as a cold draft crept into the room and crawled across the floor.

"When my mother was diagnosed with cancer, not only did it completely change the dynamic of our family, it also changed my mother physically. My mother was a classy woman who received attention from men and women by the way she carried herself, and she was definitely easy on the eye. Not saying that in a vain way, but my mother just had this sweet spirit about her that radiated from within, and it made her that much more attractive. There was a pure glow about her that is hard to explain unless you were in her presence. Not only was her spirit sincere, but she was a naturally beautiful woman who didn't need make-up whatsoever.

"After she was diagnosed with breast cancer, the doctors performed a mastectomy on her left breast. We thought she had beat it, then a few months later cancer resurfaced. The doctor offered my mother chemo but she felt her faith was strong enough to heal so she declined. My mother fought cancer longer than I had realized. She passed from this earth when I was 17, but had been battling cancer since I was 13…right around the same time I gave myself to Chad. It started in her breast, and eventually spread to her lung and her hipbone. It hurt me so bad to see her hurting… to see her lose her vigor. This once physically strong mother of mine now had to walk with a cane. I saw the agony in her face as she tried to force a smile and fight to come to our school and athletic events…meanwhile still trying to keep our house in order."

A tear trickled down Rose's cheek as she spoke about this emotional period of her life. Before she knew it, her eyes were consumed with fluid to the point where the images on the television became distorted and colors bled together.

"I don't know what was going on with these doctor's because I was too young to understand. That, and a combination of me being self-absorbed and drowning everything that was occurring with her in the middle of my own teenage drama. I just remember my grandparents talking about she beat it, then the doctor tacking on six more months. My mom beating that, then they gave her additional months. This went on for about four years. When the cancer spread and started eating away at her physically, it broke her spirit completely. You could see a difference in her demeanor, as well as her physical presence. This once beautiful woman now looked completely different from the woman that used to flour my hands and teach me how to make pies while standing on a kitchen stool.

"After my mom passed, I just stared at her in the casket in disbelief. It was unbelievable to me how the physical shell of what was supposed to represent my mother looked no different from me randomly attending a funeral of someone I didn't know. I was upset at the funeral home because it looked nothing like my mother, but I knew after cancer removed the life from her, they didn't have much to work with."

Rose walked over to her kitchen counter so she could wipe her face.

To divert her attention, Rose rummaged through her crystal container of hard candy and chewing gum.

"Would you like a piece of candy Candy?" Rose joked. "I can't get this taste of pizza and tea out my mouth. It didn't really mix well."

"No thank you, I'm fine."

Rose proceeded to unwrap the gum, then took a few bites while she enjoyed the immediate release of flavor.

"You know what, I absolutely love the first 60 seconds of chewing gum. It truly is an enjoyable experience for me. You know, my mother used to always keep gum in her purse. She was very self-conscious of her breath and always wanted it to be fresh, so after every meal she would chew a piece. It was so cute."

Candice smiled as Rose was reminiscing about her late mother. She felt it was best to not ask questions, and just give her time to vent.

"To answer your question…why did I start Rozi Cosmetics? After my mother died, a few weeks passed and my siblings and I went to her house to start the daunting task of going through her clothes and personal items. I sat on the bed as my sisters argued over what clothes they wanted, and tried to sneak certain articles out when the other wasn't looking. While one of my sister's was going through the closet, the other was sneaking into the kitchen to steal some of my mother's recipe cards, which in both cases are so wrong. Why would you take a piece of my mother's legacy and not share it?

"In any case, I was young at the time, but understood it was just their own special way of grieving and holding on to this great woman. During one of the fights between my sisters, I walked over to my mother's dresser and grabbed her hair brush. My mother would sit there at night and brush her hair 100 times. There were strands of her hair still intertwined in the brush and I took one and pulled it out. This may sound crazy, but I stood in the mirror which was attached to the dresser and held the strand of hair next to mine. I wondered how I'd look if I had hair as pretty as my mom's. I then took the strand and placed it under my nose to smell it. My mother's hair had this sweet distinctive smell. Nostalgia overtook me and made me break down. My eyes were consumed with tears and the last thing I remember was how distorted I looked in the mirror through my glossy eyes. I took a tissue and cleaned my face, and noticed that even with the tears gone and everything being visible, I still looked distorted. My perception was damaged and I was no longer happy with the way I looked anymore. It was like the guilt from my past almost made me feel dirty and ugly, and all of a sudden I didn't feel pretty anymore. My self-confidence had never been so low in my life."

"That is nonsense Rose. You are one of the prettiest women I know. Look at you. Your face is gorgeous, and your body is just incredible. Why would you think that?"

"I was a chunky chick back in the day. And even though some people said I was cute, sometimes when traumatic things happen to you, it breaks you down mentally. My sisters kept arguing with one another, and after they realized I would not side with either party, eventually left me alone in the room. I stood there for 15 minutes staring at myself, and thinking about my mother's last days. I thought back to the times I spent with Chad, how that was about the same time she was diagnosed, and wondered if I didn't waste my time on him and spent more time helping my mother out, would she still be here? I blamed myself and went through my memory to recall all instances I was disrespectful. The burden of my actions pierced my heart.

"I prayed, and asked God why He didn't heal her. What was the point of having faith if there is no deliverance? I was confused, frustrated and hurt. I cried again, then at that moment something happened. I can't really explain what it was, but I realized that I had to stop feeling sorry for myself and do something. I didn't want to feel ugly anymore and I didn't want anyone to go through what I did…having their mother be unrecognizable. I was talking to myself, and God, and whoever else would listen to me at the time. I made a promise that if I were ever put into the position where I had the opportunity, I would create make-up so that women wouldn't feel ugly like this anymore. Not to say it would make all your problems go away, but feeling good about the way you look physically can sometimes help with the emotional scarring."

"I read in an article somewhere that you birthed this vision through pain, but I had no idea."

"I went to college and obtained my degree, but I always kept up on cosmetic trends by subscribing to various magazines, reading, and doing research. It had become more of a hobby than anything…next to exercising. When I was not studying or working out, I sold make-up for a couple huge chains to earn some extra cash, and to learn the ropes. I never thought I would make a career out of it, but it was my passion and I did extremely well. Time passed and I met Troy. Troy was a guy I also knew since high school and he came from an affluent family. I won't bore you with another relationship gone bad story, but it didn't work out with us due to infidelity on his end, so we got divorced. Instead of wasting my settlement money, I sold the house and all the assets awarded to me because I wanted no part of him, and started fresh. Troy hurt me so bad, and I felt seemingly the same level of pain and period of mourning as when my mother passed. I channeled that anger, decided to stop living for others, and do something for myself. I took some time off and studied and researched. I cut a lot of people out of my life who were just there because I was beneficial to them and worked on my business plan. I hired a consultant to help me with this plan as I was aware I didn't know everything. I proposed my plan to several investors, including my ex-father-in-law, and I guess you can say the rest is history."

"That is awesome. So where did the name Rozi come from? Was that just wordplay on your middle name – Rose?"

"Actually, on our honeymoon in Africa, one of the places we traveled to was Kenya. We were speaking to the locals, and they referred to me as Rozi, which is Swahili for flower or rose. The enunciation of my name in a foreign language just stuck with me, and ended up becoming the trademark one of the first mineral makeup companies on the east coast. That's my story in a nutshell. My divorce was painful, but at least it pushed me into doing something I always wanted to do."

"I pray God doesn't make me go through all that to make my dreams come true," Candice stated in a light-hearted, yet exhausted tone as the night began to digress to morning.

Eventually the two ladies both passed out on the pile of pillows on the floor. The next morning they ate breakfast, then Rose drove Candice home.

* * *

Candice entered into her living room feeling rejuvenated like she just went through a team building camp. She walked over to her mother, who was folding clothes on the couch, and gave her a big hug.

"I love you Mommy."

"I love you too sugar. Where is this coming from?"

"Oh, no place."

"Candy, now remember I am your mom. What do you want? I know you have to want something because you are acting nice."

"Dang, why can't I show my mom some affection without a motive?"

"I suppose so baby," Lisa said sarcastically as she threw a folded t-shirt on the pile.

"Seriously mom, I know I have been hard to get along with lately. I was frustrated moving here, going to this new school, and just all the drama I have been going through there."

"Well baby if you ever need to talk, I am here for you."

"I understand that Mom, but you don't need any additional stress. I don't fully know what you are going through, but I know that between Daddy, Grandma passing, and these bills that you don't need any petty high school drama added to your list."

"Candy, listen to me. I have seen a lot of things in my day. When I am tough on you, that is because I don't want you following in my footsteps and making the same bad decisions. Sometimes I just get so frustrated that I don't know how to communicate that well. If you ever need to talk, I am here for you. I don't ever want you to think I am too busy for you."

"I appreciate that mom. I just wanted to apologize. I really haven't been the best kid I could be. I will try to help out more, and even get another job if you need me to. I only have two more years in this house, and there is no reason why we can't make these the best years thus far. I know a lot has happened to our family, but hey we still have each other. I don't want to fight with you…I want to use these two years to bond with my Momma."

Lisa turned her head to the side as she felt her eyes tear up while listening to her babygirl grow right in front of her.

"Candy, you don't know how much that means to me to hear you say that."

* * *

A few months passed, and Candice was true to her word. She developed a plan to help her mother. Instead of getting a part-time job, she took her mother's hobby, making jewelry and crafts, and created her a store on eBay. The store took off, and before they knew it, they had steady income coming in. Through time, the supplemental income helped her mother pay down their debt, and provided an overflow to contribute savings and other investments. The women were able to spend more time with one another and bond. Candice's love for her mother helped heal her physically and emotionally. Her new determination to do right bled into her school work as her diligence raised her GPA to a 3.8. She appeared to be back on the path she set to obtain a scholarship, thus lifting the burden from her mother. Candice also found the time to compile the list of attributes she wanted in a man that her uncle inspired her to create.

Chapter XIII

Shears

The temperature this day was in the low 80s, but there was a nice breeze. Candice was outside pulling up weeds with her mother. As her mother crawled around wearing her new knee pads she purchased from the hardware store, Candice thought of several jokes, but decided to keep them to herself.

"Hand me the shears Candy."

As instructed, Candice grabbed the long wooden handle lawn shears and handed it to her mother. She watched as her mother used the shears to prune and cut excess grass around her flower bed. When done, Lisa used the shears to edge the walkway. Candice zoned out and started thinking about her life, conversations with Rose, and her boyfriend. As she stared at her mom working diligently, she woke from her daydream and noticed the pathway became more visible. Candice received a revelation in that moment.

"Mom, would you mind if I took a rain check? There is really something I need to do."

Lisa saw the concern in her daughters face, and nodded giving her approval. Candice began to walk down the street as she pieced her thoughts together. She often took long walks to clear her head, and for exercise. She also ran cross country, so distance was no problem for her. While the air whipped through the trees and her hair, she took a deep breath, and turned at the two mile marker towards her destination.

After a few minutes of walking, Candice finally arrived at her target; Andre's house. She walked up the four steps and knocked on the flimsy metal screen door. Andre came to the door with his shirt off rubbing his stomach.

"Hey girl? What is this about? I didn't know you were coming over?"

"Why? You expecting company?"

"No, no…nothing like that. Come on in."

"I'd prefer if you came out here. I need to talk to you."

Andre grabbed a shirt from the couch so he wouldn't hear complaints from his elderly neighbor for walking around half-naked as she calls it. He put on some worn down house slippers which looked thicker than they actually were because of his crew socks.

"So you going to tell me what this is about?"

Candice took a big breath, then sat down on the bottom step.

"I woke up this morning, and it just felt so nice outside that I figured I would help my mother out with some yard work. So I was out there with my mom working in the garden and…well, it really doesn't matter."

"Candy, what are you talking about?"

"You see, I spoke with my uncle, right. And he was telling me that I should make a list of things I want. You failed the inspection."

Andre's ego took a direct blow and he became upset because he felt the direction this conversation was headed.

"Inspection? What are you talking about? That doesn't make any sense. What is going on?"

"Ok, I will just come right out and say it. Dre, I love you and you will always have a place in my heart, but this is not healthy for either one of us. Both of us are at two different places. I have goals, you have goals. I see a path you can't necessarily see, and I need to start pruning to make this path clearer. I am not trying to be mean, but let's just call this what it is."

"Call it what it is? What are you trying to say Candy? Be straight up with me."

"What I am trying to say is you are about to go to college next year, and I will still be stuck in this town. You are going to be around a bunch of loose, drunk women who will throw themselves at you, and I am not trying to get my heart wrapped around a man who will most likely tear it into shreds. What I am saying is be free and go. I love you, but I need to work on some things in my life. I have two more years till I graduate, and I need to get some things aligned."

"Don't worry about school. You are smart…you will get a scholarship. Where is all this coming from Candy."

Andre's last ditch effort fell upon a guarded heart.

"See, that is your problem. It is always about you, and what you want. You don't care about my well-being. You have no clue about our financial situation at home. Yes, I could possibly get a track scholarship, but what if I blow out my knee? I have to make sure all my bases are covered... academics, finances, mind, body and spirit. I need to get myself right with the Lord Dre. I can't continue to go down this same path."

"Oh, so you one of those Bible-toters now, huh? You going to go to hell for speaking to me?"

"Don't be like that Dre. Just respect my decision as I have always respected you."

Andre was completely caught off guard. Even though he made idle threats to leave Candice if she didn't put out, he never anticipated she would leave him first. He wanted to be mad, but because of Candice's demeanor, he initially had nothing to say. Simmering in a stew of ignorant rebuttals, Andre was on the verge of spewing out anything to plead his case, but was interrupted when a white Honda Accord pull into the driveway... it was Camille. Candice's jaw slightly dropped in awe.

"Oh, so I guess it doesn't matter anyways, huh? This is great. You hittin' my best friend now?"

"It's not like that Candy. She was just coming over to..."

Candice blocked Andre's voice out. At this point there was noting he could say that would make her feel any better. Camille jumped out the car, and tried to act oblivious to what was going on, however her guilty eyes told a different story.

"Hey girl, what you doing here?"

"Don't worry Cammy, you don't have to kiss up to me. I am not going to fight you over him. It really is not worth it. You have him all to yourself."

"Have him? It is not even like that girl. I was just..."

"Camille, it is not that serious. Just shut up. We broke up, so he is all yours. Good luck. Dre make sure you strap up. She smashed *all* the homies!"

Candice dusted the seat of her pants off, and walked away. She was hurt by the betrayal, but liberated that she finally broke it off with Andre.

* * *

On her way home, Candice walked to the local convenience store. She grabbed a beverage, and when she walked out, she was surprised to be greeted by Rose.

"Hey lady! What are you doing here?"

Candice walked over and gave Rose a hug.

I was on my way to workout, and stopped to get some water. What are you doing over here? You need a ride somewhere?"

"I was just out walking getting some fresh air. I will be fine."

"It is no problem. I am going that direction anyways."

"If you are sure it won't be a problem."

"Girl, jump in the car. I will be right back. I need to go get me something to drink."

Candice sat in the passenger side and slid down in the seat absorbing the comfort of the leather interior. As she fell into a trance staring at the twirling incense hanging from the rear view mirror, her peripheral vision refocused on Rose exiting the store.

Rose began driving, and noticed Candice was distant.

"Everything ok with you?"

"Yea, I suppose. Just sad I guess. Sometimes you never really know who your friends are…especially if you throw a man in the equation."

"Something you want to talk about?"

"Can you go to jail for driving with a learners permit with no adult?"

"What are you talking about Candy?"

"Have you ever thought about killing another woman? Like seriously."

Rose figured what was going on, but wanted be sensitive to Candice's feelings.

"What happened Candy?"

"Nothing. Nothing I really want to talk about," Candice said in a short tone. She tried to suppress her revengeful thoughts and not come across mean to Rose.

"Rose, I cut him off."

"Cut who off?"

"Andre"

"Really. Is that a bad thing?"

"I don't know if it was the right decision…but it feels right."

"What made you decide to end it?"

"It is hard to explain. See, I was working with my mom in the garden today. She has this walkway she has been talking about all spring. I couldn't really see the hype, but she visualized how it would look. It is hard to explain, but it's almost like she saw it before she physically saw it. My mom had a vision…a vision no one understood but her. She never gave up on it, and she didn't try to tackle it all at once. She took baby steps to achieve her goal and chipped away at it. Little by little, paycheck by paycheck, she took portions of our resources and put it towards that goal. Today she took some shears and cut things out of the path. I never knew that something as small as edging, or cutting that little bit of grass out, would highlight that pathway in the way it did. When I saw that, it hit me. I thought about our past conversation, and how we talked about getting rid of people not aligned with God's word. I sat there and it was plain as day. My path could be so clear if I just get out some shears and cut some things out of my life."

Rose was taken back by the wisdom if this young girl. In her attempt to minister to Candice, Candice ended up ministering to her.

"Well here we are. Look Candy, keep your head up. I don't know exactly what happened, and it is none of my business. I see so much potential in you, and I believe you made the right decision."

"Thank you Rose."

"No, thank you."

"Thank me for what?"

"Whether you know it or not, you have been a blessing to me. You are so young, but there was so much wisdom and encouragement embedded in your words. I needed to hear that myself."

Candice smiled, then jumped out the vehicle. Rose put the car into drive but after a few feet slammed on the brakes.

"Candy, come here real quick," she yelled.

Candice hadn't quite made it to the porch yet, so she jogged back over to the car.

"What's up?"

"You know, I was just thinking. I don't know what happened today, but it sounds like you need to getaway. And from what you tell me about your mom, she doesn't get to relax either. How about I cancel my workout, and we all just go hang out at the spa, my treat? We can get our hair done, get massages, and just do girly stuff to pamper ourselves. You think your mother would be game?"

"I don't know what to say. I can't accept this Rose, and I know my mom is…"

"Candy, you have been a blessing to me, and helped me in more ways than you know. Just let me do this for you."

Candice had never been to a spa before and was excited. She ran into the house out of breath, but with a voice full of excitement which convinced her mother to come along. The three women headed off to a spa on the outskirts of town which Rose had become familiar with. She treated Candice and Lisa to the package which included the hot stone massage, pedicure, manicure, facial and spa lunch. The girls had a good time together pampering themselves.

As Rose dropped Candice and Lisa off, Candice once again thanked her for the day in the spa.

"Oh yea, before I forget I want to give you something."

"Candy, I told you before…you don't owe me a dime."

"Believe you me Rose, if I had a dime I'd give it to you. This is just something I wanted you to check out. You can throw it away when you are done because I made a copy on my computer."

Candice reached into her purse, and handed Rose a piece of college ruled notebook paper which had been folded into fours.

"What is this?"

"I was speaking with my uncle a while back, and he was telling me how I should approach men like an interview. He told me to make a checklist, or what I call my 50 Point Inspection, and initial every line my potential interest falls into. Poor Dre barely made 5 on my list, and I was being flexible with that."

Rose thought the gesture from Candice was cute. She admired her signs of maturity and politely thanked Candice, then waved as she drove off. Once out of sight, she opened her glove compartment box, and threw the worn paper inside.

* * *

The evening rolled around and Rose was still simmering on the afternoon with Candice. Now relaxed from her spa treatment, she decided to make a trip to see her grandfather. She let the top down on her convertible as she weaved through the country roads on the 40 minute drive to his home. The nostalgic feeling one gets who was raised in a country environment all resurfaced when she heard the crackle as her car drove up the stone and gravel driveway. Welcomed by a 14 year old dog, Rose rubbed him lovingly, then swung the scrawny screen door open. It creaked, then snapped back into place.

"Daddy, you home?"

Rose had referred to her grandfather as "Daddy" since he was the closest thing to a father she knew. She never knew much about her father other than he contributed to her birth.

"Daddy, you here?"

"I'm in the back room baby."

Rose dropped her purse on a nearby chair and walked into the backroom. Her grandfather was sitting at an old table working on putting a ship into a bottle. She gave him a big hug around his neck and kissed him on his cheek.

"Still working on those crafts, huh?"

"Well, I have to do something to keep me busy. Too hot to work in my woodshop today."

"Nothing wrong with that. So, how have you been feeling? Are the aides treating you right? Are you taking your medicine?"

"Yes, yes and yes…to everything you asked. I am good sugar."

"Daddy, why won't you come stay with me? You know I have plenty of room."

Rose has had this conversation with her grandfather for several years now. Her grandmother passed a few years ago; right around the time Rose was going through a divorce. She selfishly thought it would be good if they stayed together so they could prevent one another from being lonely, but her grandfather thought otherwise. She still persistently brings it up at least once per visit. Not so much from a standpoint of needing something from him, but out of worry for his health and a desire to take care of him. No matter what pitch she gives, she is met with resistance.

"Your grandmother and I raised our family in this home and worked hard to pay it off. We raised 6 kids and 4 grandkids and 1 great grandchild. I have every intention on letting my spirit leave the earth right here in the home stained by many years of my blood, sweat and tears. Your grandmother's memory is in here. I can still smell her sweet scent when I fall asleep at night. We made so many memories together in this house. We would just sit and talk for hours out on the porch about our families and everything. I remember the first year of our marriage, your grandmother was upset we had to go eat Thanksgiving over her brother's house because his wife could not cook. This was back before our family was big enough to hold our own Thanksgivings. I believe granny was pregnant with your oldest uncle at the time. We went there and all I can remember was those sweet potatoes. I took a bite into one, and that son of a gun was like a thick sliced raw carrot. Sweet potatoes aren't supposed to crunch. Safe to say your great uncle lost a lot of weight married to that woman."

Rose laughed hysterically. She loved the antics of her grandfather and enjoyed sitting back listening to him tell stories. She had a flashback from her younger years when he would sit in the rocking chair and read the Christmas story from the Bible to all the grandkids.

"Your grandmother was an absolutely beautiful woman. You rarely find women like her anymore. I watched her so intensely because I had never laid my eyes on something so graceful. I sit in that rocking chair over there, and I can remember her precise movements. I remember how she would let her hair down at night and brush it 100 times in the mirror. I remember everything about her. I remember how she would clean each item in the house and how she did it. I remember watching her light up when she received a new photo of a grandchild and how she would clear a space on the mantle for it. I remember all the children she sat in the kitchen and fed with this same baby spoon. I remember the romantic meals she made when we had no money. I remember the love that radiated from her when she walked into a room. I remember the look on her face when we moved into this house, and I also remember the look on her face when it burned and we had to rebuild it. As long as I have breath in this body and I can get around, I am going to stay right here. Along with her family, this home was her other love. When I die, I want her loving aroma on me."

Rose was overwhelmed by the amount of love her grandfather displayed for her grandmother. She wanted a man to treat her in that manner, but was growing resentful and not buying into the idea that good men exist.

'We were still having sex, you know.'

"Daddy!"

Rose's grandfather loved to say off the wall comments to get reactions.

"I am telling you the truth. And I didn't have to use any medicine either!"

Rose shook her head and was so tickled her smile stretched from ear to ear.

"Why are you trying to get me to move in so bad? You aren't letting these young men pinch on you, are you? They get fresh let me know. I still have my pistol and I know how to use it."

Rose looked at the frame of this brittle old man, and found it cute he was still willing to defend her honor.

"That's ok Daddy. I think I can hold my own. Thank you for wanting to protect me though."

"What brings you this way? What's on your mind?"

"Nothing really."

"I haven't lived this many years and not learned how to read people.... especially my bloodline. Something you want to talk to me about?"

"Nothing really, I am just tired."

"Tired of what Rosie?"

"Nothing...Hey, speaking of Rose, I have a question for you. I understand Mom named me Edith after Grandma, but why the middle name Rose?"

"Your mom didn't tell you?"

"She passed when I was 17 years old Daddy."

"Oh my Lord, 17 years of age? I didn't realize you were that young." Rose's grandfather took his glasses off, and cleaned the lenses on his shirt. "My, my, it has been a long time. I sure miss that girl. You remind me so much of her."

"You said my mother didn't tell me? What didn't she tell me?"

"Your mom used to have these dreams. I just can't believe she never told you."

"Told me what Daddy? Is it bad? Why do you keep avoiding my question?"

"No, nothing bad at all. When your mother was pregnant, she would have these dreams. It was that way with all of your siblings. If I remember correctly, she told us she saw you in front of thousands of women speaking words of encouragement."

"She thought I was going to be a motivational speaker?" Rose asked in her inquisitive tone.

"I don't know what her dreams meant. That is for you to try to figure out. I am just telling you what I know."

Rose's grandfather was finally finished buffing his glasses and adjusted them back on his face.

"She also saw that you would be financially well off and she also saw the bad. She saw that some man would come and break your heart. That the pain from that experience would be the seed to your destiny."

"I don't know what to say about all that. Seed to my destiny? I suppose so. So where did *Rose* come into play?"

"In every dream that she had, there was always a purple rose there, so that is where it comes from."

"A purple rose? Why purple? Was that her favorite color?"

"The purple rose represents protection, or a maternal love. Maybe nurturing has something to do with your destiny as well."

"Maybe. I just get tired Daddy. Tired of trying. Yes, I have built a nice living for myself, but something is missing. I am missing that fulfillment at the end of the day. I fooled myself into believing that if I worked hard and made it so I wouldn't have to rely on a man for money, that it would fix all my problems. I am well off beyond my dreams, but there is still a void. People always said money doesn't solve all your problems and I never understood what they meant until now."

"I know this is hard to believe given some of the people you run across daily, but God has a purpose for each and every one of us. Rose, you have to find your purpose. Let that consume your desires. Learn how to glorify God in all you do and He will bless you with all your hearts desires."

"Sounds good Daddy, but they just don't make men like you anymore. You can be a good person till you blue in the face, and that still doesn't mean a good man will fall from the heavens and land on your plate."

Rose's grandfather produced his distinctive laugh where his entire body shook.

"You have always said things that tickled me ever since you were little. Yes, men will probably not fall from the sky in an obvious manner, but when it is of God, the man will sweep you off in such a manner it will feel like he fell from the heavens. The problem is, no one wants to work on themselves. You work on yourself, then let God do the rest."

"I suppose so." Rose interrupted as she felt he was getting a tad bit too personal. Growing her business, she had learned to guard herself and really shrug criticisms off. Though it was effective in the work place, it was detrimental to her personal relationships.

"I am running late. I brought you some dinner. I put it in the fridge and also made you some cobbler for dessert. Tell that one nurse aide, the one that feels they always have to do number two in the bathroom, to not to eat it all up this time!"

Rose's grandfather escorted her to the door. He gave her a routine hug followed by some inspirational words.

"Baby, one last thing before you go. God blessed you and put you in a position with tremendous responsibility. Not because of the money you make, but because your platform allows you to touch a lot of people. You have a voice that can influence many. Allow yourself to be positioned so God can use you, and you will find the edification you seek. There is nothing more satisfying than walking in your purpose."

Rose nodded her head silently acknowledging that she heard her grandfather, then exited his home.

Chapter XIV

My New Man

Rose walked to the podium towards a girl who was short in stature and barely visible. She thanked her for the introduction, adjusted the cordless microphone on her lapel, and began to speak.

"Today I am here to talk about a good man. Let me tell you, this man of mine is like none other. He covered my past with His blood and propelled me into my future. A future of having a beautiful family that operates in line with the Word of God. My Heavenly Father, knowing all that I have done in my past, every dark evil sordid detail of it, saw fit to still bless me as I turned back to Him with a wonderful, beautiful daughter and dedicated husband. God is awesome and He can do anything."

In the middle of her speech, there was an incredible blaring feedback on the microphone which caused the audience of all females to cringe. The noise made Rose cover her ears. As the sound penetrated through her hand barrier, there was a loud thud. Rose looked up to find a coffee table knocked over. It took her a second to realize she was dreaming, and fell off the couch.

Man, I must have dozed off on the couch. What was that dream about? A man? A daughter? I must really be desperate or something. Either that, or I really need to stop eating food after 6pm.

Rose maneuvered on her knees, and laid her head across the seat of the couch. She felt if she moved slow enough, she could avoid a headache from waking up abruptly.

"Lord, what is wrong with me? Am I going to die lonely?"

She thought back to the conversation she had with Terry a few months ago about forming a relationship, and immediately began praying.

"Lord, I want to be back in Your favor, but I don't know how. I am sorry, and repent for going astray. I am sorry for not listening when I felt you were speaking to me. I am sorry for being rebellious and trying to go at this thing my way. Lord, I messed up. I am a complete mess, and I need You to restore me."

Rose placed her hand on the coffee table, and grunted while pushing herself up. She walked to her bookshelf in her office, and pulled her Bible off the shelf. As she slid the Bible out, a thick layer of dust dissipated in the air.

I ought to be ashamed of myself. I literally haven't pulled this Bible out in years.

Ok Lord, I need a sign. I am going to open this Bible, and I want you to speak to me right now.

Rose opened the Bible to Lamentations 5:7 – *Our fathers have sinned and are not; and we have borne their iniquities*

"Ok, this is not really what I had in mind. I don't even have a father. Let me try something else."

Rose flipped through her Bible again searching for another passage. She arrived at Romans 10:9-10 – *If you confess with your mouth the Lord Jesus and believe in your heart that God has raised Him from the dead, you will be saved. For with the heart one believes unto righteousness, and with the mouth confession is made unto salvation.*

"What does that mean? I am already saved. Lord, if you want to give me a message, this is the time. What am I supposed to do? I am not hearing anything?"

Now frustrated, Rose closed her Bible.

* * *

A few days passed, and Rose kept trying to extract revelation from the Bible by flipping through and randomly picking scriptures. After the third day, Rose became so frustrated trying to hear from God that she flung her Bible across the room with such velocity it smacked her leather office couch knocking over the decorative pillows. Immediately the phone rang. She walked to her cellular and flipped it open.

"Hello"

"Hey Rose, this is Terry. You were on my mind, and thought I'd give you a call."

"What is up with that? You just get off the phone with Jesus or something? He tell you He was mad for me throwing His book?"

"Woman, what are you talking about?"

"Nothing. I was just sitting here reading the Bible, but I am getting a little frustrated."

"What seems to be the problem?"

"I don't know. I just feel a little frustrated with my walk right now, and sometimes it seems like it is hard to hear from God."

"What are you doing to communicate with Him?"

"I don't know what you mean what am I doing. I pray, I read my Bible, I listen to gospel, I have been going to church. What else am I supposed to be doing?"

"Rose I don't have a direct answer for you. Many times we pray, then move before we hear an answer."

"I suppose so. It is just a tad bit annoying at times. You try to do right, but don't see any rewards for your diligence."

Rose thought back to her mother, and how her mother displayed faith and was not healed.

"A lot of people don't live their life to the fullest and attempt to conquer their dreams because of fear. They give fear a prominent position in their lives, and allow it to have a stronghold over them. Never let fear impede your happiness. You know my grandfather used to have this old sign hanging in the living room that said – Fear knocked, faith answered, no one was there."

"I understand what you are saying. It is just hard. Why does everything have to take so long?"

"Rose, you like working out, correct?"

"Of course I do."

"I used to love going to the gym, but after the kid and additional responsibilities, I am not anywhere near in the shape I used to be in 15 years ago. I haven't dedicated the necessary time to achieve those fitness goals. I mean I look at myself sometimes in the mirror, and my love handles look like an accordion."

Rose burst into laughter.

"The point is, nothing comes overnight. When you workout, results don't happen immediately. When you diet, results don't happen immediately. So when you study the Word, and pray, sometimes things don't happen immediately…visually anyways. Just like working out, most changes start happening on the inside before you see results on the outside. You have to learn how to be patient and grow. Through these times, God will mold you and teach you, but you have to allocate the necessary time to form a relationship with Him. That means working out spiritually by praying, meditating and studying your Bible. If you put yourself into position, God will reveal himself."

"I guess so. I am an intelligent woman. I know that God exists, but sometimes it just seems like people are overly dramatic at church falling out and whatnot. Is that really necessary? You can have a relationship without crying or acting out for attention. That is just how I see it."

"Rose, I love you like my lil' sister. I don't have all the answers you seek. We can engage in debates regarding the sincerity of church members all day. Who is to say who is being real, and who is fake? What I can say is when you invite Jesus into your life, there will be some times you will sit there and be so overwhelmed with joy that you feel a rush come over you, and tears will stream from your face. What you need to do is not worry about anyone else around you. Focus on yourself. Dedicate time alone to God. Position yourself to hear from Him. Surround yourself in things that can feed your spirit. Gospel music, listening to sermons, the people you surround yourself with. Sit down and pray before you read your Bible for clarification and wisdom, and God will reveal Himself to you. If you are having a hard time understanding your Bible, pick up another translation. There are so many translations that there truly is no excuse."

Rose knew Terry was right, and encouraged his scolding, yet wanted to avoid it at the same time.

"Well Terry, I have to get up off here. Got a lot of paperwork to do. Thanks for the advice. I will go to the bookstore tomorrow maybe and see if I can find something to help with my study habits."

"Anything you need, just let me know. If you want to pray, or come over and we can all have Bible study, just let me know."

Rose wanted to grow closer to Christ, but at her own pace. She felt anxiety as her last bit of flesh wanted to resist.

"We'll see Terry. Kiss Tonda and tell her I love her. Tell Ro I will call her tomorrow."

"Alright Rose. Take care."

"You too!"

* * *

Rose sat on the couch reading fiscal reports from last year. As she adjusted her glasses, she felt this was a good time to take a break. She walked over to the fridge still thinking about her conversation with Terry, grabbed a bottled water, then plopped down on the couch to watch CNN.

"Wow, is this what my life has been reduced to? Sitting at home working watching CNN? I need to do something fun. I work too hard not to play."

No sooner than Rose completed the thought, her cell phone vibrated. She briefly looked at the caller ID display, then flipped the phone open.

"Hello."

"Hey girl, it's me Ang. What you doing?"

"Just took a break from looking at these reports."

"I know you are not working on a Friday night. I was calling to see if you wanted to take a break. A couple of the girls and I are going to The Lounge. Supposed to be live tonight, and you know there are some cute men there."

"Sounds good, but I should really stay in. I have a lot of work to do."

"Rose get out of here with that. You have all day tomorrow to work. Just come out and relax. Hang out with the ladies. Get a drink or two, flirt with some men, then leave."

Rose figured there was no harm in going out to a club, plus it had been a while since she heard a live band, so she prepared a one-woman exhibition to the deepest recesses of her closet as if she were searching for King Tutankhamen's tomb within the pyramid, retrieved one of her sexy ensembles, and headed out.

Rose arrived at the club, did one last check of hair and makeup in her mirror, then straightened her skirt as she approached the entrance. Just so happen she knew the doorman from high school so she bypassed the line and was escorted directly inside. Her eyes performed a scavenger hunt for her friend as the strobe lights bounced across the club, and music rattled the walls. The stench of smoke and alcohol saturated the air worse than the state fair aroma this particular night. It had been 3 years since Rose came to The Lounge. It used to be a nice jazz bar with a live band, but apparently it had been taken over by new owners, and boasted a hip-hop theme. Fifteen minutes in the club, Rose spotted Angie sitting at a table with two young men. It was apparent that Angie had one two many drinks as she was sitting on one of her acquaintance's lap while the other bit his lip looking Rose over like her body held the secrets to the fountain of youth.

"Hey girl, this is my new friend." As she gazed at her new interest, she stroked the side of his face in a sensual manner, "What is your name again sweetie?"

Rose was unable to hear his name, nor did she care due to the ringing in her head caused by the music which thumped through the place. The combination of the bass making her heartbeat feel irregular, and aroma of colognes, perfumes and funk mixed together started to give Rose a slight headache. *I must be getting old, because I used to like loud music. Now it just agitates me.*

"Rose, sit on down. I want to introduce you to Sean's friend, Bryan."

Bryan was a semi-attractive man, and prior to speaking the only flaw Rose found was remnants of tea or coffee as his teeth were discolored. Even though he boldly displayed her pet peeve, she attempted to be cordial.

"Hi Bryan."

"So your name is Rose, huh? That is a pretty name, for beautiful, delicate flower like yourself."

Rose tried not to roll her eyes, but the combination of Angie screaming every time Sean tickled her or whispered something dirty in her ear, and Bryan trying to get close to talk was starting to become an overload. Yet and still, she tried to make the most out of the moment.

"Can I get you a drink?"

Rose thought maybe a drink would take the edge off, so she responded, "Sure, why not."

Moments later Bryan came back to the table with two drinks in his hand.

"I couldn't tell if you were on brown liquor, or white so take your choice. Goose, or cognac?"

"I will take the vodka. Thank you."

"My pleasure," Bryan sat down in his seat and took a sip of cognac. His eyes glossed over as this was his fourth drink of the night, and he tried to remain cool while he bobbed his head to the music.

"Bryan is it? So tell me Bryan, what do you do for a living?"

"Funny you say that, because I am in-between jobs at the moment."

"Oh Lord," Rose recited not realizing her thoughts were traveling outside of her head.

"It's not like that. I was just going through a rough patch with my daughter's mom, you know. Little domestic dispute jump off. I went over to pick my daughter up, and there was some weed on the table. I'm heated right. So I go to the backroom and she got her head buried in some dudes lap…while my daughter was in the other room, ya feel me? Well, safe to say I was livid but I am a man about mines, so I pistol whipped homey. Real talk, just protecting my daughter from an unstable environment. So my babymom gets mad and calls the cops on me. I'm already on probation and my gig was like a favor for my PO, so it kind of set me back." Bryan took another sip of cognac, then continued.

"I can't let this get me down though. I think God has a purpose for me. Maybe it was meant for me to lose my gig so I can be an entrepreneur. I was thinking about starting up my own daycare around the way. But to set it apart, attach a barbershop. That way you can drop off your little shortie, then get a lineup. Win-win situation for all."

Rose's brain shut off after Bryan referred to his daughter's mother as a *babymom* and did not hear one word thereafter.

"Bryan, how old is you?" Rose stated in a sarcastic tone taking shots at his grammar. The sad part was Bryan didn't catch the joke.

"I am 24, but I am real mature for my age and I love older women. My last woman was 32, so I know I can handle you. True, we'd have to get down at your crib for right now. This situation livin' with my moms is just temporary, you know, till I gets back on my feet."

Rose couldn't believe she put herself in this position again. *This is not even funny. I am too dag on old to be acting like Stella like Angie is. I don't need sex or a fling, I need a real man. Shoot, a God-fearing man…which is something I most likely will never find here. I should have just stayed at home. Now I am irritable and my head hurts.*

"I am sorry, this is not working. Ang, I will call you girl. I have to go."

Rose heard Angie in the background yelling for her to wait, along with rejected comments from an intoxicated Bryan. Shimming through the thick youthful crowd while attempting to avoid inconspicuous hands reaching out fondling her breasts and buttocks along the way, Rose finally made it out to her car.

Can't believe those perverts! Why do guys grab women without their consent? That is some old junior high foolishness. What was I thinking coming here? This club scene was the same when I was in my early 20s…nothing at all has changed.

Sitting in her car, Rose placed her head on the headrest and let out a deep sigh.

This would be the ideal love story. I am frustrated with the club, and so is my knight in shining armor who just so happened to walk out in the parking lot and see his damsel in distress. He politely knocks on the window pane, asks what is wrong, and engages me in intellectual conversation.

Rose opened her eyes, and was disappointed her dream was not reality. She looked around the perimeter of the club, and there were guys standing in groups drinking, gawking at women as they passed by.

This is ridiculous. I can't believe I let Angie talk me into coming out here again.

A long dehydrated ride home, Rose was elated to pull into her driveway. As she reached up to grab the garage door opener from the visor, it was nonexistent.

Now where did I put that dag on opener? I am always losing it.

Rose scurried her hands frantically under the seat as her bladder was full.

Where is this stupid thing. Argh. I am going to pee on myself.

After searching the normal locations, Rose opened the glove compartment box, and the opener fell out...along with Candice's list. Rose chuckled again thinking about how this young girl was trying to teach her about relationships.

That was cute of her. Guess homegirl said I am old and need to get my act together. But heck, what could it hurt at this point?

Rose was about to discard the paper, but to humor herself she opened it up:

50 Point Inspection Checklist

1. ___ Man who loves and respects God
2. ___ Honest
3. ___ Loves me like 1 Corinthians 13:4 (does not boast etc.)
4. ___ Saved
5. ___ Obedient to the Word of God
6. ___ Respects his parents
7. ___ Respects my parents
8. ___ Willing to communicate with me
9. ___ Not too prideful and willing to ask for help
10. ___ Honest (I think this needs to be on the list twice)
11. ___ Open with his feelings
12. ___ Doesn't pressure me to have sex
13. ___ Strong physically and mentally
14. ___ Not possessive
15. ___ Attends church
16. ___ Has personal relationship with God and desires to please Him
17. ___ Has a strong prayer life
18. ___ Is willing to pray for me
19. ___ Is willing to seek God for guidance
20. ___ Likes children
21. ___ Doesn't have illegitimate children
22. ___ Passionate about something positive

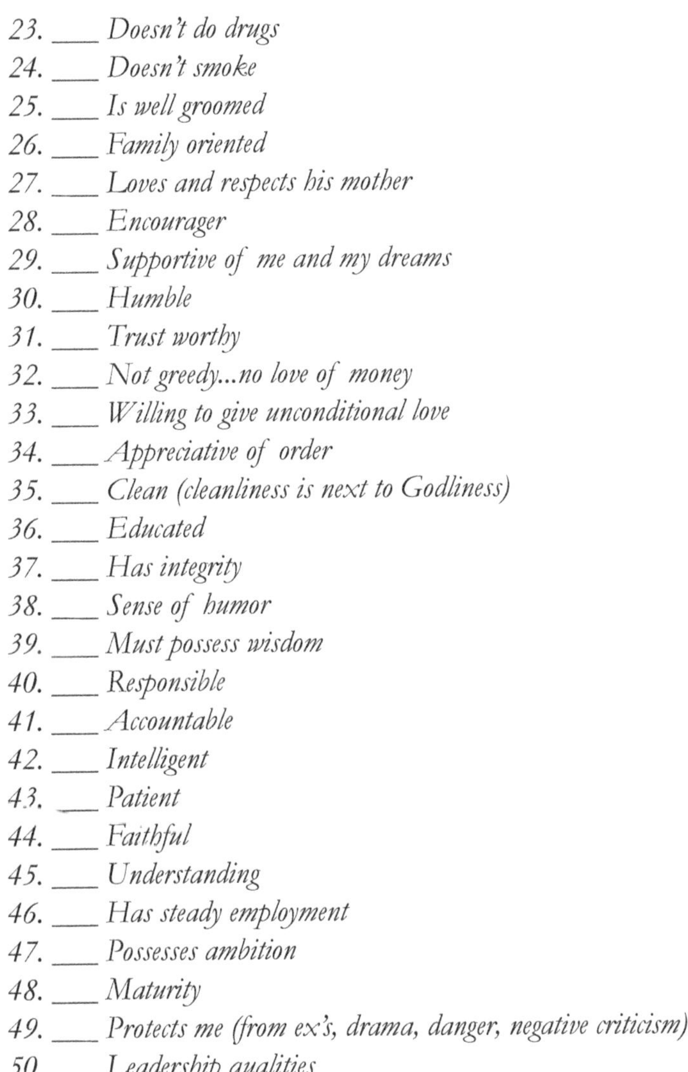

23. ___ *Doesn't do drugs*
24. ___ *Doesn't smoke*
25. ___ *Is well groomed*
26. ___ *Family oriented*
27. ___ *Loves and respects his mother*
28. ___ *Encourager*
29. ___ *Supportive of me and my dreams*
30. ___ *Humble*
31. ___ *Trust worthy*
32. ___ *Not greedy...no love of money*
33. ___ *Willing to give unconditional love*
34. ___ *Appreciative of order*
35. ___ *Clean (cleanliness is next to Godliness)*
36. ___ *Educated*
37. ___ *Has integrity*
38. ___ *Sense of humor*
39. ___ *Must possess wisdom*
40. ___ *Responsible*
41. ___ *Accountable*
42. ___ *Intelligent*
43. ___ *Patient*
44. ___ *Faithful*
45. ___ *Understanding*
46. ___ *Has steady employment*
47. ___ *Possesses ambition*
48. ___ *Maturity*
49. ___ *Protects me (from ex's, drama, danger, negative criticism)*
50. ___ *Leadership qualities*

Rose was dumbfounded. She walked into her house, relieved herself, then sat on the couch thinking about Candice's list. She stared at her reflection in the gray tint of her television which was turned off, and began talking to herself.

"Here I am an old chick, and this young girl has learned how to set standards for herself. I sat there and preached to her about having boundaries and not settling for less. And what did I do? Sit here and let friends peer pressure me into going out to some club and an environment I know I am not interested in."

A sudden wave of emotion hit Rose, and tears raced down her face.

"At what point in your life do you become tired? Tired of making the same mistakes over and over with men and relationships. It is like I have been stuck in the wilderness for years now. Is something wrong with me? I am exhausted. I have been going at this thing my way for way too long now. God, I submit to you. If a girl half my age can get tired and set boundaries then so can I. I will do whatever it takes. If that means I won't ever have a man or get married then I am ok with that. It hurts too much to go against Your will so have Your way with me. I just want to do right by You. I repent for my behavior lately and I am sorry for trying to do things my way. I respect, honor and reverence You, and want to please You. Use me as you see fit Lord."

Rose's heart opened up to God at that moment and she rededicated herself to developing a relationship with Him.

* * *

Three weeks passed, and it was another lonely Friday night for Rose. As usual her phone rang with Angie attempting to coerce her to a club.

"Ok, I know the last time was not ideal, but you have to admit that he was awfully cute. And those young boys are so adorable in bed. They try so hard."

"Ang, maybe a different day and era, but right now I am looking for more. I am fooling myself if I think I will find Mr. Right in a club."

"There is nothing wrong with just going out to a club. Don't be a prude."

"Maybe not, but that club scene is just not for me anymore. The man I am looking for won't be out at the club with a beer in his hand. If me filtering my men by location means that I will remain single and lonely then so be it. I don't know what happened that night, but something changed in me. I started to feel all warm all over and…"

"Girl, that was that liquor in your system."

"No Ang, this was different. I broke down and prayed, and felt warm all over. I began crying, and it just felt so cleansing. In that moment, I realized that maybe it is not in God's will for me to be remarried right now and I have to learn to live with that, versus making foolish decisions based off emotion. I have a lot of work to do on myself first before I can even remotely begin to start looking in that direction. I am not getting any younger, and I don't want to spend my remaining days on this earth chasing after some non-existent dream. I have been reading my Bible and

I know God has my best interest and will bless me with my hearts desires. Not only that, but there is just so much work to do as far as ministering to people and trying to help others hear about the goodness of God. I think I have been abusing my position and not really giving back as I should. Sometimes…"

Angie muted Rose out completely. She really didn't like hearing anything about God as she grew up as a PK, or preacher's kid. Angie constantly heard her father speak to her about scripture and the direction of her life, but she was so rebellious and content on doing things her way. From married men, to flat out Mr. Wrong, her father always tried to guide her but Angie would not listen. She deliberately disobeyed him and never took his words of love into consideration. Rose envied Angie for having a father who cared.

"You sound like Daddy now. Well you got to do you. Just thought I'd be cordial and offer. Hey, it's been fun but I have to run."

The two women hung up the phone understanding the fault line in their relationship had cracked and divided them. How they had been friends for years, they were traveling in two different directions.

Rose knew she had to monitor her personal interactions with Angie and distance herself. As she sat there, she felt at peace with her decision. She opened her Bible and continued reading about Hannah. Rose read this story before but while reading the text at that moment it captured her like it hadn't before. She continued reading the passage, said a prayer, then sat there meditating. During the process she thought of Candice, and began to smile, so she grabbed her phone to give her a call.

"Richards's residence."

"Hello, may I speak to Candice please."

"This is her, may I ask who's calling?"

"This is Rose."

"Hey Rose! I am sorry, I didn't recognize your voice. What's up?"

"Nothing much really. I was just thinking about you, and thought I'd drop a line. How is everything going with school?"

"Oh, it's going. I am just ready to get through so I can get out of this town."

"I know that feeling," Rose stated under her breath, even though the gravitational pull of the town brought her back. "Hey, I also wanted to thank you for that list you made with the 50 qualities you want in a man. That is a good way to filter out nonsense."

"Oh, no problem at all. I suggest you come up with your own list though because you and only you know what you want out of a man."

Rose took the phone away from her ear, and stared at it while smiling. She was so tickled by Candice giving her relationship advice.

"So what are you getting into tonight Rose?"

"Nothing much. I have just been sitting here reading my Bible."

Embarrassed because she hadn't read her Bible in weeks, Candice truthfully confessed, "I have to be honest. I haven't read mine in a while. I joined this youth prayer group but I don't know…something is just missing with them. I know that is no excuse but I will get back on track. What are you studying?"

"I am actually reading about Hannah," Rose responded.

"Hannah. Ironically, the last time I went to that Bible study we were just talking about that. That is the one where she was married to that guy and then he married another woman and had kids with her. Where Hannah couldn't have kids for some reason and then the second wife… what was her name again?"

"Peninnah."

"Yea, Peninnah. The second wife Peninnah would rub it in Hannah's face that she had kids knowing Hannah couldn't have any. Man, I would have popped that heifer straight in her mouth."

"Candy!" Rose stated while listening to a young clone of herself on the other line.

"What? I am just saying. You know I can't have kids, you then come behind me, have kids, then taunt me? Naw, it is not going down like that."

"Candy, you are a riot. You know, I thought about that as well, but tonight while reading, the story hit me differently. Really put yourself in her shoes. Hannah had a husband who truly loved her. The passage says that after he would make a sacrifice, he would give Hannah double portions of meat because she had favor in his eyes. Hannah appeared to have everything she wanted…that was except for a child as the Lord closed her womb. Keep in mind in those days, they shunned those who were barren, or couldn't have children.

"So I was reading this tonight and it got to the part where it talked about Peninnah having children by Elkanah, and how she knew Elkanah loved Hannah more. Peninnah was jealous so she provoked Hannah to the point where Hannah wouldn't eat. It said that this went on for years and years. Just think about that. She let this woman get her so mad that she wouldn't even eat. It became so bad that it bled into their marriage, but Hannah was so brokenhearted that she couldn't even respond to her husband's frustration. She let the words of Peninnah break her spirit and infiltrate other areas of her life."

"Well that is her fault for being stupid. She should have bounced. I'll be darn if I stay in some foolishness like that and be miserable."

"It wasn't that simple in that time Candy. I think there are so many lessons to be learned from this passage. Proverbs 18:21 tells us that death and life are in the power of the tongue. I think sometimes we, as women, get so caught up with listening to another scornful female that it blocks our blessings because it cuts us off from hearing from God. We get so upset that it disrupts us physically and spiritually. We allow another woman to come in and basically take all our power. They use words to plant seeds of doubt, worry, confusion, frustration, anger…and we allow it to take root."

"I can agree with that."

"Like I said, I read this before, but today this passage spoke to me. What really stood out was verse 9. Hannah was praying and looking a hot mess. So much in fact that they thought she was drunk. I mean, this situation really tore her up. The Bible stated three words that were so powerful to me in the 9th verse. It said – *So Hannah rose.* Just think about that. She got pushed to her limits. Pushed so far that she gathered herself, rose above the situation, and in the following verses poured her heart out to God. She was depressed, dejected, and dispirited but God intervened in her life.

"I believe that the message here is God sometimes allows things to happen to get us to a certain point in our prayer life. A point where we solely rely on Him with everything. A point where we open up our hearts and pour them out to God sincerely. I believe that is the point where God wants us to be. As soon as Hannah got to that point, that is when God blessed her with a son. When you get some time, just read the text in the first chapter of I Samuel."

"You know what Rose, I needed to hear that. Thank you."

"I have to thank you as well Candice. I must admit my call was selfish in nature as I wanted to thank you for who you are. Thank you for the seeds you planted in me." Rose started shaking her head from side to side. "Do you know I went to a club a few weeks back?"

"Really? I mean, I shouldn't say it like that 'cause you are a cool woman, but just doesn't seem like your cup of tea."

"You are absolutely correct Candy…it is not my cup of tea. I knew that before I went and I suppose I was in rebellious mode. You know that mode where you know right from wrong, but chose to do wrong anyway.

Well long story short, I went and had a terrible time. I actually left early. So I got home and was looking at your list and thinking about my life and the stupid stupid stupid mistakes I made in relationships…and just started to cry and pray."

"Like Hannah, huh?"

"I guess in a sense. I had let my past mistakes beat up on me so much that I just broke down and recommitted myself to God. I don't know why I am telling you this…I guess just to tell you thank you for being one of the positive people in my life. You know it is hard to go against the grain in society when everyone is doing something a certain way, but Romans 12:2 tells us not to be conformed to the ways of this world but transformed through the renewing of our mind. We have been called to go over and beyond. We have to stop making emotional decisions and start thinking logically about relationships and other choices we make because like it or not, we are different from the world. We have to use spiritual discernment and learn from our past mistakes so we stop falling in these same pits.

"The problem we have is we want to obtain Godly wisdom, but continually walk outside His will. That is not how it works and a lesson I had to learn the hard way. First we have to get our relationship right with God, then He will bless us with the wisdom we seek. He will place conviction so deep within your heart that you have no problem standing up for what you feel is right. Just because everyone is having sex, or drinking, or doing whatever doesn't mean that we have to. I know this was a long-winded response to get to this point, but I just wanted to thank you for being one of the ones that went against the grain. You ministered to this old lady, and I love you."

"I love you too Rose."

Chapter XV

The Attendant

A year and a half passed, and Candice was ready to graduate early. She was accepted into Boston College with a full ride presidential scholarship and she was also recruited to be on the track team. During those last years of high school, her relationship with her mother blossomed. Whenever she felt herself getting upset with her mother she thought about the pain in Rose's voice when she spoke about losing her mother as a teen, so Candice tried not to be argumentative and to live each day as if it were the last. Through Candice's love, she ministered to her mom and helped her to heal from the pain of the divorce and its circumstances. Not only was Candice a blessing to her mother, but to everyone's life she touched.

Rose's testimony helped to influence Candice and the decisions she was making, but on the same token Candice aided her in healing from some old wounds. Through Candice's actions, Rose took the time to reinvest in herself and form a relationship with God. It didn't happen overnight, but through time she developed a peace which hadn't been present in her life before. During this period of time she was so consumed with her work and other activities that she didn't pursue relationships with other men. Her appetite for life was full and she learned that whatever state she was in to be content.

* * *

Rose was in route to the office. Running low on gasoline, she pulled into a local gas station. She passed this station on numerous occasions, but never filled up there. Feeling courageous and slightly desperate to prevent running out of gas, she swiftly maneuvered into the filthy gas station.

As Rose stepped out of her automobile, she attempted to pay for her gas by sliding her credit card. She tried several times, but it kept beeping and instructing her to see the attendant inside.

"Why is this stupid thing not working?"

Rose noticed there was only one guy working, and his torso was hidden underneath an old rusty GMC Suburban.

"Excuse me sir. I went inside, and no one was in there. Is anyone else working?"

The man slid from under the car, and wiped his hands on his one-piece mechanics outfit. As he stood erect, Rose found herself delighted as a tall, muscular man now stood before her. His body showed signs of perspiration, however there was actually a clean scent that came from him, and his breath was accented by winter mint inspired gum. Rose noticed he had good oral hygiene. Bad oral health was her pet peeve. She had been known to be in important sales meetings and be distracted by someone with dingy teeth or bad breath.

"I am sorry Miss, but we are short staffed today. What can I do for you?"

"Well, this stupid thing won't take my card."

"Let me see it."

The assertive worker walked over to the gas pump, and wiped the card on the only clean portion of his clothing prior to inserting it.

"Sometimes these things act silly, and you just need to wipe them. Don't worry…I don't stink or anything."

Rose laughed as she already made that observation. The worker attempted two times before the card was actually accepted.

"Well thank you!"

"I am so sorry for the inconvenience and for time you lost. I tell you what. It is a hot day…how about you go get yourself a beverage. It's on the house. I will pump your gas for you in the meantime."

Wow, a gentleman. That was awfully nice of him. Then again, this is his job.

"That is ok, I don't want to get you into trouble with your manager." Rose responded.

"Oh, I am sure he won't mind."

The worker insisted that Rose grab herself a beverage. Something about this man intrigued her, but she couldn't quite place a finger on it.

"Are you sure? I don't want to get you fired."

The worker smirked.

"I don't think that will be a problem."

Rose found his gesture cute, plus she wanted to get a better look at him from inside the store instead of gawking at him face to face, so she walked in to grab two bottled waters. With her cute walk now in force, Rose worked it as she walked back to her BMW.

"I thought you could use a water too. You have been working in that hot garage all morning."

"That is very considerate of you Madam. May I ask your name?"

Rose looked the gentleman over from head to toe. *Madam? Do I look like I run a brothel? Ok, be nice Rose, he was just being cordial.*

"My name is Edith, but my friends call me Rose. Yes, I know already… my name is old."

"I actually think it is pretty. My name is Herb, but I go by my middle name, Scot…with one T. As you can see, it isn't the most attractive name either so I am not one to talk. So Edith Rose, tell me, what do you do for a living?"

Rose was reluctant to tell people what her position was so she concealed it. She feared men would either approach her in one of two ways. They'd either be intimidated and make everything a competition in order to compensate for their bruised ego, or they'd try to be manipulative and see what they can get out of her. After years of bad blind dates, Rose became apprehensive of letting people know too much information about her personal life.

"Oh, it is a boring job…I deal with cosmetics and whatnot."

"That actually sounds interesting." Scot twisted the cap of his water and released a surprisingly loud *kisk* sound as the seal was broken and air escaped. He took a sip of his water, then continued. "I don't want to hold you up. Looks like you were in a rush."

"No, not at all actually."

"Rose, do you have any plans for this coming Friday?"

Rose kept a smile on her face while strategizing her next move. *Shoot, I knew this was coming. Why didn't I just get in my car? He is cute, I will give him that, but a gas station attendant? What would my friends say? Oh, whatever. Why not? Couldn't be any worse than men I met in the past.*

"Nothing actually, why do you ask?"

"I was wondering if you wanted to go out to dinner possibly?"

Rose paused as to play hard to get, yet maintaining a smile the entire time. Scot's confidence began to grow.

"I think that would be nice, Herb."

"Please call me Scot."

"No problem. You can call me Rose by the way. All my close friends and family call me Rose."

"I feel important to be in that circle of close friends that can address you as Rose. Can I call you, or get your e-mail address?"

"This is a new era, isn't it? People now ask for e-mail addresses," Rose responded.

"I know. I just wanted to make you comfortable. Some people don't feel comfortable giving out their home number. Heck, my sister usually Google's her dates and runs background checks before she goes anywhere."

Rose laughed.

"Do I need to Google you?"

"Feel free too. I don't have anything to hide. In the meantime, how will I contact you to arrange this date?"

"Do you have something to write my number on?" Rose replied.

"You can just recite it. I have an extraordinary memory."

"Oh really? Now that is interesting. You aren't going to have me sitting at home hungry on Friday, are you?"

"Of course not Rose. I am just going to act like I remember, then after you drive off, run into the shop real quick and write it down."

Rose chuckled again.

"Seriously, I have a good memory. Don't exactly know why, but I have always been able to remember things in incredible detail. Especially things which are important to me. Just a gift I suppose."

Rose was intrigued by this man, so she recited her number, then waved as she drove off.

* * *

Time elapsed and Rose arrived at the office. As she was greeted with the normal banter, Angie noticed a different glow on her. She followed Rose into the office and shut the door.

"Who is he girl?"

"Who is who Ang?"

"Stop playing with me. You know how long we've known each other. The man you met. I haven't seen this look on you since…well, you know who. You either met a new guy, or had some killer sex last night…or a combination of both. Which is it?"

Rose blushed.

"Ok, it is nothing serious. And I told you I am not having sex. I made a promise to God that I would close down shop until I get married. And if that never happens, then oh well."

"I hear you, but whatever. So back to this man. Ooo girl, give me all the details. What was he driving? What does he look like? What did he have on? And more importantly, does he have a brother?"

Rose knew where Angie was steering the conversation.

"He had on clothes, and I didn't see his car."

"Girl, what is up? What happened? What did he say? Rose, you holding out on me."

"Nothing really. No pickup lines or anything, we just talked. He was very charming, tall, and very handsome."

"Whoo girl, you get all the good ones. You leaving all the good parts out though. You know I am an old freaky broad, so you have to give me more data. What he have on? Casual clothes or a suit?"

"Does it matter?"

"I am trying to get a visual, and you making it hard. You know I haven't had any in quite some time, so I have to live through my friends. There is no shame in my game, now details please."

"He had on his work outfit?"

"Work outfit? I don't understand. Where does he work?"

Rose sighed.

"Look, he works at the gas station."

Angie sat back in her chair. The smile which once occupied her face turned into a face of disappointment and confusion.

"Hold the hell up. You did what again? Gave your number to who?"

"Don't be like that Ang."

"Be like what? Do you even know who you are? I love you because you are my girl and modest, but do you know how much this company is worth? All you did? And you are talking to a who? A gas station attendant? What is wrong with you? You want a man that you have to take care of? I understand times are hard, but come on now. Even I am not that desperate."

"See, that is why I didn't want to say nothing to you. Sometimes it ain't about what a man has, but how he treats you. And I don't necessarily see a man on your arm while you are sitting here scolding me."

"That sounds good and all, but heck I want a man that is fine and got money. What is wrong with that? I'll be single before I settle for less. I worked too hard to go back."

"Go back to what? You didn't have anything to begin with. Angie, I am telling you from experience, I been down that road. All that money won't bring you happiness if he is not treating you right and going to sleep with your family members. Troy's family had all that money and it did not help our relationship out one bit."

"I guess. I never had that problem, so I can't speak on it. Just protect yourself girl. He probably has seven kids or something. Don't let this man come in and hustle you for your money."

"Don't worry…I think I can handle my own. How about you stop sleeping with married men instead of worrying about me? Meeting these men on cruises and their wife's are totally clueless. You have enough issues to worry about yourself instead of trying to give me advice."

Angie took the hint, and walked out of the office without saying a word. Rose didn't mean to be so rude, but her patience with her long-time friend was dissipating and at this point Angie's ignorance had reached an apex.

* * *

Friday rolled around and Scot called to make arrangements to come pick Rose up. While Rose was preparing for her date, she thought about the worst case scenario. *He appears nice, but Lord, please don't let this boy pick me up in a Sanford & Son truck.*

As Rose put on her lipstick, her doorbell rung. She walked to the door, and without looking in the peep hole to verify who was there, swung the door wide open. To her surprise, her knight in shining armor was standing there, well groomed and shaved.

"Wow, you clean up well."

"So do you Rose. I know this is corny, but here is a rose. It is a rare breed called Careless Love."

"That is not corny at all, it is actually very sweet. Careless love, huh? Interesting. Are you dropping me hints?"

"Let's just see how the night goes," Scot confidently smiled. He wrapped his arm around Rose, and escorted her to his vehicle which she was delighted to see wasn't a dumb truck but a BMW X5.

The conversation along the way to the dinner was good. The two flirted but kept it relatively clean. They joked about Scot's taste in music; his radio was broke due to his nephew jamming Disney CDs into the player.

After a thirty minute drive, they arrived at their destination. Scot exited the vehicle and walked around to escort his female companion out. She thanked him and held his hand as they walked into the restaurant. The maitre d escorted them to their table which was a secluded booth with dim lighting. The couple ordered their drinks then jumped into conversation to prevent any silence from occurring.

"So tell me about yourself Scot. How did you get into the gas station business? Forgive me for my ignorance, but I don't know what you call it."

"That is ok. Well, it is a long story actually. The short version is my father is actually an electrical engineer. When he was younger his father passed away and left him some property. My dad ended up selling the land, then acquired a gas station. He wanted to teach my brother and me about business, so in high school he allowed us to manage it. My brother and I grew it to four stations."

"I am impressed. Business savvy I see."

"I took some time away from it to go to college, but I still handled the books. Once I graduated, I decided I wanted to get back in there and be more hands on. Short story of my life. So tell me about you. You say you work in cosmetics, but I never seen anyone drive a car like that working for a cosmetic company unless they either own it or inherited some money."

Rose usually wouldn't have responded or would have tried to deter the conversation, but she felt comfortable in Scot's presence and there was a vibe present that put her spirit at ease.

"A is the correct answer."

"Sounds like you are business savvy as well. What is your story?"

"Nothing really. I always wanted to create a makeup that looks natural and doesn't make women look like clowns or like makeup is caked on their face. Short story I conducted research, was wise with money from my divorce settlement and ended up growing the company to what it is. I paid back all my investors with interest, purchased my own office building as well as my own factory. I have to say, God has truly been good to me."

"That is awesome. I mean, not the divorce…I can only imagine that was painful…but at least something good came out of it."

"I agree." Rose carefully sipped her red wine and stared into his eyes to dicern any faults or flaws. She had been down this road of making rash decisions and wanted to make sure she didn't make another bad one. "Tell me Herb Scot, why is it a man as fine as yourself is still single?"

"That is a hard question to answer. I won't say I am the easiest person to be with. I am very driven and I believe in taking care of business first before pleasure. That being said, I can't pinpoint it. I was married for short period of time…"

Scot paused as it was apparent it was bothering him.

"You don't have to explain, that is ok," Rose blurted out knowing it was not true and she longed to hear his response.

"No, it is ok. You see my wife and daughter were coming to surprise me at work. It was my birthday and they were bringing me a cake and balloons. On the way there, their car was hit head on by a drunk driver. My wife died on the spot and my daughter died later on that night in ICU. She was only 7 years old."

Rose sat with her mouth hanging wide open. She wasn't expecting him to be so blunt and to the point, and definitely wasn't expecting the story which he just told her.

"Oh my God. I don't know what to say."

"It is ok, you don't have to say anything. To answer your question, after that incident, I didn't date for a few years. My family kept telling me to get out there and find someone because I became a workaholic but it is hard for a man like me to attract a woman in my line of work because women I have encountered are very superficial. Working at a gas station is not necessarily a prestigious position for them to go back and tell their friends and I feel that when I meet a female, I shouldn't have to wear a shirt telling her I own the gas station. She should see that I am sincere and at least respect me for having employment. And as far as church, I just don't feel comfortable meeting women there. I go to church to worship, not to pick up women."

Scot's responses were tallying up major points with Rose.

"Let me apologize on behalf of women because I know how we can be. Sometimes women just search for security and we have been trained to recognize it physically, before spiritually. Something I am trying to work on."

"So you judged me from my job?"

"No, not at all. I thought you were very attractive and I admired how you were so friendly. I mean just offering me a beverage and being considerate. It is the little things that get to me. What I was talking about was recognizing pure spirits on people. I have had a history of attracting a certain type of man, and I am trying to get back on track with my walk with the Lord. I just want to make sure I don't get off that track again because this is the first time in quite some time I have had such a peace about me."

"Rose, I assure you I am not trying to get you off path. I just want to learn more about you, but I am more than comfortable with us taking our time. I think we are both at the age we have made enough mistakes to know that jumping into something doesn't solve your problems. Let's just play it by ear and see where it leads us."

"That sounds like a plan…under one condition."

That you keep your shirt on, because your body is amazing. Ok, don't say that aloud Rose.

"That you take me to church with you next time you go."

"But of course. I would love to have you on my side Rose. I think you will enjoy it."

The two continued to talk and had a pleasant evening. Scot took Rose to a park and they held hands while gazing at the stars talking about life, death, goals and dreams. Rose felt so comfortable in Scot's presence. It was almost as if they met before and he just understood her. Nothing ever felt so right. His eyes felt like they were peering into her soul; a feeling Rose had never experienced before.

After walking around, it was obvious the temperature outside dropped as a chill went through both their bodies. Scot walked Rose back to the car, drove her home, then walked her to the door.

"Why did you leave your car running? Don't you want to come in?"

"Rose, I truly enjoyed myself. The way I am feeling right now, I seriously doubt this will be the last time we see one another. I think I would like to end the evening right here on this doorstep under the moonlight. It is nice and brisk. I feel chill bumps as I know you do but moments like these make for memorable first kisses."

Rose completely forgot about the cold, and allowed her lips to gently touch Scot's. He wrapped his arms around her and the warmth from his body sent tingles through her spine. Scot pulled back, kissed Rose on her check, then walked away while wiping his mouth in the sexy, masculine way.

"Now that is a memory. Bye Rose, I will call you tomorrow."

"Bye Scot."

Scot walked back to the steps and leaned in to give Rose one additional kiss on her cheek. Rose grabbed him and wrapped her arms around his neck and kissed him again. When they stopped, Rose's eyelids took a second to retract.

"Ok Rose, you are really messing with me now. I am going to go. I will call you tomorrow."

"Bye baby."

Rose watched as Scot strutted back to his car. She noticed her kiss made his walk more confident. She smiled as he drove off, then walked into her home still glowing from her first date, and anticipated new love interest.

Chapter XVI

Rose Program

Rose landed her charitable hooks in another program by funding a non-profit youth organization for teen girls. Candice came up with the concept R.O.S.E; which was an acronym for Raising Our Standards & Expectations, and helped organize the project. Now two years strong, Candice invited Rose back to be their guest speaker. It was also a ceremony to introduce new leadership as Candice was well into her second year of college and could no longer handle the workload of the organization. She found an adequate replacement and retained a board seat.

The room slowly filled with young ladies and middle age women. The turnout was bigger than Candice expected and she was excited about the growth. She walked to the podium to commence the engagement.

"Can I have your attention please? If you could please find a seat, as we are about to get started. I understand it is getting late, so we will try not to hold you too long. We also have some refreshments which will be served shortly after we are done.

The women all managed to find their seats, and the chatter in the room ceased. "Good afternoon ladies!"

"Good afternoon," the women responded.

"Welcome to the R.O.S.E. Program."

Candice had a speech on the podium, but as she looked over the room she felt a spontaneous urge to speak from the heart so she closed her folder.

"I had a speech I prepared ladies, but you know what, I think I will just talk. After all, the idea of this is to be a session where we can feel free to speak to one another. I want to tell you a short story. Years ago I met a woman. A woman who, if you approach life and view people from a status level, you'd wonder why a big whig CEO would spend any time with a peon like me. Why would she care about what I am going through? I mean, here I am a 14-year old, and I have a million-dollar chick taking me out to lunch, treating me to spa's, and showing me the finer things in life. When I met her, I would have never imagined that she would be the financial backing behind my vision.

"One day I was at home alone meditating about what was going on in my life. While I gazed at the sky, this revelation came to me. Rose's relationship with me was like an analogy of the relationship some of us have with our spiritual Father. There are times when we get down on ourselves. These are points in our lives when we face discouragement, and start to question ourselves and our relationship with Him. I used to think - *Why would God care for someone like me? What can God do with some old damaged goods like me? Why is He even giving me the time?* I have been in depressed places in my life where I felt I was being punished. I had so many goals and dreams but I felt I was climbing an uphill battle. Trust me ladies, God wants to show us the finer things in life. He wants to be the backing behind our visions. He wants to bless us, but in order to do that, we have to get ourselves together first.

"This program is a stepping stone for us to get there. It won't provide you with all the answers, but will be a support system for you. To be a safe haven where we can bond as sisters, rather than tear each other apart due to jealousy and insecurity issues. Women were created to be givers of life, not perpetuators of chaos and conflict. Our organization serves as a sisterhood where you can get the help you need. For those of you who are new, we will provide you with the tools needed. We have regular prayer groups, we assign mentors, and have numerous study materials…but ultimately, all these resources mean nothing if you don't have a desire to change. You have to make the decision to change yourself, and be adamant about it. You only have one life to live, so live it to the fullest."

Candice looked over at Rose and winked as she took her last line from their previous conversations.

"Now the key-note speaker I am about to introduce is a woman that many of you know already. What can you really say about her? She is successful, beautiful inside and out, and someone I am proud to say is a good friend of mine. I present to some, and introduce to others, Edith Rose Hughes."

The women clapped as Rose approached the front of the room. She hugged Candice, then walked in front of the clear podium. At that moment she realized her mother's dream as she stood in an auditorium full of young ladies awaiting her encouraging word.

"Good afternoon daughters of God!"

"Good afternoon," the women responded.

"I said good afternoon daughters of God!"

"Good afternoon," the women responded now with more intensity and excitement.

"That is good. That is what I like to hear. I pray all is well with you. I won't take up much of your time. I just wanted to drop a few words of encouragement for you.

"You know ladies, I am excited about this organization and the growth since its inception. As you know this program was created help you grow in your relationship with God and help you to transform your mind so that you can handle future relationships with men. It is also here to serve as an avenue to promote abstinence in order to protect your life, health, and your future as well as to form a support group of your peers. For those of you who have already become sexually active, we don't judge you and welcome you as well. This program is for all women. We want to foster an environment where females of all ages can take a vow of celibacy until marriage and do things God's way. No matter if you made mistakes in the past or not, it is never too late!

"See, many of you know who I am, but few of you know my story. You'd be surprised the things you don't really know about people. This program was birthed through a conversation I had with a real good friend of mine a couple years ago."

Rose looked over and threw a wink back at Candice.

"Now look what it has grown to. I am standing here in a room of 300 beautiful young ladies."

Rose took a sip of water which sat on the podium.

"The other day I was on sitting on my back deck while looking at nature just meditating and admiring God's handiwork. As I sat there, I began to reflect over my life and I came to realize that even though there are differences physically in younger and older women, we are more alike than anything. Many of us older women sometimes forget how tender your heart is when you are young and how we are supposed to be nurturing…instead of being judgmental. According to Titus 2:3-5, it is our responsibility to mentor and teach the younger generation of women. Sometimes we lose sight of that.

"Let me start by saying I know it is very hard for women your age. You have so many influences; friends, videos, advertisements, movies, church, family, teachers, and school life in general. There is peer pressure and the desire to be popular, attractive, or just well-liked. Then you have situations where your body changes and there are new hormones and feelings. You have a desire to be grown but still want to enjoy the teenage life and benefits. It is a tough period of time, and I am not here to belittle it by any means. My goal today is to speak to you out of the kindness of my heart, and to let you know there are those who care. You are not alone, and you aren't the only one who has been through what you are going through.

"As a woman in general, no matter what your age, we are affected by the pressure society places on us. We continually watch advertisements for many products which portray women who seem to have all the perfect material possessions, the perfect children, the perfect relationships, the perfect careers, and the perfect ability to balance it all. Those types of images overtake you in every commercial and every magazine stand you pass. Then you have the requirements and the demands that imperfect men place on females concerning what we should look and act like. All of these sources will kidnap your confidence if you allow them, and hold it hostage for eternity if you do not do something to combat them.

"Where do we start you ask? Well, one of the hardest things for females to do is release the guilt of sin, the weight that we feel from doing those things that are against God's will and purpose for our life. We may not want to do wrong, but sometimes we fall victim to our feelings and our flesh. Even though Jesus paid the ultimate sacrifice, some of us don't know how to deal with the guilt, nor the consequences, for the actions we set forth. Some of us are hemorrhaging so bad from our past experiences that it is hard for us to move forward. We have to get a grasp on how to handle relationships because like it or not, what has happened in our past is affecting our present and unchecked will continue to negatively impact our futures. The men that we have been with in the past have been a direct reflection of us, our level of wisdom, our ability to discern, and how we carry ourselves. They are a direct reflection of our intelligence level, our desperation, our attitudes about life, our character, and what we were willing to accept.

"Trust me when I say I understand how it feels when you have baggage. I understand how just everyday living can carry a weight which seems too much to bear. I know what it means to act out in rage. I know what it feels like to not know what to do with the hurt and pain another individual has caused you. I know what it means to place demands on others out of fear and having control issues.

"There are some of you in here that feel image is everything and you must look good at all costs and protect that image. The problem is there is a price of protecting that image. What price are you paying to cover up your past and the pain you feel from it, verses taking steps to truly heal from it? This program was created because there is a need for women to peel back layers and reveal their scars so healing can occur. Something in you should get tired of going in circles and want to make a change. When you can be transparent with your fellow sisters, and just be real with no fear of rejection or judgment, then you can finally reveal and work on who you truly are. What many of us fail to realize is that in order to get peace, joy and victorious living, we must first lay ourselves out before God.

"I stand before you today completely transparent. I lost my virginity at age 13 to a man in a cold, dirty, damp basement on a plaid recliner. It was not romantic at all, and nowhere near how I thought my first experience would be. After it happened, I thought that was a precursor to the rest of my life. To make it worse, I found out he slept with someone else a day before… literally hours before me. I gave myself to this guy, and what did I get in return? Following that unwise choice, I continued to see this man off and on up until college. I never once as a young lady stopped to really question why I was making the string of bad decisions I was making. Instead, I just continued on a path of following my feelings verses truly seeking wisdom.

"As I look at other men I dated, and married, I see how the negative experiences in my first relationship and interaction with men polluted my other relationships. The first person I opened up and gave myself to left a hairline fracture across my heart that slowly broke me over the years. Many females have this same experience. But you know what? God is awesome. After I made a conscious choice to follow His Word and His will for my life, He saw fit to restore me and bless me with a husband and a beautiful daughter - who I named Elisabeth which means oath of God or God's promise. I named her that because I felt that it represented the oath I made with God to change myself. After I aligned myself with His will, everything in my life started to fall into play. All that He promised came to fruition.

"Yes, I had money and success prior to, but I was not happy. Money will not solve all your problems, believe me. And no, everything did not magically change overnight. What I will tell you is that once I turned my life over to Christ, started living according to the Word, and allowed Him to heal my mind, body, and spirit, He blessed me with treasures it seemed my heart was not big enough at times to contain. I have a beautiful, healthy daughter, and this is coming from a woman who thought she wouldn't have children. Not only that, but I did not have to settle for a babydaddy. I didn't have to run to a sperm bank, or do something desperate to force God's hand. When I finally decided to patiently wait for my promise, God blessed me with a devoted husband. He is such a good man, let me tell you. He shows me love as it was intended. He is an honest, smart, God-fearing man. And I know I shouldn't say this nor be thinking this at the time, but there is nothing sexier, nothing more attractive than your man possessing a heart to willingly, openly worship God!

"Let me be clear on this though. I didn't find this man of my dreams until I took time…and I mean a good amount of time…to work on myself. It did not happen overnight! If you don't hear anything else I say, listen to me when I say Jesus alone is more than enough. Instead of focusing on relationships with men, I made a decision that I needed to learn how to develop and restore my relationship with God through His Son Jesus. I did this through repentance, prayer, Bible study, meditation, worship, praise, and honoring God with my life by using my gifts and influence for His kingdom. God touched my circumstances and changed my life.

"My focus determined my ability to receive from and hear from God. I had to do some spring cleaning and get rid of those things and people that were sent to distract me, and get myself on the course God laid for me and my purpose. Anyone or anything not aligning itself with the Word of God I cut out my life! My time alone with Him allowed transformation to occur. It brought about a peace that became a part of my daily life experience and assured me that all I need is God.

"Through opening up about my first encounter in the basement and my testimony of what has occurred in my life since then, I have been able to use it to help other females and propel me towards my destiny. Metaphorically speaking, that basement in which I lost my virginity represents every bad experience in our lives. The hours of weakness, the periods of pain, the times we did things in the dark we didn't want anyone to know about, the things that emotionally corrupted us, and damaged our spirits. For the men that abused us physically, mentally and spiritually. For the innocence lost. It represents all our mistakes and decisions that haunt us. For children born outside of the protective boundary of marriage, for the abortions many females have had to live through, or the STD's contracted when we were acting irresponsible. For times we were emotionally traumatized, so we decided to damage our bodies doing things like cutting ourselves, becoming hypersexual, or developing eating disorders.

"That basement represents things that happened to us as a result of our choices, but also those experiences that were not our fault and out of our control like rape, molestation and incest. I come today to speak words of encouragement to you. When you put your faith and trust in God, and put forth effort into consistently living according to His Word, He can heal and restore you from your past. It is the Word that will produce healing in your spirit, health in your flesh, and restoration in your life. Now I will be honest, everything will not be perfect at all times in your life but your relationship with God will give you the ability to rise above all the situations that have or will happen in your life. I believe God put me in this position of sharing my testimony to give you ladies hope and to physically show that you can rise from all these situations…just as I rose from the basement."

ABOUT THE AUTHOR

When not spending time with his family, Jerome mentors young men and volunteers as a youth football and basketball coach. Under his coaching and tutelage, many young people have developed a new found love of sports, as well as increased levels of confidence and personal responsibility. A native of Dayton, Ohio, he now resides in Dallas, TX with his wife Marla and six sons.

ALSO AVAILABLE FROM
The Real Life Series Publishing Co.

Marriage As Advertised
by Jerome J. McCarthy
Fiction/Novel
ISBN-13: 978-0-9800083-9-5

Enhancing Your Journey:
Quarterly Prayer Journal
by Marla A. McCarthy
Non-Fiction/Self-Help
ISBN-13: 978-0-9800083-5-7

Create The Life You Want Now:
Quarterly Goal Journal
by Marla A. McCarthy
Non-Fiction/Self-Help
ISBN-13: 978-0-9800083-3-3

The 10 Commandments of Friendship
by Jerome J. McCarthy, Marla A. McCarthy
Non-Fiction/Self-Help
ISBN-13: 978-0-9800083-7-1

The 30 Day Intimacy Challenge for Married Couples
by Jerome J. McCarthy, Marla A. McCarthy
Non-Fiction/Self-Help
ISBN-13: 978-0-9800083-7-1

Loving Me:
10 Ways to Renew Your Mind, Body & Spirit
by Marla A. McCarthy
Non-Fiction/Self-Help
ISBN-13: 978-0-9800083-0-2

R.O.S.E.

Raising Our Standards and Expectations:

Transforming Your Ability To Handle Relationships

by Marla A. McCarthy

Non-Fiction/Self-Help

ISBN-13: 978-0-9800083-8-8

Inquires should be addressed to:

The Real Life Series Publishing Co., LLC

PO BOX 1563, Keller, TX 76244-1896

www.TheRealLifeSeries.com

info@thereallifeseries.com

www.ingramcontent.com/pod-product-compliance
Lightning Source LLC
Chambersburg PA
CBHW020947310726
48980CB00001B/92

* 9 7 8 0 9 8 0 0 0 8 3 4 0 *